ON STAGE

RAY BRADBURY
ON STAGE

A Chrestomathy of His Plays

Primus
DONALD I. FINE, INC.
New York

Library of Congress Catalogue Card Number: 91-55178
ISBN: 1-55611-305-6

Manufactured in the United States of America

10 9 8 7 6 5 4 3 2 1

Designed by Irving Perkins Associates

With love to the memory of my friend and teacher
Charles Laughton
and to the actors who brought these plays to life:
F. Murray Abraham
Len Lesser
Joby Baker
Joe Montegna
Fred Villani
Talia Shire
Henry Darrow
who helped tailor the Ice Cream Suit.
And to the Anthem Sprinters:
Bobby Ball
Monte Markham
& Gary Walberg.
And to Harold Gould
who described the Chicago Abyss,
and Anne Loos
who made it rain forever.
And to
Charles Rome Smith
Terrance Shank
& Kirk Mee
who directed traffic and richly earned their applause.

CONTENTS

THE ANTHEM SPRINTERS

and Other Antics

CONTENTS

The Great
Collision of
Monday Last

CHARACTERS

THE OLD MAN (MIKE)
THE YOUNG MAN (MCGUIRE)
HEEBER FINN
KELLY
FEENEY
QUINLAN
KILPATRICK
THE DOCTOR
PAT NOLAN
MR. PEEVEY
FLYNN
DONOVAN
CASEY

The curtain rises upon darkness. Later on, we will make out certain details, but now, in the dark, we hear someone whistling and singing, off away somewhere, an Irish ditty of some vintage or other; "Sweet Molly Malone" will do as well as any. The voice fades, then comes back, dies off into a kind of pumping gasp, and at last we see why, as onto the stage, wobbling badly, exhausted, pedals an old man on a bike. He more falls than gets off the damned thing in midstage and lets the beast lie there at his feet as he takes off his cap and wipes his brow, shaking his head.

THE OLD MAN: Old Man, you're not what you once was!

He puts away his handkerchief, puts on his cap, bends to heft the bike, is still too winded and lets it fall.

Ah, lie there, brute that you are!

He takes out a bottle and eyes it sadly. There is but one last fiery gulp in it. He downs it philosophically and holds it up to let the last tiny drop fall off on his tongue. As he is doing so, we hear a car approach, stage left. Its lights flash out in a beam to spot THE OLD MAN, *who fends off the light with his free hand.*

Enough of that, now!

The lights go off, the motor cuts, a door opens and slams. THE YOUNG MAN *enters, stage left.*

THE YOUNG MAN: Is anything wrong?

THE OLD MAN *(blinking, peering):* You made a blind man of me is all. Who's there? *(Squints)*

THE YOUNG MAN, *uncertain, takes half a step.*

THE YOUNG MAN: Oh, you don't know me—

THE OLD MAN: That's certain! *(Squints)* Is that an American voice I hear?

THE YOUNG MAN: I just got off the boat—

THE OLD MAN: He just got off the boat! He did indeed! Come closer!

THE YOUNG MAN *approaches.*

There! Me eyes are better. An American face to go with the American voice.

THE YOUNG MAN: May I be of assistance . . . ?

THE OLD MAN *holds the bottle up so it can drain its emptiness on the air.*

THE OLD MAN: Well, there's assistance *and* assistance. It came over me as I pumped up the hill, one or the other of us, me or this damned vehicle *(He kicks the bike gently),* is seventy years old.

THE YOUNG MAN: Congratulations.

THE OLD MAN: For what? Breathing? That's a habit, not a virtue.

THE YOUNG MAN: Let me give you a lift.

THE OLD MAN: No, a moment's rest, thanks, and me and the beast will be on our way. We don't know where we're going, Sally and me—that's the damn bike's name—ye see, but we pick a road each day and give it a try.

THE YOUNG MAN, *who has been watchful and warming to this, now says, with real affection:*

THE YOUNG MAN: Does your mother know you're out?

THE OLD MAN *(surprised):* Strange you say that! She does! Ninety-five she is, back there in the cot! Mother, I said, I'll be gone the day; leave the whisky alone!

He laughs to himself, quietly.

I never married, you know.

THE YOUNG MAN: I'm sorry.

THE OLD MAN: First you congratulate me for being old and now you're sorry I've no wife. It's sure you don't know Ireland. Being old and having no wives is one of our principal industries! You see, a man can't marry without property. You bide your time till your mother and father are called Beyond. Then when their property's yours, you look for a wife. It's a waiting game. I'll marry yet.

THE YOUNG MAN: At *seventy?*

THE OLD MAN *(ruffling):* I'd get twenty good years out of marriage with a fine woman, even this late, do you doubt it!

THE YOUNG MAN *(impressed):* I do not!

THE OLD MAN *relaxes.*

THE OLD MAN: Now, what are you up to, in Ireland?

THE YOUNG MAN: I'm looking for the Irish.

THE OLD MAN *(surprised, pleased, then mystified):* Ah, that's difficult. They come, they throw shadows, they go. You got one standing before you, now!

THE YOUNG MAN *(smiling):* I know!

THE OLD MAN: You be a writer, of course.

THE YOUNG MAN: How did you guess!

THE OLD MAN *(gestures):* The country's overrun! There's writers turning over rocks in Cork and writers fishing in dinghies off Dun Laoghaire and writers trudging through bogs at Kilashandra. The day will come, mark me, when they will be five writers for every human being in the world!

THE YOUNG MAN: Well, writer I am, and Irish I'm after. What shapes the Irish to their dooms, and runs them on their way?

THE OLD MAN *eyes* THE YOUNG MAN *with not exactly suspicion, but . . .*

THE OLD MAN: You're in the country two hours and already you sound like an actor in the midst of the Abbey Theatre stage!

THE YOUNG MAN: Do I? Well, my family's all from Ireland, fifty years ago. So I came to see their town, their land— their—

THE OLD MAN *(wincing):* Enough! I got the sense of your jabber! Come here!

> THE YOUNG MAN *steps closer.* THE OLD MAN *takes his shoulder.*

All right now, you say you want to bag the Irish in his lair? find him out? write him down? I'll take you to that place where you can spy on him unbeknownst! And where you'll see an event that's Irish as Irish can be—unseen before by outlander's eyes, or if seen not believed, or if believed not understood!

THE YOUNG MAN *(eagerly):* An Event? a fair? a circus?

THE OLD MAN: A *sort* of circus, you might say . . . an unusual circumstance, the meeting of Fates is better! Hurry on, man, or we'll miss it!

> THE OLD MAN *starts to trot, with his bicycle.*

THE YOUNG MAN: My car—

THE OLD MAN: Leave it there. It's not far.

> TO MUSIC: THE YOUNG MAN *follows* THE OLD MAN *off into the wings, right. They reappear almost immediately, left,* THE OLD MAN *on the bike this time, pumping unsteadily along.*

THE OLD MAN *(pointing):* Do you see those men there, walking on the road?

THE YOUNG MAN *(running behind):* Yes!

THE OLD MAN: That's *not quite* the Irish!

TO MUSIC: *They vanish offstage right and reappear, left,* THE YOUNG MAN *still jogging after the old one on the bike.*

(Pointing) Do you see all them young fellows on their bikes pumping uphill?

THE YOUNG MAN *(breathless):* Yes!

THE OLD MAN: That's *almost* the Irish.

TO MUSIC: *They vanish stage right, then reappear, left,* THE OLD MAN *seated on the crossbars of the bike,* THE YOUNG MAN *pumping.*

(Pointing) Do you see that sign, now?

THE YOUNG MAN *(gasping):* Yes!

THE OLD MAN: Hold everything! *Stop!*

The bike wobbles and collapses. Both leap off barely in time. THE OLD MAN *points dramatically.*

That's the Irish!

A door has slid out of the wings, right. A sign has come down out of the flies. THE YOUNG MAN *reads it aloud.*

THE YOUNG MAN: Heeber Finn's. *(His face takes fire)* Why . . . it's a *pub!*

THE OLD MAN *(all innocence):* By God, now, I think you're right! *(He runs to the pub door)* Come meet my family!

THE YOUNG MAN: Family? You said you weren't married!

THE OLD MAN: I'm not! But a man, seventy or no, has got to have a family. Right? Well!

THE OLD MAN *rams the double wicket doors, plunges through. At this instant the scrim goes from front to back lighting. Instantaneously we see the inside of Heeber Finn's pub, the men at the bar, and Finn himself working the spigots. Once the lighting is established, the scrim can go up out of the way.*

At the sound of the doors flung back, the men at the bar jerk.

It's *me,* boys!

HEEBER FINN, *behind the bar, sighs.*

FINN: Mike! Ya gave us a start!

ANOTHER MAN: We thought it was—a *crisis!*

THE OLD MAN *is pleased with the savor of that word.*

THE OLD MAN: Well, maybe it is! This is my friend!

He points to THE YOUNG MAN. *Now he points to the others.*

. . . and these, you might say, are what I use for a family . . .

THE YOUNG MAN *is touched by this fancy, and nods to all. The men murmur in friendly fashion, nodding.*

FINN: Has your friend a crisis, then, Mike?

THE OLD MAN *sobers dramatically.*

THE OLD MAN: He's come to see the Irish, clear!

FINN *pours from a bottle.*

FINN: See it or drink it?

THE YOUNG MAN: A—bit of both.

FINN: Well spoke. To your health.

He shoves the glass across the counter, winking. THE OLD MAN *leans, peering, toward the door.*

THE OLD MAN: Fine! it's dark early. Ah, that lovely mist! Now, peel an eye, Young Man. There's great events preparing themselves out in that fog, of all kinds and sorts even *I* can't tell you; right, boys?

The men assent. THE YOUNG MAN *drinks, gasps.*

THE YOUNG MAN *(peering):* What should I look for?

THE OLD MAN: Let nothing pass unquestioned! *(Turns)* Give 'em another, Finn, to focus his eyes.

FINN *pours.* THE YOUNG MAN *wisely lets it lie.* THE OLD MAN *trots to the door, half opening same to let in a wisp of fog, which he fingers.*

Will you look? Why, you could wear the dainty stuff about your neck! A fine night. *Anything* could happen! and always *does!*

He inhales the fog, the lovely dark, smiles at the aroma, lets the doors shimmy shut, and comes back to the bar to sip his drink.

Mind, now, maybe you'll have to wait for some other night—

FINN *(incensed):* Can you name one night in history wasn't a night of earthshaking consequence at Heeber Finn's?

THE OLD MAN *(scratches head):* I can't.

FINN: You can't. *(Turns)* Son, do you play darts?

THE YOUNG MAN: Yes.

FINN: Good! Do you lie?

THE YOUNG MAN: Lie?

FINN: Can you tell untruths, man? Big ones, small, all sizes?

THE YOUNG MAN *(dubiously)*: I'll try.

FINN *(pleased)*: I'm sure you will! We——

Suddenly THE OLD MAN *quickens, catching hold of elbows to right and left.*

THE OLD MAN: Hist!

All down the bar, everyone freezes.

(Whispering) That was *it!*

Every head, on a single string, turns toward the door.

THE YOUNG MAN: What . . . ?

THE OLD MAN: Ssst! *Listen* . . .

All lean. All hear—something, far away.

(Eyes shut) That's it . . . yes . . . yes . . .

Everyone stares. Footsteps batter the outside step drunkenly. The double wing doors flap wide as a bloody man in his thirties staggers in, capless, holding his bloody head with a bloody hand. He stops, blinking numbly at the crowd.
THE YOUNG MAN *stares, amazed.*
All down the bar, the men lean toward the intruder. The intruder sways, trying to find words, eyes glazed.
THE OLD MAN *moves forward, frantically curious, gesturing his hand as if bidding the man to speak up, speak up!*
The bloody intruder finally gasps for breath.

THE INTRUDER: Collision! Collision on the road!

Then, chopped at the knees, he falls down. The men glance at each other.

ALL: Collision!

HEEBER FINN *vaults the bar. His landing breaks the spell.*

FINN: Kelly, Feeney, quick!

All run toward the "body." HEEBER FINN *is first, with* THE OLD MAN.

THE OLD MAN: Easy does it!

FINN: Quinlan, out to the road! Mind the victim! Kilpatrick, run for the Doc!

A VOICE: Wait!

ALL *look up.*
THE DOC *steps out from the far end of the bar, from a little dark cubby where he has been standing alone with his philosophies.*
FINN *is surprised.*

FINN: Doc, you're so quiet I forgot you was there! Out you go!

THE DOCTOR *plunges out the front door with half a dozen men. The fog streams in past them.*
THE YOUNG MAN *looks down at the "victim" on the floor. The "victim's" lips twitch.*

THE VICTIM *(gasping, whispering):* Collision . . .

FINN: Softly, boys.

They lift "the victim" and carry him over to lay him on the bar.
THE YOUNG MAN *comes up to stare at the man lying there, and at his image in the mirror behind the bar . . . two dread calamities for the price of one.*

THE YOUNG MAN *(puzzled):* But . . . I didn't hear any cars on the road.

THE OLD MAN *is proud to reply:*

THE OLD MAN: That you didn't!

He beckons. With a high sense of melodrama, THE OLD MAN *escorts him to the swinging doors, opens one for him.*

A scrim has come down as they move toward the door.

As they emerge into the "outside," the "world," the lights go off behind the scrim and come on in front of it. This particular scrim is a mist, a fog, a gray background across which they may wander, looking out over the apron at the night, the weather, and the men foraging beyond. There are wisps of fog or mist moving in from either side, from the wings, and from below in the pit.

THE OLD MAN *stands next to the young one, on the steps of the pub, sniffing the weather appreciatively.*

You'd almost think that Ireland was gone. Oh, but it's there, all right.

THE YOUNG MAN *stares into the fog, continuing his thought.*

THE YOUNG MAN: . . . nor did I hear a collision.

THE OLD MAN *(shouting beyond):* Try the crossroad, boys! That's where it most often does! *(Quieter, he turns to* THE YOUNG MAN*)* Ah, we don't be great ones for commotion, nor great crashing sounds. But collision you'll see if you step on out there. *(Points stage left)*

THE YOUNG MAN *moves stage left, probing into the fog, groping.*

Walk now, don't run! It's the Devil's own night. You might head-on into Feeney, too drunk to find any road, no matter what's on it. You got a match?

THE YOUNG MAN: A match?

THE OLD MAN: Blind you'll be, but try it!

> THE YOUNG MAN *strikes a match, holds it out in front of him.*

That's pitiful poor, but on you go, and me behind you. Careful now, *walk!*

> *Both move in a great circle about the stage.*

Hist, now!

> *They listen to a rally of voices approaching.*

Here they come!

A VOICE *(hidden in fog):* Easy now. Don't jiggle him!

ANOTHER VOICE: Ah, the shameful blight!

> *Suddenly from the fog, stage left, a steaming lump of men appear bearing atop themselves a crumpled object.* THE YOUNG MAN *stares up, holding the match. We glimpse a bloodstained and livid face high up there. Someone brushes the lit match, which snuffs out. The catafalque rushes on.*

A VOICE: Where's Heeber Finn's?

ANOTHER VOICE: Bear left, left, I say!

> *The crowd vanishes.* THE YOUNG MAN *peers after. He hears a chilling insect rattle approach in the fog. He strikes another match.*

THE YOUNG MAN: Who's there?

A VOICE: It's us!

ANOTHER VOICE: With the vehicles!

THE YOUNG MAN *blinks at the old, who nods sagely.*

A VOICE: You might say we got—the collision!

Two men trot out of the fog, bringing with them under their arms two ancient black bicycles, minus head and taillights.

THE YOUNG MAN *stares at them. The two men with the bikes smile, proud of their task, give the bikes a heft, tip their caps, and trot off away again, vanishing in mist, toward Finn's, just as the last match dies forever.* THE YOUNG MAN, *stunned with the simple facts, hangs his mouth open, turning to* THE OLD MAN.

THE YOUNG MAN: What?

THE OLD MAN *(winks):* What? What, indeed! Ah, the delightful mysteries!

And he runs off into fog. THE YOUNG MAN, *musing, follows.*

THE YOUNG MAN: Men . . . *bicycles* . . . collision? Old Man, wait for *me!*

THE YOUNG MAN *runs, finds the front door to Finn's, and plunges in. The lights come on inside Finn's, the fog-scrim vanishes.*

Inside Finn's, THE OLD MAN *turns to welcome the arrival of* THE YOUNG MAN.

THE OLD MAN: Ah, there you are! *(lowers voice to a whisper)* We got the "bodies" on the bar.

THE YOUNG MAN *peers over the crowd at the two "bodies" laid out in pale ruin on the long bar,* THE DOC *mov-*

ing fretfully between the two, shouldering the crowd aside.

THE OLD MAN *whispers:*

One's Pat Nolan. Not under employment at the moment.

THE OLD MAN *peers and nods at the next.*

The other's Mr. Peevey from Meynooth. In candy and cigarettes, mostly.

THE OLD MAN *raises his voice.*

Are they long for this world, now, Doc?

THE DOC *mutters, swabbing a marbled face.*

THE DOC: Ah, be still, won't ya! Here, let's put one victim on the floor.

THE DOC *moves.* FINN *stops him.*

FINN: The floor's a tomb. He'll catch his death down there. Best leave him up where the warm air gathers from our talk.

THE DOC *shrugs and continues working.* THE YOUNG MAN *whispers in* THE OLD MAN'S *hairy ear.*

THE YOUNG MAN: But I've never heard of an accident like this in all my life!

THE OLD MAN *(fascinated with* THE DOC*):* That you didn't!

THE YOUNG MAN: Are you sure there were absolutely no cars?

THE OLD MAN: None.

THE YOUNG MAN: Only these two men on their bikes?

THE OLD MAN *(turning):* Only! *Only!*

THE YOUNG MAN *(embarrassed):* I mean—

THE OLD MAN: Great gods, man, what do you *know* of buycycles?

THE YOUNG MAN: Just—

THE OLD MAN: Just nothing! Clear the way!

> THE OLD MAN *fists a path to the two bikes leaned to the wall.*

Flynn! Donovan! Lend a hand! Casey, the other bike!

> *He kicks the backstand of the bike down. He swings astride a bike. The men grab front and back to steady it.* CASEY *does likewise with the second bike.*

Where am I now?

THE YOUNG MAN: In Heeber Finn's—

THE OLD MAN: *No!* I'm on the Meynooth Road . . . idling home lazy as you please . . .

> *He pumps. The back wheel, being free, hums quietly at a nice easy pace.* CASEY *pumps, too.*

(Listens) I hear a church bell. I know I'm late for meals. So what do I do?

THE YOUNG MAN *(trying):* Go faster?

THE OLD MAN: Now you're with it, lad! Faster I go! Where before I was toddling along easy at twenty or twenty-five, now here I work up a drizzling sweat at—

FLYNN: Forty an hour!

THE OLD MAN: Forty-five! Fifty!

> *He pumps furiously, bent down in concentrated passion.*

Now with a long downhill glide I hit sixty! So here I come, with no front or taillights.

THE YOUNG MAN: Isn't there a law against that?

THE OLD MAN: To hell with government interference! So here I come!

CASEY: And here *I* come! the other way!

Both pump furiously, heads down.

THE OLD MAN: The two of us, no lights, heads down, flying home from one town to the next, thrashing like Sin himself's at our behinds! Both going opposite ways—

CASEY: But both on the *same side* of the road!

THE OLD MAN: Always ride the wrong side of the road, lad, it's safer, they say! But look on those boys, fair destroyed by all that official palaver. Why? One remembered it, the other didn't! Better if the officials kept their mouths shut! For there the two boys lie, dying!

THE YOUNG MAN *stares. The wheels hum, whining!*

THE YOUNG MAN: Dying?

CASEY *(pumping)*: Well, think on it, man! What stands between two able-bodied hell-bent fellas jumping along the path from Kilcock to Meynooth?

THE OLD MAN *(pumping)*: Fog! Fog is all. Only fog to keep their skulls from bashing together. So look now! Here we come, *bang!*

THE OLD MAN *jerks his bike up in the air with a grand whining, humming flourish, as does* CASEY.

There we go, nine feet up in the air, heads together like dear chums met, flailing the mist, our bikes clenched like two tomcats. Then we all fall down and just lay there, feeling around for the Dark Angel.

They let the bikes fall and stand over them, looking down at the imaginary wreckage.
THE YOUNG MAN *looks from them to the bar.*

THE YOUNG MAN: Surely these men won't—

CASEY: Oh, *won't* they? Why, last year alone in all the Free State, no night passed some soul did not meet in fatal collision with another.

THE YOUNG MAN *(aghast):* You mean to say over three hundred Irish bicyclists die every year, hitting each other?

THE OLD MAN *bows his head as at the grave of a friend.*

THE OLD MAN: God's truth and a pity!

HEEBER FINN *eyes the "bodies."*

FINN: I never ride my bike nights. I *walk.*

THE YOUNG MAN: Why . . . let's get them to a hospital, then, quick!

THE OLD MAN *is mildly irritated at this interruption of their round-robin discussion.*

THE OLD MAN: One thing at a time, please. You was saying, Finn . . . ?

FINN: I walk!

CASEY: But even walking, the damn bikes run you down!

THE OLD MAN: True!

CASEY: Awheel, or afoot, some idiot's always pantin' up doom the other way, they'd sooner split you down the seam than wave hello!

THE YOUNG MAN *(touching* THE OLD MAN*'s elbow):* The victims here—

THE OLD MAN: One moment, lad. *(Shakes head)* Ah, the brave men I've seen ruined or half-ruined or worse, and headaches their lifetimes after.

He looks at the bicycles on the floor between them, and trembles, his eyelids shut.

You might almost think, mightn't you, that human beings was not made to handle such delicate instruments of power.

THE YOUNG MAN *(still dazed):* Three hundred dead each year . . .

CASEY: And that don't count the "walkin' wounded" by the thousands every fortnight who, cursing, throw their bikes in the bog forever and take government pensions to salve their all-but-murdered bodies.

THE YOUNG MAN *(nervously):* I hate to bring it up but should we stand here just *talking?*

THE OLD MAN *(wounded, as are the others): Just* talking! We're debating the problems and making the decisions! Look there, do ya see?

They look.
    THE DOC, *quite obviously enjoying his moment of power in center stage of the crowd, walks back and forth between the two creatures on the bar. The crowd looks after him from right to left. He is building his moment of suspense. He squints one eye, closes both, rubs his chin, scratches his ear.*

THE MEN *(restlessly):* Ah . . .

THE DOC *realizing he has gone almost too far, feeling his audience begin to drift away, now snatches their attention back by straightening up and exhaling briskly.*

THE DOC: Well, now!

The men quicken.
THE OLD MAN *whispers to* THE YOUNG MAN, *grabbing his arm.*

THE OLD MAN: He's ready for his pronouncement!

THE DOC, *veteran of much medical play-acting, rocks on his feet, and points at the first "body."*

THE DOC: This chap here—

The crowd leans toward the chap.

Bruises, lacerations, and agonizin' backaches for two weeks runnin'.

Everyone nods at the shame of it. THE DOC *now turns to the other and makes his face grim. The men lean that way.*

As for this one—

He pauses.

(In a dramatic whisper) Concussion.

ALL: Concussion!

The quiet wind of their voices rises and falls in the silence.

THE DOC: He'll survive if we run him quick now to Meynooth Clinic. Now then—whose car will volunteer?

The crowd looks at itself, then turns as a staring body toward THE YOUNG MAN. *He feels the gentle shift as he is drawn from outside the ritual to its deep and innermost core. He looks about, thinking perhaps there may be another volunteer. Then he walks to the door, half opens it, and looks out.*

THE YOUNG MAN *(counting):* . . . twelve . . . fourteen . . . sixteen bicycles . . . and, two hundred yards down the road . . . one automobile . . . *mine.*

THE OLD MAN: Praise God, that's fortunate!

THE YOUNG MAN *turns sheepishly. The crowd leans toward him.* THE YOUNG MAN *nods, once.* THE DOC *quickens with gratitude.*

THE DOC: A volunteer!! Quick, lads, now, hustle this victim —gently—to our good friend's vehicle. Take his keys. Drive the car up outside!

THE YOUNG MAN *holds out the keys as someone runs by, seizing them. The men reach out to lift the body and freeze when* THE YOUNG MAN *clears his throat. All look to him.* THE YOUNG MAN *circles them with his hand, tips his cupped hand to his mouth, and nods at* FINN. *The men gasp.*

CASEY: He's right, of course! It's a cold night. One for the road!

HEEBER FINN *lines up the shot glasses lip to lip and sprinkles them all quickly with the passing bottle. Hands seize the glasses. One of the victims is taken off the bar and set in a chair, where, reviving, his face like a white cheese, he feels a glass put in his trembly hand.*

THE OLD MAN: Here, lad, now . . . tell us . . .

CASEY: What happened, eh . . . ? eh?

The drinks are gulped. The second victim is hefted. The men head for the door. THE YOUNG MAN, *amazed, watches them go, his drink in his hand.*

THE OLD MAN: Finish your drink, Mr. . . . ?

THE YOUNG MAN *(faintly):* McGuire.

THE OLD MAN: By the saints, he *is* Irish!

THE YOUNG MAN *looks—at the recovering victim, at the bar, the mirrors, the two bikes against the wall, the fog seeping in through the door, then, at last, at* THE OLD MAN, *and the depths of the drink in his hand.*

THE YOUNG MAN *(thoughtfully):* No . . . I don't think I am.

He swigs his drink and heads for the door with THE OLD MAN *dogtrotting after. At the door he stops, for a voice is speaking behind him. He does not turn, but listens. Behind, over his shoulder, the recovered "victim" is sipping his drink and talking to two men bent earnestly to listen.*

THE VICTIM *(hoarsely, dramatically):* Well . . . I'm on me way home, blithe as you please, see, and—

THE YOUNG MAN *steps through the doors quickly. The pub lights go out. Outside, the fog-scrim appears, mist drifts in from either side. We hear voices off and away, and the approach of* THE YOUNG MAN's *car, driven by someone. The car stops, just out of sight.*

A VOICE: There we are!

ANOTHER VOICE: Now, easy, inside with the poor victim!

THE YOUNG MAN *muses, with* THE OLD MAN *beside him, in the night.*

THE YOUNG MAN: Old Man, do you ever have auto wrecks, collisions between people in *cars?*

THE OLD MAN *(insulted):* Not in our town!! If you like *that* sort of thing, now *(Nods scornfully east),* Dublin's the very place for it!

THE YOUNG MAN *looks east, nods, moves toward his car offstage.*

Look now, McGuire, a last bit of advice. You've driven little in Ireland, right?

THE YOUNG MAN *nods.*

Listen. Driving to Meynooth, fog and all, go fast! Raise a din!

THE YOUNG MAN: In this fog? Why?

THE OLD MAN: Why, he asks! To scare the bicyclists off the path, *and* the cows! Both sides! If you drive slow, you'll creep up on and do away with dozens before they know what took them off. Also—when another car approaches —douse your lights, pass each other, lights out, in safety. Them devil's own lights have put out more eyes and demolished more innocents than all of seeing's worth. Is it clear, now?

THE YOUNG MAN *nods.*

You got a cap? I see ya haven't. So—

THE OLD MAN *produces a tweed cap from his coat pocket.*

THE OLD MAN: Put this on! Bicycling, driving, or especially, walking, *always* wear a cap. It'll save you the frightful migraines should you meet Kelly or Moran or some other hurtling full tilt the other way, full of fiery moss and hardskulled from birth! So you see, there's rules for pedestrians, too, in our country, and *wear a cap,* is Number One!

THE YOUNG MAN *pulls the cap down and looks to* THE OLD MAN *for his approval, which he gets.*

THE OLD MAN: Well now, get along, lad.

THE YOUNG MAN: Aren't you riding with me?

THE OLD MAN: Ah, no, I got the beast here, I must check on the mother.

He picks up his bike and slings a slatty leg over it and pulls his cap down.

THE OLD MAN: Well, sir, did you find what you came for? did you see the Irish, clear?

THE YOUNG MAN: I saw but didn't see . . . lost one thing and found another . . . now, *that's* gone, too. Tell me, how did you guess all this would happen tonight, here? How did you know?

THE OLD MAN: I didn't! Some other night it would be some other thing! Like I said, anything could happen, and always does! That's Ireland for you. And it's waiting out there for you now, in the fog. Go find it!

THE YOUNG MAN *runs off, stage right.*

THE YOUNG MAN: I will!

We hear the motor revved, offstage.

THE OLD MAN *(shouting off):* Remember what I said! Douse your lights!

The lights go off, stage right.

THE OLD MAN *(shouting):* Go fast!

Offstage, we hear the furious gunning of the motor.

THE OLD MAN: Keep your cap on! Tight! *(Yanks his own cap, hard)*

THE YOUNG MAN *(offstage):* See you again!

THE OLD MAN: God willing!

We hear the car roar off and away. The sound fades. When it is gone, THE OLD MAN *is alone on his bike. He prepares himself, clears his throat, and sings going off, stage right.*

THE OLD MAN: "She wheeled her wheelbarrow . . ."

At which moment, a shadowy bicyclist (FINN) *comes through the other way. They almost collide.*

THE OLD MAN: Damn! Watch where you're going!

FINN: Hell! Look what you're doing!

THE OLD MAN: Heeber Finn, it's you!

FINN: Old man, it's you!

THE OLD MAN: God Bless!

FINN: God Bless! *(Takes up the song, sailing away)* "She wheeled her wheelbarrow . . ."

THE OLD MAN *(sings):* ". . . through streets wide and narrow . . ."

They vanish, pumping, but to reappear, wave, pass, and go off in darkness, alternating lines of song, vanishing at last as the mist and dark take over:

HEEBER FINN: ". . . singing cockles . . ."

THE OLD MAN: ". . . and mussels . . ."

HEEBER FINN: ". . . alive! . . ."

THE OLD MAN: ". . . alive! . . ."

BOTH TOGETHER: ". . . Ohhhh! . . ."

By this time the curtain has hushed down on the mist and the play is at . . .

THE END

The First
Night
of Lent

CHARACTERS

The Young Man (Douglas)

Mike (The Old Man)

Heeber Finn

Timulty

Nolan

O'Connell

Purdy

Kelleen

Sean (Telephone Operator)

Curtain up on darkness.
THE YOUNG MAN strolls along in the dark to a single spotlight where he stands debating with himself, hands in pockets, head down.
Off somewhere, a harp begins to play a few bars of "Molly Malone" or some such ditty.
THE YOUNG MAN raises his hands.

THE YOUNG MAN: Please. No harp. That will only muddy the waters and stop us from thinking clear about Ireland.

The harp rushes to the end of the next few bars, as if to get it all in, then ceases. THE YOUNG MAN nods, not surprised at this maneuver, and continues, looking out at the audience.

Does anyone understand the Irish?
No.

35

Will anyone *ever* understand them in all of time?
No.
Can there be some system or method to size and sort them, tincture their ganglions so we can slide them under a microscope and see what makes them dance? *(Shakes his head)*
No history can date them, no psychiatrist's couch lure them, no song explain them. And yet, as others tried, now so must I.
Did I ever know one solitary Irish fellow well?
I did. His name? Mike.

MIKE *sticks his head out of the wings, left.*

MIKE: Ya called, sir?

THE YOUNG MAN: In a moment, Mike—

MIKE: Take all the time in the world!

MIKE's *head vanishes.*

THE YOUNG MAN: I knew Mike for two hundred consecutive nights—

MIKE'S VOICE *(offstage):* Two-hundred-*one!*

THE YOUNG MAN: —two-hundred-one consecutive nights of one fall, winter, and early spring when I went to Ireland to write a film. I lived in Dublin, and every day when I finished ten new fresh pages of script, I would hire a taxi out to Kilcock, show my director my work, and at midnight go back to Dublin. How? By hiring the only taxi for miles around. So, every night I'd call the village exchange.

He picks up a telephone. And perhaps to one side, now, spotlighted, we can see SEAN, THE TELEPHONE OPERATOR, *bent over the village switchboard.*

SEAN: Are ya there?

THE YOUNG MAN: Hello, would you—

SEAN: Ah, it's *you,* Mr. Douglas.

THE YOUNG MAN: Who's this?

SEAN: Why, Sean, of course!

THE YOUNG MAN: Sean?

SEAN: The wife's got the uneasies. I took over the village *ex*-change for tonight.

THE YOUNG MAN: Good . . .

SEAN: A fine night.

THE YOUNG MAN: It is.

SEAN: It must be up to at least fifty degrees on the damn thermometer.

THE YOUNG MAN: All of that.

SEAN: Warm for this time of year.

THE YOUNG MAN: I always said, Dublin is the Riviera of Ireland.

SEAN: Did ya, now? I must remember to tell the wife. I suppose Heeber Finn's is where you're calling?

THE YOUNG MAN: If you don't mind, Sean.

SEAN: Mind! I'll put ya through like a bolt of lightning!

> *There is a hissing crackle. From the phone now pours a veritable millrace of voices, laughter, tinkling bottles, toasts, brags, and general multitude of hilarity. In the background, through a scrim, we see Finn's, and the crowd there at the bar.* THE YOUNG MAN *listens, fascinated.*

(At last) I have reason to believe you are through to Heeber Finn's, sir.

THE YOUNG MAN *(listening):* I don't doubt it, Sean.

We see FINN, *behind the bar, maneuvering drinks and the phone.*

FINN'S VOICE *(shouting):* Heeber Finn here! Who's on the other end!

SEAN: Heeber, it's *himself* from the big house!

THE YOUNG MAN *starts to speak but is cut across.*

FINN: Mr. Douglas, is it?

SEAN: The same!

FINN: Always glad to hear from Mr. Douglas.

THE YOUNG MAN *starts to speak, but—*

SEAN: Did you know he was a writer?

FINN *(awed):* I *did* not!

THE YOUNG MAN *opens his mouth, nodding.*

SEAN: He is! Writes them science and fiction stories!

FINN *(dismayed):* How's that?

SEAN: You know; them shiny magazines with the green monsters chasing raw naked women over the Martian Hills on the covers!

FINN *(pleased):* So *that's* what he's up to!

THE YOUNG MAN *opens his mouth, but—*

SEAN: He is also writing the fillum with the title *Moby Dick.*

FINN: *Is* he?

THE YOUNG MAN *nods, defeated. He does not try to open his mouth any more.*

SEAN: *You* know the story, about the Whale!

FINN: And Jonah in his belly!

THE YOUNG MAN: No—

SEAN: *No,* man. Ahab!

FINN: What?

THE YOUNG MAN *(getting it in fast):* Ahab!

FINN: Who else is on the line, Sean?

SEAN: Himself!

FINN: Ahab?

SEAN: Mr. Douglas, ya dimwit!

FINN: Hello, Mr. Douglas!

THE YOUNG MAN: I——

FINN: Now, who's this Ahab?

SEAN: Ahab is the captain that hunts the White Whale, man!

FINN: A fine story. Are ya there, Mr. Douglas? I said . . .

THE YOUNG MAN: Mr. Finn. Could you find Mike, the taxi driver, for me?

FINN: He's good as found.

> *There is a long silence. We watch and hear the mob at Finn's and* FINN *himself calling off and away:* "Mike, Mike!"

SEAN: It's a fine night, Mr. Douglas.

THE YOUNG MAN *(by rote):* A bit warm for this time of year.

SEAN (*admiring the other's sense*): Just what *I* was thinking——!

We see a man jog through the crowd, rear, and grab the phone.

ANOTHER VOICE (*breaking in*): Hello, Mr. Douglas?

THE YOUNG MAN: Mike?

ANOTHER VOICE: No. He'll be here when he finishes his game of darts!

We see MIKE, *rear, playing the game out.*

THE YOUNG MAN: Never mind, just tell Mike——

We see MIKE *forging toward the phone.*

ANOTHER VOICE: Hold on, here comes the triumphant victor now!

THE YOUNG MAN: There's no——

MIKE'S VOICE: Mr. Douglas, congratulate me!

THE YOUNG MAN: Mike, is that you?

MIKE'S VOICE: Who else? And I won!

THE YOUNG MAN: Mike, can you drive me to Dublin, now?

MIKE: I'm halfway to the door!

There is a thud as, presumably, the phone is dropped at the other end. The crowd noises swell. THE YOUNG MAN *holds the receiver off and looks at it with bemusement, then addresses the audience again.*

THE YOUNG MAN: Halfway to the door. It is but thirty feet, I'd wager, from the bar of Heeber Finn's to the far side of the pub where the door, neglected, abhorrent, waits. Yet that thirty feet is best negotiated carefully, and may take all of one minute per foot. In other words, it may take Mike half an hour to go from the phone to the outside world and five minutes to drive the half-mile up the road to where I am waiting for him. Listen to them.

He holds out the phone, taking his hand off the earpiece so the noise swells.

Mike's on his way. He's halfway to the door, plus one foot.

And this is true. During all the above, in dim panto-mime behind the rear scrim, we see MIKE *turning in slow circles, moving his head here, there, touching this per-son, touching that, trying to finish a stout thrust in his hand, answering a jest with another, laughing at one man, scowling at a second, blinking at a third. The pan-tomime continues during the following speech.*

Do you see how patient I am? Do I yell or threaten? I do not. I learned, early on, that Mike's "headin' for the door" was no nerve-shattering process for him. He must not af-front the dignity of the men he moves among. He must admire, on his way out, the fine filigree of any argument being woven with great and breathless beauty at his elbow or behind his back. It is, for him, a gradual disengagement, a leaning of his bulk so his gravity is diplomatically shifted toward that far empty side of the public room where the door, shunned by all, stands neglected. On his way, a dozen conversational warps and woofs must be ticked, tied, and labeled so next morn, with hoarse cries of recog-nition, patterns may be seized, the shuttle thrown with no pause or hesitation.

THE YOUNG MAN *produces a long instructor's pointer or baton.*

To give you an idea of Mike's debilitating journey across the pub, here, for instance—

He points to one of the men who, approached by MIKE *now, breaks into a kind of jig or reel.*

That's old Timulty, who will dance for any reason or no reason at all.

MIKE *is appreciative of the jig and perhaps joins in a once-around.*

THE YOUNG MAN *points to a second man ahead.*

Here's Pat Nolan. A fierce outcaster of politics. A banger, a smasher and a shouter, to the wonderment of all.

Now that TIMULTY *has been gotten by,* MIKE *is confronted by* NOLAN, *who has two other men by their ties or lapels —that is, when he is not banging his own knee or smashing his fist into one palm. Now, as* MIKE *happens along,* NOLAN *sees him and, in pantomime, grabs out for him and starts bellowing on some vasty argument or other.* MIKE *is totally impressed, and nods, nods, nods.*

THE YOUNG MAN *points farther on—one, two, three.*

While up ahead waits O'Connell with his jokes.

We see O'CONNELL *laughing at his own stories, holding to someone's shoulder.*

Purdy with his harmonica.

PURDY *is guzzling his harmonica as we see him swaying there.*

And Kelleen with a brand-spanking-new poem he is just finishing . . .

We see KELLEEN, *using someone's back for a desk, scribbling furiously on a crumpled paper.*

There! Mike's almost to the door. He's got the doorknob in his hand!

Which is true. We see it!

Now, he—

At this instant, far across the pub, on the other side, a man waves and shouts in pantomime. MIKE *turns, lets go the door, waves, and, to fast harp music, jogs back through the crowd to where it all started!* THE YOUNG MAN, *dismayed, readjusts his face to the situation.*

(Philosophically) Well . . . that's how it goes.

He ambles back to the telephone, picks it up, listens.

So I do not yell, threaten, or rouse my blood.

He holds the phone out toward the audience so it can hear the tumult and the shouting inside the earpiece.

Who would hear me?

He hangs up. Silence. The pub lights go out. The pub vanishes.

While I'm waiting at the old house way out in the Irish wild, I take a little drink *(Drinks)*, get into my coat and cap *(Does so)*, and go out *(Goes)* into the night to look at the clear stars. Until at last, down through the night forest the nineteen-thirty-one Chevrolet comes thrashing, peat-turf-colored on top like Mike himself, and inside the old car—

Through the darkness from stage left comes MIKE, *gliding on a car seat with an apparatus to hold the steering wheel. The car, no more than seat, steering wheel, doors, circles the stage. From it comes the gasping, choking sound of a very old vehicle indeed.* MIKE *and his framework auto stop dead-center stage. The engine, with a hiccup, strangles and dies.*

Mike?

MIKE *(waving easily):* None other!

THE YOUNG MAN *opens the car door.*

Ain't it a fine warm evenin'?

THE YOUNG MAN *(hesitates; rubs jaw):* Mike . . . ? Have you ever visited Sicily or Spain? The south of France?

MIKE: No, sir.

THE YOUNG MAN: Paris, the north of France, even?

MIKE: I guess you'd say the furthest south I've ever been is the Tipperary shoreline, sir.

THE YOUNG MAN: I see.

He gets in. He looks at MIKE, *breathes the air, exhales, slams the door.*

Well . . . it's a fine *warm* evening, Mike.

MIKE: You hit it right on the head, sir!

We hear the motor roar, shadows and stars move on the scrim behind them, the men's bodies bounce a little.

THE YOUNG MAN: Mike, how've you been since?

MIKE *(wheeling the car slow and easy):* Ah, I got me health. Ain't that all-and-everything, with Lent comin' on tomorra?

THE YOUNG MAN *(muses):* Lent. What will you give up for Lent, Mike?

MIKE: I been turnin' it over. *(Sucks the cigarette which hangs from his lip until his face glows cherry-red)* And why not these terrible things ya see in me mouth?

THE YOUNG MAN: Cigarettes?

MIKE: Dear as gold fillings and a dread congester of the lungs they be! Put it all down, add 'em up, and ya got a sick loss by the year's turnin', ya know. So ya'll not find these filthy creatures in me face again the whole time of Lent—and, who knows, after!

THE YOUNG MAN: Bravo!

MIKE *(suspicious at this outburst; glancing over):* I see you don't smoke yourself.

THE YOUNG MAN: Forgive me.

MIKE: For what! Bravo, says I to meself if I can wrestle the Devil's habit two falls out of three!

THE YOUNG MAN: Good luck, Mike.

MIKE: And do you know something? I'll need it!

We hear the motor roar. The stars over Ireland swirl this way and that behind the car moving in darkness. At this point, THE YOUNG MAN *quietly rises up and steps down from the car and addresses the audience.*

THE YOUNG MAN: Well, now! We're on our way! But I want to make a few points . . .

He reaches out and with one hand swings the car about so it points its hood and bumpers stage left. The car purrs happily on, MIKE *at the wheel, smoking and humming to himself.*

Look upon Mike. The most careful driver in all God's world, including any sane, small, quiet, butter-and-milk

producing country you'd want to name. Mike, all innocence—a saint!—when compared to those drivers who
switch on paranoia each time they fuse themselves to their
bucket seats in Los Angeles, Mexico City, or Paris!

*We hear various cars roar by, see flashes of light, hear
honking of horns.* MIKE *philosophically watches the
imaginary cars pass, waving them on with calm good
nature.*

Compare him to those blind men who, forsaking tin cups
and white canes, but still wearing their Hollywood dark
glasses, laugh insanely down the Via Veneto in Rome,
shaking brake-drum linings like carnival serpentine out
their race-car doors!

*During the above we hear the approach of a carnival of
cars, sput-sputs, hornets, wasps, swarms of big and little
blasters and blowers, and mixed with it hilarious voices,
shouting, many horns: picnic day at Indianapolis Speed-
way.*

MIKE *smiles at it all, blinking gently, driving along between the bogs. The voices, horns, motors avalanche
away into silence.*

THE YOUNG MAN *circles the car, turning it till* MIKE *faces
another way, before he continues the lecture.*

But Mike, now . . . See his easy hands loving the wheel
in a slow clocklike turning . . .

*The car makes a vast, lovely swirl around a bend in the
road—we can guess as much by the magical rotation of*
MIKE's *arms.*

Listen to his mist-breathing voice all night-quiet as he
charms the road . . .

MIKE *(singing)*: "As I was walking
Through Dublin City . . .
Around the hour of twelve at night . . ."

THE YOUNG MAN: . . . his foot a tenderly benevolent pat on the whispering accelerator . . .

MIKE *(singing softly)*: "I saw a maid,
So fair was she . . ."

THE YOUNG MAN: . . . never a mile under thirty, never two miles over . . .

MIKE *(singing)*: ". . . combing her hair by candlelight."

> THE YOUNG MAN *steps back into the car and settles himself, looking kindly on this older man.*

THE YOUNG MAN: Mike, Mike, and his steady boat gentling a mild sweet lake where all Time slumbers. Look: compare. And bind such a man to you with summer grasses, gift him with silver, shake his hand warmly at each journey's end.

MIKE *(reaching for the hand brake)*: Here we are! The Royal Hibernian Hotel!

THE YOUNG MAN: What a fine lilting name!

MIKE *(thinks on it)*: The Royal Hibernian Hotel! Sure, it falls right off the tongue!

> THE YOUNG MAN *climbs out.*

THE YOUNG MAN: It does. See you tomorrow, Mike!

> *The car drives off into darkness.*

MIKE: God willing!!

> *The car is gone.* THE YOUNG MAN *turns and walks in a grand circle, vanishing for a moment behind a curtain but reappearing on the instant, checking his watch.*

THE YOUNG MAN: Now. Let twenty-three hours of sleep, breakfast, lunch, supper, late nightcap pass, and here I come again, another midnight . . .

He suits word to action, going in and coming out the door far stage right.

Out the door of that Georgian mansion, to tread down the steps to feel Braillewise in fog for the car which I know bulks there.

The stage has darkened during part of this speech, and in the dark, unseen by the audience, the car has returned, MIKE in it, to center stage. We hear the car faintly now. The lights are beginning to come up as THE YOUNG MAN gropes forward.

MIKE: Ah, there you are, sir!

THE YOUNG MAN: Mike. *(To the audience)* I climb in. I give the door its slam.

He slams the door.

And *then* . . .

The car gives a great spasming jerk. THE YOUNG MAN grabs his hat, grabs the dashboard, grabs MIKE's knee.

Mike!

With a thunderous roar, the car is off, vibrating. The sound is furious. The black background behind the car rushes and flurries with lights and shadows; the car spins and turns.

Mike!

MIKE *(smiles benevolently):* Yes, sir.

THE YOUNG MAN: Mike!

MIKE: Yes, *sir!*

THE YOUNG MAN *(staring):* Sixty miles an hour, Mike.

MIKE: Seventy!

THE YOUNG MAN: Now it's seventy-five!

MIKE: Is it!

THE YOUNG MAN: Eighty!

MIKE *(looks):* So it is!

THE YOUNG MAN: Eighty-five! Eighty-five!

MIKE: Can that be possible?

THE YOUNG MAN: It is, it is.

> *The car turns in a great thunder of shadowy light, in*
> *huge riverings of hill and meadow thrown on the back-*
> *drop.*
>
> THE YOUNG MAN *leaps out and watches the car with*
> MIKE *bent over the wheel gripping it hard, his smile a*
> *leer.*

It is, it was, indeed! There went Mike and me with him!
Ninety full miles an hour! From the blazing mouth of the
cannon we bounced, skidded, cast ourselves in full stoning
ricochet down the paths, over the bogs, through the trees!
I felt all Ireland's grass put down its ears when we, with a
yell, jumped over a rise!

MIKE: Ninety-five! Do you see that! Ninety-five!

> *The car whirls, rushes.*

THE YOUNG MAN: Mike, I thought—Mike!

> MIKE *puffs his cigarette feverishly. Pink light comes and*
> *goes on his creased face.*

Mike was changed as if the Adversary himself had squeezed and molded and fired him with a dark hand. There he was, whirling the wheel roundabout, over-around, here we frenzied under trestles, there knocked crossroad signs spinning like weathercocks! I studied Mike's fine face. A fine face no longer!

He moves close. The motor sounds die away so we can hear better, study better. The car still rocks and turns slightly this way and that while THE YOUNG MAN *philosophizes, standing beside it, perhaps pointing in at* MIKE's *face with a flashlight.*

The wisdom drained from it. The eyes, neither gentle nor philosophical. The mouth neither tolerant nor at peace. It was a face washed raw, a scalded peeled potato.

Thunder up for a moment. Flashing lights. MIKE *leans avidly forward. The thunder fades.* THE YOUNG MAN *is back in the car now.*

MIKE *(loud, raucous):* Well, how you been since, sir!

THE YOUNG MAN: Mike, your voice! It's changed!

MIKE: Changed?!

THE YOUNG MAN *(to the audience):* A clarion, a trumpet, all iron and brassy tin! Gone the warm fire. Gone the gentle grass. *(To* MIKE *now)* Mike, has a dire thing come into your life, a sickness, a sorrow, a sore affliction?

MIKE *(amazed, loud):* Now why would you think that?

THE YOUNG MAN *(touches the car):* And, Mike, is this the same car you drove last night?

MIKE: None other!

THE YOUNG MAN (to the audience): But it was changed, too. This car, this crusty old beggar that had been content to stroll along, careful of its breath and bones, now thundered toward Hell as if to warm itself at some special blaze there.

THE YOUNG MAN scans MIKE now, carefully.

Hold on, I got it! Mike! It's the first night of Lent!

MIKE: It is, sir.

THE YOUNG MAN: Well, then, remembering your Lenten promise, why's that cigarette in your mouth?

MIKE casts his eyes down on the smoke jiggling on his lip and shrugs.

MIKE: Ah—I give up the ither.

There is a long moment during which THE YOUNG MAN stares.

THE YOUNG MAN: The other?

MIKE (nodding wisely): The ither.

THE YOUNG MAN pulls as far back in his seat as possible to look at MIKE. Suddenly he reaches forward and twists the key in the ignition. With a great squealing, MIKE brings the car to a halt, surprised but not angry.

Why, will you tell me, did you do that?

In silence, the two sit there.

THE YOUNG MAN: Mike, for two hundred nights we have ridden together.

MIKE: True.

THE YOUNG MAN: And each night as I came from my employer's house I drank, at the door, a fiery douse of Scotch or bourbon "against the chill."

MIKE: A reasonable precaution.

THE YOUNG MAN: Then I walked out to this cab where sat a man, yourself, who, during all the long winter evening's wait for me to phone for your services, had *lived* in Heeber Finn's pub.

MIKE: You might say, it's me office!

THE YOUNG MAN *(slaps his own brow):* Fool!

MIKE: Who is?

THE YOUNG MAN: I am!

MIKE: And why?

THE YOUNG MAN: Because, Mike, because there in Heeber Finn's while you waited, you took onto yourself—a mellowness. And that mellowness distilled itself down in a slow rain that damped your smoldering nerves. It colored your cheeks, warmed your eyes soft, lowered your voice to a husking mist, and spread in your chest to slow your heart to a gentle jog-trot.

MIKE: Ah, I wish the Guinness family could hear you!

THE YOUNG MAN: It loosened your hands on the wheel and sat you with grace and ease as you gentled us through fogs and mists that kept us and Dublin apart. And all the while, Mike, the liquor *I* drank stopped me from ever detecting the scent of any spirits on *your* breath.

MIKE: What are you leading up to, sir?

THE YOUNG MAN: This, Mike! Tonight, the first night of Lent, for the first time in all the nights I've driven with you, you are sober!

He lets this sink in. MIKE *lets it sink in, too, aghast.*

MIKE: By God now, that's true.

THE YOUNG MAN: And all those other two hundred nights you weren't driving slow and careful and easy just for my safety—

MIKE: Well——

THE YOUNG MAN: —but because of the gentle warm spirits sloping now on this side, now on that side of you, as we took the long scything curves.

MIKE *(as if revealing something):* If you *must* know, yes; I *was* drunk all of them nights.

They both sit and look at each other for a long moment.

THE YOUNG MAN: And now you've given up liquor for Lent?

MIKE *(nods righteously):* You've noticed the improvement?

There is a moment of critical silence.

THE YOUNG MAN: Drive on, Mike.

MIKE *starts the car with a roar. They thunder on, rocking silently,* THE YOUNG MAN *studying the older.*

MIKE: And here we are! Dublin's Fair City!

He stops the car. THE YOUNG MAN *gets thoughtfully out. He looks around at the imaginary city. He speaks to the audience.*

THE YOUNG MAN: Dublin's fair city. Oh, who *really* knows the Irish, say I, and which half of them is which? Mike?

(Turns to look at the man) Which Mike is the real Mike? Which is the Mike that *everyone* knows? *(Gasps, shakes his head as at a foul vision)* I will not think on it. There is only one Mike for me. That one that Ireland shaped herself with her weathers and waters, her seedings and harvestings, her brans and mashes, her brews, bottlings, and swiggings. If you ask what makes the Irish what they are, I'd point on down the road *(Points)* and tell where you turn to find Heeber Finn's. *(Turns)* Mike?

MIKE: Sir?

THE YOUNG MAN: Wait here a second!

> THE YOUNG MAN *runs offstage. He comes running back out a moment later, something hidden under his coat.*

Will you do me a favor, Mike?

MIKE: Name it!

> THE YOUNG MAN *winces at the loudness of that voice.*

THE YOUNG MAN: Here.

MIKE: What's that, sir?

> MIKE *blinks at the bottle* THE YOUNG MAN *has brought from hiding.*

THE YOUNG MAN: A bottle of whisky.

MIKE: I rarely see a whole bottle of it. That's why I didn't recognize—

THE YOUNG MAN: Mike, this is the first night of Lent, right? Now . . . on the second night of Lent—

MIKE: Tomorrow night?

THE YOUNG MAN: On the second night of Lent, when you come to pick me up, in Kilcock, will you *drink* this, Mike?

MIKE: Do you know what you're doing?

THE YOUNG MAN: Tempting you, Mike.

MIKE *(sore torn between):* You are indeed.

THE YOUNG MAN: Take it, Mike.

MIKE: Ah, God, it's Lent.

THE YOUNG MAN: Only the first night.

MIKE: You said that before, but with repetition it makes sense.

THE YOUNG MAN: Give something *else* up!

MIKE: Ah, Jesus, in all of Ireland, there's not so much joy, beauty, and riotous pleasure about you can count them on more than five fingers! Gimme the damn thing!

THE YOUNG MAN: Good old Mike!

MIKE *(eyeing the bottle):* Do I drink it *all?*

THE YOUNG MAN: Or as much as will turn Mr. Hyde into Dr. Jekyll!

MIKE: How's that?

THE YOUNG MAN *(rephrasing it):* Enough so Mike will come for me tomorrow night, instead of you.

MIKE: Mike instead of *me? I'm* Mike. Michael Finneran Seamus Kelly!

THE YOUNG MAN: *Are* you?

> *He peers in at the fellow.* MIKE *gets his meaning, uncorks the bottle, takes a long swig.*

MIKE: Ah!

He takes another swig as THE YOUNG MAN *beams.* MIKE *leans out, his voice immediately softer, mellower.*

Is that better?

THE YOUNG MAN: Mike, Mike you're back!

MIKE *(nods slowly):* I was long away.

THE YOUNG MAN: You were!

They clench hands in a great shake, steadfast, true.

MIKE: Here now, take these precious bits of pure gold!

He shoves over his cigarette pack.

THE YOUNG MAN *(taking them):* Thanks, Mike.

MIKE *(gently):* Ah, shut up.

THE YOUNG MAN: See you tomorrow?

MIKE: If we're both alive.

THE YOUNG MAN: Do you doubt we will be?

MIKE *(with a last swig):* Strange—I'm thinking now—I'll live forever.

He drives off, waving beautifully. THE YOUNG MAN *watches the car go. He lights one of* MIKE's *cigarettes, studies it, studies the smoke on the air.*

THE YOUNG MAN: The Irish? The Irish. Here they come out of the mist. There they vanish into the rain.

He calls into the growing darkness.

Michael Finneran Seamus Kelly! *Who* and *what* are *you?*

He listens.

No answer. And *(Checks watch)*—already, look! It's the *second* day of Lent! So—what am *I* giving up?

He looks at the cigarette pack, rips it open.

What indeed?!

He tears the cigarettes apart, sprinkles the tobacco about, beaming. A harp plays in the darkness offstage. THE YOUNG MAN, *hearing it, laughs and shrugs.*

All right, all right! Let the harp play all it wants! I'm done, finished, through!

He moves briskly for the exit stage right as the harp lilts up playing a zestful reel. Just before exiting, THE YOUNG MAN *turns about once, and maybe clicks his heels. When he is gone, from the darkness* MIKE *reappears on his throne, in his car, swinging back out in one long wonderful slow curve.* MIKE's *smile is mellow. The motor is quiet. The harp plays gently now, as* MIKE *vanishes back into the Irish dark, and on away toward . . .*

THE END

A Clear
View of an
Irish Mist

CHARACTERS

HEEBER FINN

KATHLEEN (HIS WIFE)

OLD MAN

CASEY

TIMULTY

NOLAN

FATHER LEARY

HOOLIHAN (THE SALESMAN)

NOONAN

O'HARA

KELLY

At the rise of curtain we see the bar of Heeber Finn's pub somewhere deep in Ireland's fogs and rains, deserted in the early-morning hour. For a change, a rosy glare comes through the stained-glass windows to either side of the bar; the day has begun with rare weather.

HEEBER FINN *enters, breathing the good air, scratching himself, yawning, fully dressed for a day of business. He looks about at the silent room.*

FINN: Ah, there you are, waiting for it all to begin. What will happen today? Only God knows in the morning. By ten tonight *I'll* know. Some day I should set it down.

He moves about, arranging the chairs.

HIS WIFE *(entering):* Set what down?

FINN: All that happens, Katy, in a single day with the doors open and the world flocking in.

HIS WIFE: Would you rather write it or live it?

FINN: Since you put it that way—living's best.

HIS WIFE: Live and *work*. I wish you'd do more of that. There's much needs mending here. That chair leans favoring the left, the table leans favoring the right. . . .

FINN *(polishing)*: Playing with these spigots is my work!

HIS WIFE: And you play them fine, like the organist at the Variety Cinema in Cork, but—

FINN: *But,* Woman! It's opening time!

HIS WIFE *(checking)*: Ten seconds after.

FINN *(hustling)*: Wait till I get set up! Peep through the door! What do you see?

She peeps.

HIS WIFE: A band of hoodlums, as is usual, elbowing each other and smacking their lips.

FINN: Well, what are you waiting for?

HIS WIFE *(peeking through a chink)*: It does me good to make them stay out in the cold a bit overtime.

FINN: You've a hard heart!

HIS WIFE: I thought you only worried about my soft behind.

She fiddles with the latch. There is a groan of relief from outside.

Ah, listen to them craitures stir, will ya? Like so many cows in need of milking!

She fiddles the latch again, smiling. Another groan from outside.

They're fairly seething!

FINN: Inhuman woman, let be!

She unlocks, unbolts, and lets the Red Sea in.

HIS WIFE: One at a time! No hurry!

THE OLD MAN *(entering indignant):* One at a time? No hurry? What does she mean?

CASEY: Out of the way, Woman!

TIMULTY: Lift me to the bar, I'm too weak to make it alone!

NOLAN: I'm famished!

FINN: Come get it, Men!

THE OLD MAN: Finn, why the delay? You opened twenty seconds late!

HIS WIFE *(snorting):* Twenty seconds! The shame of it!

She exits.

THE OLD MAN: Has she got the humors?

FINN: When *hasn't* she?

NOLAN: Women!

THE OLD MAN: I'm glad you said that. Why is it, when a ship goes down, it's always women and children first to the lifeboats? Shouldn't it be the other way round?

CASEY: Oh, my wife wouldn't mind going down with the ship. The question is: Would the ship mind going down with *her?*

THE OLD MAN: I think we have found a proper subject to converse on for the day.

All drink, assenting.

CASEY: Break out the cards, we'll have a game!

All move away into the next room, dragging chairs, flourishing a deck of cards, carrying their drinks, laughing and warmly joyous. After the brief riot, there is a little storm of silence in the pub. THE WIFE *appears with a basket, on her way out to shop. She peers into the next room, sniffs.*

HIS WIFE: Well, the avalanche is fair started down the mountain!

FINN *eyes her but she will not be eyed and goes off, away.*
Another silent moment. FINN *polishes glassware. Then:*
The doors open. It is FATHER LEARY, *from the church across the way.*

FINN: Father Leary, come in! We don't see you often!

FATHER: I'm glad to hear that. I was beginning to worry.

FINN: Will it be the Same?

FATHER: First you say you don't see me often, then you ask if it'll be the Same!

FINN: No offense, Father. What'll it be?

FATHER: The Usual.

FINN *(pouring):* Begging your pardon, Father, but what's the difference between the *Same* and the *Usual?*

FATHER *(drinking): Same* is too blunt, cold, hard a word. *Usual* is—well—more savory, at ease, you can roll it about on your tongue. *(He savors the word)* Us-u-al. Do you see?

FINN: As far as I need to, Father. And how's business? I mean—the Church, are people finding their way there through all the fog lately?

FATHER: If they don't, I'll build hellfires to give them light.

FINN: Oh, you can do that, all right. You know, Father, I was thinking just the other day, you and me—is much alike. No offense.

FATHER *(pausing in midsip):* It's too early to tell. Go on.

FINN: I mean, the things you hear in the confessional and the things I hear behind the bar. There is a rough equivalation, now.

FATHER: Very rough.

FINN *(sotto voce):* And neither of us can *breathe a word.*

FATHER: Come now, Finn, you'll be putting on lace next.

FINN: Father, no word that's spoken goes back across this bar. I'm proud of my own peculiar vow of silence. If the church ain't open, Heeber Finn's is.

FATHER *(controlling himself beautifully):* You must be absolutely groaning with truckloads of sin.

FINN: I got me share.

FATHER: You don't imply now, do you, that you're in competition with the Church? Eh?

FINN: Heaven forbid! And forgive my pride, but maybe I've eased your burden a bit, Father.

FATHER: Do you mean by that that some sins get waylaid here that I never hear about?

FINN: I only imply, Father, that I oil their tonsils so they can tell it better by the time they get over to you, thus cutting down the fearsome time you spend cooped up in the box—

FATHER: Why, you're almost an annex to the Church, it seems!

FINN: Now look what I've done—made you mad.

FATHER: I'm not mad, Finn, just surprised, and mad at myself . . . for I thought I was over being surprised at the duplicity of man. You did come on me sudden, though, and I'd best leave.

He reaches in his pocket.

FINN *(hastily):* Put it in the poorbox, Father.

FATHER: I will!

FINN: Come again for the—er—Usual, Father!

Half out the door, FATHER LEARY *turns, frowning.*

FATHER: Not the *Usual,* man! *(A beat)*—The *Same!*

The wickets slam. He's gone.
   FINN *busies himself, stacking glasses and wiping the bar. As he does so, from a distance a high clear tenor voice is heard, approaching. There is also the sound of footsteps coming near. The song being sung is as follows:*

THE SALESMAN'S VOICE *(Off):* "All through life
Mid storm and strife . . .
With maid or wife,
It's the thinkin'

Not the drinkin'
Makes it go."

> *The voice stops. The wickets open. A* SALESMAN *stands looking in and about the pub.*
> FINN *has frozen at the words of the song. He does not turn now as the stranger advances easily toward the bar.*

THE SALESMAN: Though I must admit, there be occasions when the very wheels of Juggernaut are kept turning with drink. A Guinness, please.

> *This friendly sally does not unfreeze* FINN *at all; he draws the drink without looking up.*
> THE SALESMAN *looks at* FINN *and senses diplomacy is needed.*

I see that your spine is all one piece because of my song.

FINN *(turning at last):* The song was a touch subversive of my business.

THE SALESMAN *(sings):* "It's the thinkin'
And the drinkin'
Makes it go."
Is that better?

FINN *(putting the drink on the bar):* Why didn't you sing it that way to start?

THE SALESMAN: I'm a proud man.

FINN *(letting the drink go):* Pride's no sin, if it has to do with your business. What line are you in?

THE SALESMAN: I guess you'd call me a Salesman of Philosophy.

FINN: Now, how do you sell *that?*

THE SALESMAN: Here!

He swings a small case onto the bar.

Do you know the saying "Infinite riches in a little room"?

FINN: I know it now.

THE SALESMAN: Well, in this little case is the "furniture" I'm selling.

FINN: For a doll house, then?

THE SALESMAN: No, to decorate the palace of man's mind!

He opens up the case and puts forth a single item on the counter.

FINN *(confounded):* That's *it?*

THE SALESMAN *(proudly):* That's it! Fine hand-painted bone porcelain.

FINN: Don't look like much to me. *(Moving around front)* Furniture, you say.

He stops. He approaches the little object slowly, peering at it. It is about eight inches long and three inches high. There is a single word on it, a word in white letters on a black background.

(Spelling out loud) T . . . H . . . it says . . . I and N and K. THINK! Is that all?

THE SALESMAN: I'm inclined to say it's everything!

FINN *(half-suspicious):* What does it *mean?*

THE SALESMAN: Just what it says, friend. Think. *Think.* THINK!

THE SALESMAN's *voice grows in timbre and volume each time he says the word. Then he subsides and sips his Guinness.*

FINN (*uneasily*): Ye-ess, I see what you're getting at. But what do you do with a bit of furniture like that? To what purpose is it?

THE SALESMAN: To what purpose? God save me!

Before FINN *can stop him, he is around the bar and placing the little sign on top of a Guinness barrel.*

There! Now, pretend you're your own best customer, and I'm yourself, the bartender. You got your drink in your hand.

He nudges the drink. FINN *takes and holds the glass.*

You sip your drink.

FINN *sips.*

You raise your eyes——

FINN *raises his eyes.*

And what do you see?

FINN: "Think"?

THE SALESMAN: Right! You drink some more.

FINN *drinks.*

You stare at that little sign . . . and . . . first thing you know . . . you're . . .

FINN: Thinking!

THE SALESMAN: Ah, now you got the sun up. You're standing in the light!

FINN (*sips, stares; sips, stares*): Ah . . . ah . . . yes . . . I see.

THE SALESMAN: I *know* you *do!*

FINN *looks at the man with fresh admiration.*

FINN: You be a kind of intellectual, then?

THE SALESMAN: I—er—*knocked* at the door of Trinity College!

FINN: What stopped your plunging through?

THE SALESMAN *refills both glasses, playing bartender with a fine air.*

THE SALESMAN: Well, I shaped it up in my mind. Hoolihan, I said to myself, why put off helping others half your life? Why not start this day? How? I said. Well, I said, what's mainly wrong with the world? What? I said. No one stops to think any more, I said. And for lack of stopping to think, what happens?

FINN *(leaning toward him):* A great lot, one supposes.

THE SALESMAN: Wars, famines, depressions, murderous impulses, bad livers, short breaths, unwanted children, and marriages best kept running on whisky for fear of seeing the true aspect!

FINN *(enchanted):* Say that again.

THE SALESMAN: If you don't mind, I'll let the echoes die.

FINN: Right! That's a beautiful thing there, the little bit of porcelain and that single word. Already I feel a popping in my ears, like I'm on a mountain! It's amazing how full of thoughts I suddenly am.

THE SALESMAN: Think what it'll do for your customers, then, and the brand of talk they'll spray at one another! In one hour, in this room, the humidity will rise ten points!

FINN: All I do is leave it set right there, eh?

THE SALESMAN: Right there. Nothing to wind, nothing to grease or oil, nothing to get out of whack. A simple machine it is, and'll make men's minds "GO"!

FINN: I'll take one! Wait! You *are* selling them, aren't you?

THE SALESMAN: Not exactly. You can rent this for just ten shillings a month!

FINN: That's dear!

THE SALESMAN: If it raises your business twenty shillings a month, you're still ten ahead!

FINN *(amazed):* Will it *do* that?

THE SALESMAN: Who can deny thinking men blow off steam, and what makes steam? Water! And what is beer and ale and stout but mostly water?

FINN: You've gone below the surface, I see.

THE SALESMAN: Study pays. Try it. If it don't work out after four weeks, I'll buy the damn thing off you at half-price or —er—thereabouts; you'll be little out of pocket!

FINN *is still grudging.*

Hold on, let me sweeten the deal.

He pulls forth three more objects and sets them up on the bar.

Rent one, you get them all!

FINN *stares.*

FINN *(reading): STOP! CONSIDER! THINK! DO!*

THE SALESMAN: Ain't that a fine quartet?

FINN: Explain them to me!

THE SALESMAN: Well, before you can *THINK,* you got to *CONSIDER* what you want to think about, right?

FINN *(nods):* The fog parts.

THE SALESMAN: *After* you consider what to think and think it, thinking's no good, is it, if you don't *DO?*

FINN: By God, you're right. You might as well arrange a flower bouquet and throw it in the River Liffey as think and not *do.* But you've not explained the first—

THE SALESMAN: The first is *most* important! You must *STOP* whatever else you're doing, scratching your ear and notching your belt or whatever, mustn't you, in order to *CONSIDER THINKING* and *DOING?*

FINN: That's it, bull's-eye on! I'll take the lot!

> FINN *gestures frantically, for he is still "customer" outside the bar, while behind the bar is* THE SALESMAN.

Ring up *No Sale* and take out ten shillings before I regain my sanity!

> THE SALESMAN *is to the register like a shot. Bang! A bell rings, the red* NO SALE *sign jumps up.*

THE SALESMAN: How about another?

FINN: Don't mind if I do!

> THE SALESMAN *pours for both. They hoist them.*

THE SALESMAN: To the Brave New World of this afternoon!

FINN: So soon?

THE SALESMAN: You'll note the difference within hours. To thought-provocation, to the pub called *Heeber Finn's,* to the Oracle at Delphi in a way, to this cavern of philosophers—

FINN: Tavern of philosophers—that has a ring to it.

THE SALESMAN: Cavern.

FINN *(nettled):* *Cavern*'s what I said! A cavern brimming over with philosophers, eh?

THE WIFE *(walking through):* Philosophers? Is that the same as hoboes?

She is gone.

THE SALESMAN: Who was that?

FINN *(eyes shut):* I dread to tell you.

THE SALESMAN *(nods understandingly):* *(Recovers briskly)* To Finn's then, where people stop! consider! think! and *do!*

FINN: I'll drink to *those* damn things, any day.

They drink.

THE SALESMAN *(walking):* Well, I'll be off!

FINN *(worried):* You won't sell any more of these in the village, now?

THE SALESMAN: Nor in the next. I like to drop one stone in the pond and watch the lovely ripples—*spread! (He illustrates)*

FINN *(awed):* Your father was a poet.

THE SALESMAN *(eyebrows up):* Uncanny! You guessed it! Good day!

FINN: And a fine one to *you,* Hoolihan!

HOOLIHAN *exits.*

THE SALESMAN *(singing):* "In life, in strife,
With maid, or wife

It's the *thinking,*
Not the *drinking,*
Makes it . . . *Go!"*

He is gone.
Now FINN, *alone, exhales with pleasure. He mops off each of the little ceramic signs, exhales on them, shines them again—then, like a painter, looks about at the empty bar, looking left, left center, center, right center, right.*

FINN *(to himself):* Now where is best for each . . . ?
Well . . .

He snatches one and places it far over at stage right. The sign reads STOP!

When they come in the door they should see this right off!

What's next? Well, when their little eyes move on over along, the next thing they should see is *CONSIDER,* right? Right!

He places CONSIDER *right center.*

New let's think where to put *THINK.*

He picks THINK *up, deliberates, puts it back down on top the Guinness tap-barrel.*

Right where he had it is best! And last of all, *DO* should go over by the door on the other side, so people, on the way out, will *do* things. Right? I think it is!

He locates DO *where he has said he'd put it and stands back again to survey his tasks finished.*
    At which point his WIFE *happens through. He flinches as if he had expected her to throw scalding water on him and makes elaborately casual attempts to look*

calm, collected, and not guilty of putting out hard money for strange devices.

He saunters toward the bar, turning in a circle past his WIFE, *who also turns in a circle, suspicious of the smell of him.*

THE WIFE: Well?

He reaches the bar, polishes the first sign, STOP!

FINN: Well, indeed!

He moves over to polish the second, CONSIDER. She turns away and huffs out. He flings down the rag.

Damn, she didn't see! Or did she see and disapprove? All right, steady, Finn, a calm mind in a calm body, eh? *(Pours)* Here's calmness. *(Drinks)* Ah.

At which point the doors fling wide, and a man enters, somewhat in his cups. He freezes and stares.

FINN *looks at the man, follows his gaze to see what he is looking at and finds it is the sign: STOP!*

The man sways there a moment, blinking, debating, then wheels about.

I——

The man charges back out, gone.

Now, what the——? Well, where was I? Oiling the stormy seas. Another drop of oil, eh?

He gives himself a drop. He rearranges one of the signs, smiles at it, pats it.

The same half-drunk man enters again, is again transfixed at what he sees, wheels, and goes out.

I'll be . . . Now that's most peculiar. That *was* Tom Noonan, wasn't it? *(Shrugs)* Ah, he'll be back.

We can see NOONAN, *outside, warming up for another try. He steels himself, takes a deep breath, and bursts through the doors again. He is half across the barroom floor, at full steam, when his eyes fix to the dire sign and he cries in loud dismay, almost a wail:*

NOONAN: *Stop!*

and circles around to flail out and is gone again, this time for good.

FINN *(going after him):* Tom Noonan, oh, *Tom!* *(stops, bewildered)* Gone. Did he say "Stop"? Yes. Must have misunderstood. That one sign wasn't meant for *him.*

He goes over and peers at the sign.

(Muses) Stop . . .

He is wracked with indecision. He picks up the sign, puts it down, picks it up again.

Well, it might be best, for the first few hours, anyway, to turn this one around so no one can see it, right off. Later, I'll turn it back. It's not really the most important sign, anyway, is it? No!

He turns the sign around so we can't read it.

There! Now we still have *(Points)* CONSIDER! THINK! DO! *(Rubs hands)* All right, world, I'm ready for you! I'd best tell the boys to come in and—

FATHER LEARY *enters, or rather, almost backs in through the door.*

There you are, Father Leary!

FATHER *(bemused):* Am I? So I am. On my way to Mrs. Kelly's I just saw Tom Noonan on the street.

FINN *(suddenly uneasy)*: Noonan? Tom?

FATHER: Run up to me and insisted right there on the curb I take his confession!

FINN *(attempting cheer)*: *Did* he? That's nice.

FATHER: Nice, but not like Tom. He wouldn't take no. Held onto my elbow, he did. So I shut my eyes and pretended not to know and heard him out!

FINN: Fast thinking, Father!

FATHER: The Archbishop would jump straight up if he heard.

FINN: I won't tell him.

FATHER *(looking sharp)*: Do you *know* him?

FINN *(pulling his horns in)*: Now that you mention it, no . . .

FATHER *(baffled)*: It was over in a trice and Noonan gone. Said he'd stop this and stop that and stop two of those and three of the next-worst. I can't tell you *what* he said he'd stop, of course, but stop it was, all up and down the line.

FINN *has backed over to the counter to hide the sign with his back. He is edgy.*

FINN: Think of *that*.

FATHER: I *am* thinking of it, Finn.

FINN *has the "machine," the sign, in his hands behind his back now.*

What's that behind your back, Finn?

FINN: Why, Father, it's—

Crash! The damn thing has fallen to the floor. FINN *turns to look at the shards. He bends to pick them up.*

Why, it's kind of a—jigsaw puzzle, Father.

FATHER: I like puzzles.

FINN: Ah, you couldn't work this one—

FATHER: Let me try.

> FINN *reluctantly puts the pieces on the bar.*

That don't look so difficult, now, Finn.

FINN *(to himself):* More's the pity.

FATHER: Eh?

FINN: Will you have a drink while you work it, Father?

FATHER *(working):* This piece would seem to go here . . . Eh? Yes, Finn, bless you, man . . . and this piece here. . . .

> FINN *pours.* FATHER LEARY *tinkers.*

. . . as I was saying. Noonan now . . . right on the street! Nothing wrong really, I suppose, confessing him in the open, God's everywhere . . . but still . . . it shook me . . . why should old *Tom?* Stop *this* I will! he said, and stop *that!* and stop the others! *(He tinkers with the bits)* Put this piece over here . . . and move this about . . . There . . . it seems to be a word, Finn.

FINN *(mock surprise):* Fancy that.

> LEARY *shoves some more bits about.*

FATHER: S would seem to be the first letter of the puzzle.

FINN: Are you sure?

FATHER: S . . . T—that's a T, ain't it? *(He moves a last shard in place)* O . . . P.

FINN *(brightly):* "Stop!"

FATHER *(disquieted):* I can read, Finn.

FINN: I've always spoke well of your education, sir.

FATHER *(musing):* "Stop," Finn. *Stop.* Have you heard that word before in the last three minutes?

FINN: You may have used it, sir.

FATHER: Tom Noonan, didn't *he* use it, too?

FINN: We mustn't talk of it, Father. The vows of the confessional—

FATHER: *Finn!*

FINN *(quietly):* Yes, sir?

FATHER: Was Tom Noonan in here lately?

FINN: Of recent date, Father?

FATHER: Date, hell, man. The last hour?

FINN: Well, in and out, Father.

FATHER: Which is it, in *or* out?

FINN: It became a trifle circuitous, Father, to coin a word.

FATHER: *Circuitous?* Do you infer he weaved in circles, then?

FINN: I only infer, Father, he made one arc coming and another going. Six arcs in all, Father.

FATHER: Broken down, you say he arrived three times—

FINN: And left just as many—

FATHER: In how long a time?

FINN: It was remarkable for its shortness, Father. He came and went, arrived and departed, came through the entrance and looked for the exit.

FATHER *(toying with the reconstructed sign)*: How do you account for his behavior, Finn?

FINN: His wife had been nagging him, sir.

FATHER: And?

FINN: And he had been drinking hard at it, down the road, I suppose, at Rooney's pub.

FATHER: Go on.

FINN: And they heaved him out, no doubt, and he came up this way seeking more of the Same or the Usual, begging your pardon, Father. And when he came in the door, I can only figure he saw this sign, sir.

FATHER: This *sign* made him go out and in three times, and then run to me to confess in broad daylight?

FINN: Yes, sir. I figure for thirty years now, Noonan's wife has yelled at him, STOP this, STOP that! STOP the next best and the least-worst and the half-between. "STOP!" she yells. But mostly *STOP DRINKING!* It adds up, down the years. Well, today, Noonan hears "STOP!" from Rooney's bar, too, STOP! no more ale, whisky, or whatever, STOP! and threw him out! So he comes up here, shell-shocked, it's reached the point, after thirty years of his wife screaming and Rooney yelling. And he comes in the door and what does he see?

FATHER: *S-T-O-P.*

FINN: Right, Father. And that made a little drive-shaft go loose in Noonan and he headed straight off for you, sir.

FATHER: You sound rather proud of the whole thing, Finn.

FINN: Shouldn't I be, Father? A thirty-year sinner reformed? A lost soul changed—?

FATHER *(impatiently)*: Ah, let be! *(muses)* Finn?

FINN: Sir?

FATHER: I don't know how to explain it, but I have this unearthly sensation, lately, each time I drop by that some day I'll come in and find you selling Bibles and holding services.

FINN: Perish the thought, Father. I just redecorated the place a bit.

He waves his hand at the other signs.

FATHER *(staring)*: God help us, don't tell me there's more? *(Squints)* Does that say CONSIDER, Finn?

FINN: It does.

FATHER: And that THINK, and that one DO?

FINN: What eyes, for a man your age!

FATHER: Is fifty *old*, Finn?

FINN: It's neither in nor out of the casket. You'll be around a while, Father.

FATHER: I will, Finn, I will. And now suppose you tell me what these signs mean?

FINN *(trying to recall the spiel)*: Well, CONSIDER means . . . walk around, turn about . . . run your hand, run your eyes over a thing . . .

FATHER: What thing, Finn?

FINN: *Any*thing, sir.

FATHER: Did it ever strike you, Finn, that maybe there are some things should not be considered at all?

FINN: Like what, sir?

FATHER: Well, fornication, for one, if you force me to it!

FINN: That's a brave start, sir.

FATHER: Poverty's another. It must be borne, not considered. If you have no coal and no way to get coal and *never will have any coal,* as often happens at the church, believe me, I do not *consider* coal! Women, Mr. Finn, can have no part in my life, so I do not *consider* women. Travel, I will never travel, so I do not *consider* palm trees and sandy beaches and twanging guitars. And since I do not consider the above subjects as fit, to begin with, that takes us on to your next sign, Finn: *THINK.* Since I will not *consider* certain subjects to start with, that means they never become objects of my thought. I do not *THINK* about them.

FINN: That's what the salesman said, you got to consider first, pick a subject, before you can *THINK* about it.

FATHER: He was right. And thus, through disconsideration and unthoughtfulness, Finn, I am never tempted to climb the ladder of a stocking—

FINN: Father, you shock me!

FATHER: Sorry! Ladder of a *silk* stocking! Nor do I perspire for strawberry shortcakes, breathe hard for swimming in warm equatorial waters, or ask for more than this rough stuff on my back. If you consider too much, you think too much, and if you think too much you wind up *DOING,* Finn. Doing. Doing!

FINN: You're right, Father, that's how women, and other things, get done.

FATHER: Finn!

FINN: Sorry. It was off my tongue before I knew.

FATHER: It was! Now! *(The gimlet eye)* The salesman that sold you these, was he from the *north* of Ireland?

FINN: I think not.

FATHER: Were these articles *made* in Orange territory?

FINN: Why don't we look, sir?

He hastens the three objects over and puts them down before FATHER LEARY, *who peers.*

What do you see, Father?

FATHER: Hold on, I left my glasses at the rectory.

FINN: Borrow mine, Father—here!

He holds them out. FATHER LEARY *hesitates.*

Don't be afraid, Father. You won't see the world much different through these than through your own.

FATHER: I wouldn't be so sure, Finn! Do you see near or far?

FINN: A bit of both, Father. But it's best I leave the damn things off. Without my glasses, the world looks fine, sinners look less like Africans and more like angels, the shadows they cast are short and sweet, and the sun stays up till midnight.

FATHER: God help us, that kind of vision would turn a trough full of pigs into the Last Supper. Put your glasses on, man, and keep them on!

FINN: It's best to be a little blind in this sharp world, Father.

FATHER: Shut up, and give me the loan.

LEARY *gets the spectacles at last, puts them on, peers at the "machines."*

FINN: Well, *were* they made in the north of Ireland?

FATHER: No, the western part of the U.S.A.

FINN: That's good, Father.

FATHER: Is *California* good, Finn?

FINN: The north or the south of California, sir?

FATHER *(squints):* A town with the name of—Alhambra!

FINN *(truly enlightened): Alhambra!* Ain't that Spanish? And aren't the Spanish Catholic?

FATHER: They're a *variety* of Catholic, you might say.

FINN: Might? I always thought Catholic was Catholic!

FATHER: Finn, you talk like a blatherin' infant! There's types and sizes. There's Eye-talian Catholic, which is pretty good.

FINN: It is indeed!

FATHER: There's Spanish Catholic, which is fair.

FINN: Only fair?

FATHER: And there's French Catholics, which is hardly Catholic at all. It is rock-bottom Catholic, the fringe elements of the Church. Now if you want your *real* Catholic, it's here in Ireland he lives. Not that we don't sin; we do. Not that we're perfect; we're not. But there be varieties and varieties of Catholic, never forget, and the sad reflection of my life is there was never a Pope named Patrick!

FINN *(philosophically):* Ah, well, we had a Saint!

FATHER: I'm grateful, don't misunderstand.

FINN *(peering):* Alhambra, California, sounds Catholic enough to me.

FATHER: Do you have the facts and figures on church attendance in Alhambra, California, close at hand, Finn?

FINN: I do not, Father.

FATHER: Then button your lip and fill my glass.

FINN: What'll it be, Father, the Same or the Usual?

FATHER LEARY *glares.* FINN *subsides.* FATHER LEARY *peers.*

FATHER: It says The Monongaheela Gimcrack Novelty Company Inc. Monongaheela? That's pagan Indian, ain't it?

FINN: I wouldn't be surprised, Father.

FATHER: Are you *ever* surprised, Finn?

FINN: Like you, very rarely any more, Father.

FATHER: I wish you'd stop teaming us up, Finn. *(Reads)* "A Little of Something for Everybody" is the motto of this manufactory in Alhambra, California.

FINN *(savoring it):* "A Little of Something for Everybody"——

FATHER: Now, if that doesn't sound like the title for a Protestant sermon, I never heard one—

FINN: Oh, now, Father—

FATHER: Mind you, I don't say this manufactory put these signs out to make trouble in the world. No, far from it. In all innocence, I think they thought they was putting out lovely little mottoes such as *GOD BLESS OUR HOME,* which they were not. I forgive them their blind fumbling, Finn. But think of the misery they have probably spread in the world wherever these signs be!

FINN: I'm thinking on it. And I'm filled with remorse. You see, that salesman, he talked as good as you, Father. Yes, he did, he had a fine tongue, and first thing I knew I had the fevers.

FATHER: You know what you have to do now, Finn?

FINN: What, sir?

FATHER LEARY *nods at the three items on the bar, holds out his hand.*

(Groans) Oh, no.

FATHER: Oh, yes, Finn.

FINN: But I've only had them an hour, it's not been a true test, sir!

FATHER: Which is more important, the philosophy of this small town deep in green Ireland, or tuppence-ha'penny?

FINN: I wish it *was* tuppence-ha'penny, sir. Father, look—

He hands over the shards and one sign.

Take *STOP* and *CONSIDER* with you. Leave *THINK* and *DO* with me.

FATHER: Finn—

FINN: At the first sign of outbreak, unease, riot, or so much as a headache on the part of a villager, Father, you'll see these flying through the air onto the stones!

FATHER: Finn—

FINN: Twenty-four hours, then, just let me keep them *that* long. The world was made in six days, Father, but Heeber Finn sure won't undo it in one, will he?

FATHER LEARY *sighs, shaking his head, beaten.*

FATHER: Twenty-four hours, then. I don't want to be hard.

FINN *(smiling):* And you're not! You're a man of reason. Here's to you, Father!

FINN *drinks.*

FATHER LEARY *picks up the broken bits and the one sign, studies them, peers at the others, starts to say something, shakes his head, moves toward the door. At the door he pauses, his back to the bartender.*

FATHER: Finn?

FINN: Yes, sir?

FATHER: If you should need me . . . don't waste time thinking on it. Give a yell.

FINN: A helluva yell, Father.

FATHER: Come early, stay late, Finn.

And the priest is gone.

FINN *exhales and strides about the bar. He wipes his brow.*

FINN: Whew, Finn, whew! I'm shaved to the bone. 'Twill take a year for my beard to grow back! Well, what's the total? Two left out of four, but surely the most important of the whole kit. Where was I? Men! *Boys!*

He turns to shout through the door into the back room.

Is the game done? If not, bring it out here! A free round on the house!

VOICES: Free round! Outa the way, Men. Here we come, Finn!

The men surge out along the bar, gabbling, laughing.

THE OLD MAN: It's all in balances and weights, you get a man *so (Illustrates),* and thus, and he's in the ditch before he knows the fight is over!

CASEY: Women are cats, I said, born and bred in Africa, and shipped north to torment men in youth, middle age, and their dotage!

O'HARA: Meanness it is, keeps women alive long after a man, in his natural Christian goodness, has laid down with coins on his eyes—

FINN *(pouring):* Drink up!

The men drink. Each talks almost to himself. Each says, and all only half listen, their faces rosy fire.

KELLY: —worked in the pusstoffice selling stamps of all denominations . . . have you ever looked at stamps, man, close? A regular gallery of art in *one hour's* arrivals of mail from far countries . . .

The men, drinking, look around, notice the sign, THINK, *as the talk continues, pay no attention, and go on with their blarney.*

THE OLD MAN: —in the semicircular canals I heard once on the Radio Aerrean is this liquid which dances about . . . if you can tilt a man so his semicircular canals are off center, he'll get seasick, and—

KELLY: They had a fine stamp once from Portugal, and a girl on it naked as the palm of my hand and twice as limber . . .

The talk begins to die away during all the above and on through the next speeches. One by one, the men drop out of conversation.

THE OLD MAN: Then I said to him, about fighting . . . I don't remember what I said . . . hold on . . .

CASEY: My wife has six fingers on each hand and all claws. She——Well, that about describes . . . my . . . wife . . .

TIMULTY *(trailing off):* Well, the bog business ain't what it was. I've said my say, I guess . . .

KELLY *(fading away):* Then there was a stamp from . . . oh . . . but why bother . . .

O'HARA *(after a pause):* Women are mean. Put that in your pipe and smoke it.

THE OLD MAN: Well, now . . .

TIMULTY: Yes, sir . . .

KELLY: Drink . . .

They are all suddenly uneasy and shy.

CASEY: Six fingers and claws . . .

They all look at their glasses.

FINN: Drink up, boys!

THE OLD MAN *clears his throat.* O'HARA *blows his nose. They all watch him do this, for lack of anything else to do.*

TIMULTY: Old Man, tell us that joke about Nolan on the bridge.

THE OLD MAN: I can't remember.

O'HARA *clears his throat. The men shuffle their feet. The men peer around at each other.*

O'HARA: How about some more cards?

THE OLD MAN: We was *all* losing.

TIMULTY: That's hard to do, but we did it.

Another silence.

KELLY: Well?

CASEY: Well, indeed.

They move about uneasily. They peer at each other, glance at the sign, but say nothing.

THE OLD MAN *(in a spooky voice):* Hold on.

They all turn to look at him.

Listen.

They listen.

What do you hear?

CASEY: Nothing.

THE OLD MAN: That's it. Do you realize that this very moment and hour is the first time in thirty years there has been silence in Heeber Finn's pub?

FINN: Aw, now—

CASEY *(gasps):* He's right!

KELLY: By God, he *is!*

Everyone is spooked now. The men look around.

THE OLD MAN: A lull is a strange thing to an Irishman.

KELLY *(awed—sotto voce):* You can feel the damn thing, like a calm at sea.

They all feel it, together. FINN *is upset, but does not speak.*

THE OLD MAN *(whispering):* Strange . . .

CASEY: *Say* something, Kelly.

KELLY *(blinks):* What, for instance?

O'HARA *(whispering):* Ah, for God's sake, man, "what for instance," *what?* he says!

KELLY: *You* say something, Timulty.

He checks his watch.

TIMULTY: I got to get home.

THE OLD MAN *(astounded):* Home!

TIMULTY *walks, dazed, to the door.*

TIMULTY: I think so, anyway . . .

He wanders out. All look stunned at the doors as they swing shut.

FINN *(falsely hearty):* Here's another belt for everyone.

No answer. No enthusiasm.

KELLY: See you later . . .

FINN: Later?

And KELLY *is gone, too.*

O'HARA: I think I'll play solitaire . . .

He lays out the cards.

Ah, damn! I can see I've lost before I begin . . . So long, boys . . .

He leaves the cards and goes.

CASEY: For all I said of the little woman, she's mine and not well . . . I'd best go see how she does . . .

The rest follow, wordless, leaving only THE OLD MAN *and* FINN *at the bar.* FINN *comes out from behind the bar in shock, almost staggering with the blow of this great unnamed event.*

FINN: What happened?

THE OLD MAN *(puffs his pipe thoughtfully):* A strange thing, for sure.

FINN: Everybody was so happy, everybody talking, everybody bustling about like always and then, as if the Red Death Hisself had walked in all bones at the strike of twelve . . . hush . . . I never heard the likes in my life! Old Man . . .

THE OLD MAN: Hush up a bit, yourself.

> THE OLD MAN *walks about the pub, sniffing, probing, squinting.*
> *He glances now and then at the signs behind the bar and at last stops, looking at one of the signs.* THE OLD MAN *goes behind the bar and reaches up to handle the one sign.*

FINN: Don't!

THE OLD MAN: Why not?

FINN: I hate to see something shallow touching something deep, is all!

THE OLD MAN: Don't be so sure about your shallows and deeps, Heeber Finn! Have you stopped to think—*this* may be the cause?

FINN: The cause?

THE OLD MAN: Of the lull, man! Of the damn peace and quiet which suddenly befell this place? Of the becalming of this ship of yours!

FINN: *"Think"* did that? *THINK?*

THE OLD MAN: Think, Think, Think! Didn't you see their faces? I saw mine in the mirror, I watched it fall! I was talking along, fourteen to the dozen, when my eye spied that sign and my tongue went slower and I looked again and my lips tightened up on me and I read the *THINK!* again and the mud settled on the bottom of my brain! First thing I knew, I was "mum's the word," and so were the rest! I could see it come over them, they broke out in pale sweats! They been talking all their lives, man, and what did you do to them now?

FINN: I didn't do anything!

THE OLD MAN: Yes, you did; you asked them to think, think, think, what they was saying! That's more than enough to break a man's leg, his arm, his neck and then his back. Crippled them, you did. Called attention to their tongues and mouths. First time they had ever noticed they *had* tongues! First time they noticed they was actors, and they got stage fright! *Think* did it, man, think and nothing *but* think!

FINN *(lets out a loud cry of anguish)*: Ahhhh . . .

THE OLD MAN: Well may you groan. It's a sad day. Driving off old friends and pals. Scaring the wits out of them by showing them the marionette strings in their fingers and lips! How *could* you be so cruel, Finn?

THE OLD MAN *goes to the door.*

(Shaken) I *ask* myself . . . *how? How?*

He exits. FINN *is alone. He groans again and bites his knuckles, pacing the room.*

FINN: Finn, you idiot, Finn, you blathering fool! Thirty years you work to build a clientele and in one short day lop the heads and shoot the works. Lost! Finished! Done! Finn, what do you do now? Ahhh. . . .

He groans. His WIFE *comes in from the street, looks at him, looks around, moves across the pub, stops, glances over at the last sign, walks closer, peers.*

HIS WIFE: I can hardly believe my eyes.

FINN *(destroyed):* Ah, Woman, leave me alone.

HIS WIFE *(peers):* Does it say what I *think* it says, does it *mean* what it says? *(Spells)* D-O. . . . DO?

FINN: Leave off!

HIS WIFE *(turning):* Why, Finn, it shows you're taking an interest. *DO!* That does mean *ACT,* and *ACT* means work, W-O-R-K . . . does it not?

FINN *(punished but repentent):* It does. *(Shakes head once)*

HIS WIFE: Then you'll fix the roof today?

FINN *(bleakly):* I'll get the tools now!

HIS WIFE: And mend the front step?

FINN *(sinking fast):* It's good as mended!

HIS WIFE: And put a new pane of glass in our bedroom window?

FINN *(half under):* New glass, yes!

HIS WIFE: And lay new cobblestone on the path behind?

FINN (sunk): Cobblestones, glass, roof, steps, anything, everything, drive me, sweat me, kill me with work. I deserve it. I've sinned, I want to do penance! Make a list, Woman. Shall I paint the chairs, wax the bar? Sew buttons on my own shirts! I will, I will, I will!

HIS WIFE (suddenly afraid): Ah, God, it's all some joke!

FINN: I mean it! I'll chop turf!

HIS WIFE: You're not ill?

FINN: That all depends how you make illness out to be!

She brings him the tool kit from behind the bar.

HIS WIFE: Start with the steps, that's a love. Ah, Finn, you *are* a sweet man, when you want to be.

FINN (forlorn, unmoving): Sweet I am and glad you think so.

She kisses him lightly on the cheek and passes toward the back of the house.

THE WIFE (melodically): Wait for the roof till tomorrow, if you want!

She exits.

FINN (going mad): Roof . . . tomorrow . . . want! Ah, ha, Finn, ah ha! Ah, ha! There you go!

He throws the hammer through the door.

And there and there!

He throws all the tools, one by one, then the box.

Ah, Finn, there, ah ha, Finn! Look! See how it goes!

He whirls about.

What else? What, nothing? Nothing to throw, save me. And I'm too weak to fling myself out on the stones. Ah, Finn, Finn!

He almost weeps or maybe does, it is hard to tell with the groaning. Then he sees the remaining signs. He runs and grabs them.

All right for you, *THINK*, all right for you, *DO!* Here's the end, the smashing end of you! You'll make fine music on the cobbles! One, two—

He is about to throw them when the double doors open and THE SALESMAN *peers in.*

THE SALESMAN: Ah, there, Mr. Finn, sir.

FINN: Fiend of hell, get out of the way!

THE SALESMAN: Mr. Finn . . . you sound upset, sir.

FINN *hefts the clay mottoes but does not throw them.*

FINN: Upset! Since you left this noon, it has been one plague of locusts on another!

THE SALESMAN: The philosophical mottoes, they didn't work?

FINN: Work! They lost me the use of friends, the respect of neighbors, the talk and the money of ancient customers, put my wife on my shoulders along with God, the Church, and Father Leary! Hoolihan, you and your "machines" have bent and broke me. Ah! Ah! Ah!

FINN's *hands sink to his sides. The remaining signs fall to the floor without breaking.* FINN's *cries have become louder and louder; he grieves at his own wake. As he shouts his last "Ah,"* THE SALESMAN *picks up the two signs, uncertainly, whereupon the double doors flap wide and there, with imaginary sword unsheathed, stands* FATHER LEARY.

FATHER: Heeber Finn, did you call!

FINN *(surprised)*: Did I? Why . . . so I *did!*

FATHER LEARY *looks around, sees and stares at* THE SALESMAN.

FATHER: Is this the one, Finn?

THE SALESMAN *(miffed)*: Is this the one *what?*

FINN: That's him, Father.

THE SALESMAN *(faintly alarmed)*: That's *who?*

FATHER *(rubbing his hands together)*: All *right,* then. All *right.*

THE SALESMAN: *Is* it? *What* is?

FATHER *(at the door)*: Men! Inside!

There is no instantaneous response, so FATHER LEARY *lifts his voice and strikes out a pointing hand.*

Timulty! Here! Nolan, not another step! Old Man, on the double!

He holds the door wide. THE OLD MAN *peers in.*

THE OLD MAN *(squinting right and left)*: Are they gone?

FATHER: Are what gone?

THE OLD MAN *(suspicious)*: The signs, Father.

FATHER: Ah, come on, get in!

THE OLD MAN *sidles in.* NOLAN *is behind him.*

All right, Nolan, don't clog the door.

All the men shadow-sidle in, shy and uneasy, mouthing their caps with their hands. With his army assembled, FATHER LEARY *turns to the astounded and now increasingly nervous* SALESMAN.

THE SALESMAN: What's going on?

FATHER: Well may you ask! I call your attention first to the fact that the man's wearing a suit and hat the color of burning ashes and black soot.

The men all gasp and nod in agreement.

THE SALESMAN *(controlling himself):* Or, to put it another way, the suit was dyed this color in the factory and the rest is dirt from the roads of Eire!

FATHER LEARY *is now slowly circling the man.*

FATHER: His eyes are green—

THE SALESMAN: From my father!

FATHER: His ears pointed—

THE SALESMAN: From my mother!

THE OLD MAN: What's eatin' the priest? I——

NOLAN *gives* THE OLD MAN *a fierce elbow in the ribs which shuts him.* FATHER LEARY *plants himself before* THE SALESMAN.

FATHER: Do you mind doing one thing, man?

THE SALESMAN: What?

FATHER: Would you take off your hat?

THE SALESMAN: I *will* not!

FATHER: He won't take off his hat.

FINN: I heard him!

THE SALESMAN: The place is a tomb, I'd catch me death!

FATHER *(hitching up his trousers under his skirt)*: All right, then! Let us see your feet!

THE SALESMAN: They're right down below for you to see!

FATHER: Will you take off your shoes?

FINN: That's a *fine* idea, Father, his shoes!

THE SALESMAN: Ah, you're both daft! If I won't take off me hat I'm sure not to remove me shoes!

FATHER: He *refuses* to take off his shoes!

THE SALESMAN: What for, why?

FATHER: You know as well as I, man!

FINN: Slow down, Father, you've left us behind—

FATHER: Why, Finn, don't you see, beneath them leather clogs, he's got no toes!

THE MEN *gasp.*

It's all fused into one!

THE MEN *lean and stare.*

FINN: You mean—it's hooves he's got, instead of feet?

THE OLD MAN: Hooves?

FATHER: I didn't say that.

THE SALESMAN: No—but you infer it! I will not be cudgeled into displaying my fearful corns and bunions, for that's *all* that lies hidden there!

FATHER: So *you* say! Finn!

FINN: Yes, Father?

FATHER: Hang this bit of paper on the wall!

FINN: What is it, Father?

FATHER: Me own sign!

THE SALESMAN: Your sign? Now, that ain't right, Father. Unfair competition!

FATHER: Look at him quail!

THE SALESMAN: This ain't quailing. I'm mad!

THE OLD MAN: What's it say, Finn?

FINN *(peers at the paper):* Sic tran-sight—glore-rye-ah—moon-day—

FATHER *(correcting him):* Sic transit gloria mundi!

All look at THE SALESMAN.

THE OLD MAN: Look, he's gone pale!

THE SALESMAN: I ain't gone anywheres near pale! If anything, the blood pounds in me head!

THE OLD MAN: What's it mean?

FATHER: It means we're not long for this world! Post it, Finn.

FINN *hustles to nail it on the wall.*

FINN *(squinting):* You got a teeny fine hand, Father. You can't see it six inches off!

THE OLD MAN: *Sick transits,* what, what?

FATHER: *Gloria mundi!*

THE OLD MAN: And what does it mean again, Nolan?

FATHER: Everything passes away! *(To* THE SALESMAN*)* Including you, sir! Get out, begone! I banish you from Heeber Finn's. I banish you from the streets of our town and the town itself!

THE SALESMAN *(backing off):* You do indeed. It's a bunch of holy nitwits from an asylum, the town is, I'll not be back!

FATHER: That you won't.

> FATHER LEARY *advances upon the man, who backs to the door.*

Get on! Go sell your pagan bits in Kennywell, St. Bridget's and Meynooth!

THE SALESMAN: And thanks, I will!

> THE SALESMAN *backs out. The double gates slam-wriggle.*

FATHER: Watch out! Don't trip over your tail!

THE OLD MAN *(spying out the window):* There he goes! He *does* walk funny!

> NOLAN *is at the wall, squinting at the paper.*

NOLAN *(muttering):* Sic tran-sit—

> *All the men look proudly at* FATHER LEARY, *who turns to look at them.*
> FINN *puts a glass on the bar and fills it. He nods.* FATHER LEARY *walks to the bar and looks at the drink.*

FINN: Thank you, Father.

> FATHER LEARY *picks up the drink, eyes it against the light.*

FATHER: It's the least I could do, for an annex of the church!

> *He circles his drink to take in the whole of the pub. He downs the drink.*

Well, now!

He walks back to the door.

THE OLD MAN: Father! Was it wise to tell him to go sell his heathen signs to other towns?

FATHER: Ah, that's not my problem. That's the problem of the good fathers in Kennywell, St. Bridget's, and Meynooth. It's good in a way that the Devil passes by and gives us a whack and a shake and wakes us up. If I had my mind, the Fiend would make a grand tour of Ireland twice a year!

THE OLD MAN: And maybe he does, Father!

FATHER *(muses):* Yes. Maybe he does.

FINN: Is he gone, now, Father?

FATHER LEARY *peers out.*

FATHER: The road is empty. Our trial is over. All right, then! Tonight, from seven till nine, the church is open, the booth waiting, and me inside the booth!

NOLAN: We'll be there, Father!

They hold out their drinks and drink to him.

FATHER *(surprised and pleased):* By God, I think you will!

He exits.

There is a moment of silence.

TIMULTY *(sighs):* Well, this is a day will go down in Kilcock's history.

CASEY: It was a near thing. I almost went home to the wife . . .

TIMULTY: I almost put in for a job at the pusstoffice.

THE OLD MAN: When the Father saved us all.

TIMULTY *(musing)*: It will be known as the day the Fiend was thrown out from Heeber Finn's.

THE OLD MAN *(nose to the wall, squinting)*: *Sic transit gloria mundi.*

NOLAN: And what's it *mean?*

THE OLD MAN *(flaring)*: It's Latin, dimwit! That's what it means!

> FINN *has walked slow to the door to look out at the church.*

FINN: A strange man.

NOLAN: The salesman?

FINN *(shakes head)*: Father Leary. Why, I ask myself, why did he tell the salesman to sell the pagan signs in Kennywell, Meynooth, and St. Bridget's? Why? *Why?*

> *He turns to look at the others, and at the bar. Slowly, his eyes widen, his eyebrows go up, his mouth makes a smile. Suddenly he gives a great laugh.*

Ah-hah! Wife!

> HIS WIFE *appears, arms over her bosom, glaring.*

Bring more chairs! A dozen!

THE WIFE: A dozen?

FINN: Make it two dozen, three, five! And tables!

HIS WIFE: Tables?

FINN: By sundown tonight refugees will be *pouring* in here from—

THE OLD MAN *(catching on):* Kennywell?

NOLAN *(enlightened):* Meynooth?

CASEY: *And* St. Bridget's!

FINN: There's no telling where from, how many, how long! It'll be a grand weekend! Woman—Kathleen, sweetheart, have a drink.

> *She hesitates, softens, takes the drink. He gives her a buss and a pinch.* FINN *raises his glass.*

Here's to not *stopping,* but going on as always and ever, with no *consideration* for one dainty moment about *thinking* and no *doing* save as how we always done. Casey, Nolan, Timulty, lend a hand!

NOLAN: It's lent!

> *The men rush in and out bringing tables and chairs.* FINN, *in the flurry, pours a line of little glasses full. On their way in and out the men grab and swallow, hurry on.*

FINN *(sings):* "In life, in strife,
With maid, with wife!
It's the drinkin' . . . !"

THE OLD MAN *(speaks, running):* "Not *the thinkin'!*"

ALL *(sing):* "Makes it go!"

> *The Curtain falls on the beehive. And . . .*

THE END

The Anthem
Sprinters

CHARACTERS

The Young Man (Douglas)

Heeber Finn

The Old Man

Timulty

Doone

O'Gavin

Fogarty

Nolan

Kelly

Casey, Peevey, *and other assorted spectators, door-watchers, time-keepers and former champions of the Sprint.*

At the rise of curtain we find ourselves not so much in a real pub as in a sort of a sketch of a pub. A plank laid across two high saw-horses will do for a bar. Men are lined up, or rather clustered, at it, having a fine pantomime argument about something, shaking each other's shoulders, waving their hands, pulling their hats off and on their heads, yanking at one another's lapels, pounding their fists on the bar, and shouting silently, almost nose-to-nose. As the lights come up, so does the sound of the men, as if theatrically we were tuning in on the wildlife here. Four or five of the men are having the greatest to-do there at the rail. Two other men, down front, are Indian-wrestling each other. Two more are playing darts, hurling the feathered things through space at a

*target suspended far to one side. To the left a man in a
bowler hat sits on a piano stool playing a tune on empty
space. Though the piano is not there, we can hear it fine. It is
a jolly tune. So jolly that one of the men in the argument
breaks off, unable to resist, and jogs about a bit. Still another
fellow somewhere in all the melee is munching on a harmonica, his eyes soulfully shut and the banshee mourn of the
little machine in his mouth rising and falling in the smoke
and din. An ardent fan of his stands near, aching with the
melody, mouth open, watching the great musician tongue
and wheeze along the contraption. In all, there are a dozen
or so people littered about the scene. More can be added. Or
if need be, some might be taken away and never missed.*

Anyway, here we are in Heeber Finn's and FINN *himself
behind the bar, singing any tune that strikes his fancy as he
wipes glasses and foams up drinks, adding his own musical
bit to the general commotion.*

*It is a scene rather like the tumult on a pinball device when
the jackpot is struck, all the lights flash, miniature guns explode, fantastic totals jump about on the scoreboard, and all
the balls at once seem to rush wild down the ways.*

*Into this grand scene now walks our writer-hero, or for a
time anyway, villain,* THE YOUNG MAN. *He is not a nasty snob,
he is just unfamiliar with things and, like it or not, he looks
just a bit like a Tourist.*

*With his entrance, some of the activity, or at least the
sound of it, fades down.*

THE YOUNG MAN *stands dead-center of the action and looks
about, tolerantly amused. We hear a few of the cries more
clearly now from some of the men arguing at the bar.*

THE MEN *(general hubbub):* Doone!
   O'Gavin!
   Devil take O'Gavin!

Then Devil Take Doone! He's no Sport at all! Now—
O'Gavin——

At which point THE YOUNG MAN *gathers his observations
and makes his fatal comment.*

THE YOUNG MAN: Well! It sure looks like a wild night, here!

*It is as if the great blade of the Guillotine had fallen.
Silence chops across all.* THE YOUNG MAN *is instantly
sorry. Almost in midflight, the feathered dart is shot
down. The piano stops. The harmonica dies in
midwheeze. The dancer seems suddenly crippled. Nobody has turned yet to look at* THE YOUNG MAN. *Perhaps
they are only waiting for this outlander to pack his cha-
grin and go away. They will give him enough time.
Count to ten.* THE YOUNG MAN *looks around, looks at the
door, debates heading for it, but stops.*

For one man, TIMULTY, *has broken from the mob at
the bar and now slowly stalks out, not looking at* DOUG-
LAS, *only turning to survey him steadily after he has
come full in front of him, his glass of stout in his hand.*

He drinks from the glass, eyeing DOUGLAS. DOUGLAS *fid-
gets. At last,* TIMULTY *speaks.*

TIMULTY: Was that said in scorn or admiration?

THE YOUNG MAN: I really can't say——

TIMULTY: There's a confusion in your mind then?

THE YOUNG MAN *(eagerly grasping this)*: Yes, that's it!

TIMULTY *turns to glance all about.*

TIMULTY: He's confused, boys!

*There is a general murmur neither for nor against, in
answer to this.* TIMULTY *turns back.*

Are you new to Ireland, to Dublin, and to Heeber Finn's pub?

THE YOUNG MAN: Er—all *three* of those, yes!

TIMULTY *(to his friends):* He's new to all three, boys!

There is a little more affirmative rumble now, exclamations of "Oh" and "Ah well, then" and "So that's how it is" mix with the rest. TIMULTY *views* DOUGLAS *again.*

So it's an orientation program you're in search of?

THE YOUNG MAN: That's *it!*

TIMULTY *eyes him a moment longer, then waves once, idly, to his friends.*

TIMULTY: All right, boys!

The tumult and the shouting that had died, without the captains and the kings departing, now instantaneously renews itself. Darts fly. The piano sounds. The harmonica wails. The men jump hip deep into their argumentation.

DOUGLAS *views this, impressed, as if suddenly given to see the vast workings of Big Ben's machinery going full blast.*

Timulty's my name.

THE YOUNG MAN: Douglas.

TIMULTY: Is it a wild night you're looking for?

THE YOUNG MAN: Well, I—

TIMULTY: You think, don't you, there *are no* Wild Nights in Ireland?

THE YOUNG MAN: I didn't say that——

TIMULTY: You think it. It shows in your eyes. Well, what would you say if I told you you was at the eye of the hurricane! You're in the damn earthquake, half-buried to your chin and don't know it!

THE YOUNG MAN: Am I?

TIMULTY: You are! Here at Finn's pub is the Central Betting Agency for the greatest Sporting Event of Local Consequence!

THE YOUNG MAN: Is it?

TIMULTY: 'Tis! Listen! Do you hear?

THE MEN (yelling again): Two bob says you're wrong! Three bob nails you to the wall!

TIMULTY (calling over): Men, what do you think of Doone?

FOGARTY: His reflex is uncanny!

THE OLD MAN: Doone hell! My money is on O'Gavin! What a Great Heart!

THE YOUNG MAN: A Sporting Event, you say?

TIMULTY: Come along! Boys, this is Mr. Douglas, from the States.

General greetings.

TIMULTY: Mr. Douglas is in—

THE YOUNG MAN: Pictures. I write screenplays for the cinema.

ALL: Fillums!

THE YOUNG MAN (modestly): Films.

TIMULTY: No! It's too much!

THE OLD MAN: Are you staggered, Timulty?

TIMULTY: I am!

FOGARTY: Coincidence!

NOLAN: Beyond belief!

THE YOUNG MAN *(blinks)*: What is?

THE OLD MAN: Your occupation and our Sporting Event! They're in the same bed!

FOGARTY: They're twins!

TIMULTY: By God now, you'll not only bet, we'll let you judge! Are you much for sports? Do you know, for instance, such things as the cross-country, four-forty, and like man-on-foot excursions?

THE YOUNG MAN: I've attended two Olympic Games.

THE OLD MAN *(awed)*: Not just fillums, but the World Competition!

TIMULTY: Well, now, isn't it time you knew of the special all-Irish decathlon event which has to do with picture theatres?

THE YOUNG MAN: I—

THE OLD MAN: Shall we show him, boys?

ALL: Sure! Fine! On the way! Stand aside!

FINN: Out it is! This way! Doone, come on!

And before DOUGLAS *can protest,* bang! *they are out the door, the pub has vanished, and they run circling through a sort of mist.* DOONE, *who, it turns out, is the man who has been playing the invisible piano, turns last of all and, dancing around on his toes, pumping his legs like a trackman to prime himself, exits last of all, and soon catches, paces, and fronts the mob.*

FINN: Doone! Doone! There you are!

DOONE: Does an Event loom?

THE OLD MAN: It does!

DOONE *(dancing ahead):* I'm fit!

THE OLD MAN: You are!

TIMULTY: There! We've arrived!

They pull up. THE YOUNG MAN *gazes around, still not certain what to look for.*

THE OLD MAN: Will you read *that?*

A marquee with blinking lights has come on above them.

THE YOUNG MAN: The . . . Great . . . Fine . . . Arts . . . Cinema.

TIMULTY: Don't forget "Elite." It's there. But it's burnt out.

TIMULTY *throws his cap up to hit the marquee. The missing word lights feebly and flickeringly.*

THE YOUNG MAN: The GreatER Fine Arts Elite Cinema Theatre.

FOGARTY: We have a name for everything, do we not?

TIMULTY: If the Arts *need* being Greater or Finer, this is where you come.

NOLAN: Ah, look at the lights move, will ya?

TIMULTY: Like the fireflies on the meadows with the sun just set.

THE OLD MAN *(nudges the writer):* Did you *hear* him?

THE YOUNG MAN: Eh?

THE OLD MAN: Well, I mean to say, are you a writer or not? I mean, don't writers make notes of lovely things like that to put in their next book?

THE YOUNG MAN: Er . . . yes . . .

> THE YOUNG MAN *takes out a pad and pencil sheepishly. Everyone leans over his shoulder to see the words go down.*

TIMULTY *(quoting himself):* "Like the fireflies . . ."

NOLAN: ". . . on the bogs . . ."

TIMULTY: "Meadows," ya dimwit! "On the meadows . . ." That's it. "With the sun . . ."

THE YOUNG MAN *(writing):* ". . . just set."

TIMULTY: There! *(Sighs)* I'm immortal.

THE OLD MAN: Enough! We are at the place of the grand sport!

THE YOUNG MAN *(dubious):* The Greater Fine Arts Elite Cinema Theatre?

FOGARTY: Why not? Look, there's three churches in Ireland. There's them whose faith is the pubs, them whose faith is the cinemas, and then there's the Catholics.

THE OLD MAN: There's *always* a place to go.

THE YOUNG MAN: Yes, but what sport can you put in a theatre? Ping pong, basketball onstage?

TIMULTY: Doone, step forward!

DOONE, *who has been darting about on tiptoe, snorting, snuffing, dances in.*

DOONE: Doone, that's me! The Best Anthem Sprinter in Ireland!

THE YOUNG MAN: *What* sprinter?

DOONE *(spells with difficulty):* A-n-t-h-e-m. Anthem. Sprinter. The fastest. *(Bobs)*

FINN: Since you've been in Dublin, have you attended the cinema?

THE YOUNG MAN: Just once, but in London last month, I saw eight films——

TIMULTY: You're fanatic, then, as are we all, through need, on this godforsaken desert!

THE OLD MAN: In London, if you'll excuse the curse, when the fillum stopped each night, did you observe anything tending towards the peculiar?

THE YOUNG MAN *(muses):* Hold on! You can't mean "God Save the Queen," can you?

TIMULTY: Can we, boys?

ALL: We can!

THE OLD MAN: In London, it's "God Save the Queen," here it's the National Anthem, it's all the same!

TIMULTY: Any night, every night, for tens of dreadful years, at the end of each damn fillum all over Ireland, in every cinema, as if you'd never heard the baleful tune before, the orchestra strikes up for Ireland!

THE OLD MAN *(nudges the writer):* And what happens *then?*

THE YOUNG MAN *(muses):* Why . . . if you're any man at all, you try to get out of the theatre in those few precious moments between the end of the film and the start of the Anthem.

TIMULTY: He's nailed it!

NOLAN: Buy the Yank a drink!

FINN *(passing bottle):* On the house!

THE YOUNG MAN *(drinks, wipes mouth):* After all, I was in London a month. "God Save the Queen" had begun to pall. It's surely the same after all these years for you and your National Anthem. *(Hastily)* No disrespect meant.

FINN: And none taken!

TIMULTY: Or *given* by any of us patriotic I.R.A. veterans, survivors of the Troubles, lovers of country. Still, breathing the same air ten thousand times makes the senses reel. So, as you've noted, in that God-sent three- or four-second interval, any audience in its right mind beats it the hell out. And the best of the crowd is—

THE YOUNG MAN: Doone. Your Anthem Sprinter.

THE OLD MAN: Smile at the man.

> *Everyone smiles at the American, who smiles easily back.*

Now! Stand near! At this moment, not one hundred feet through that door and down the slight declivity toward the silver screen, seated on the aisle of the fourth row center is O'Gavin . . .

THE YOUNG MAN: . . . your *other* Anthem Sprinter.

NOLAN *(tipping his cap):* The man's eerie.

TIMULTY (*impressed*): O'Gavin's there, all right. He's not seen the fillum before—

THE YOUNG MAN (*looks up*): What, Clark Gable in *It Happened One Night?*

NOLAN: Ah, that was last month. They've not got around to taking down the names.

TIMULTY: This fillum tonight is a Deanna Durbin brought back by the asking, and the time is now . . .

FINN *holds up his watch. All lean toward it.*

FINN: Ten-thirty o'clock.

TIMULTY: In five minutes the cinema will be letting the customers out in a herd . . .

THE OLD MAN: And if we should send Doone here in for a test of speed and agility . . .

DOONE (*dancing about*): It's stripped to the buff I am!

THE OLD MAN: . . . O'Gavin would be ready to take the challenge!

THE YOUNG MAN: O'Gavin didn't go to the show just for an Anthem Sprint, did he?

THE OLD MAN: Good grief, no. He went for the Deanna Durbin songs and all, him playing the banjo and knowing music as he does. But, as I say, if he should casually note the entrance of Doone here, who would make himself conspicuous by his late arrival, O'Gavin would know what was up. They would salute each other and both sit listening to the dear music until *Finis* hove in sight.

DOONE (*doing knee-bends*): Sure, let me at him, let me *at* him!

DOUGLAS: Do—do you have Teams?

TIMULTY: Teams! There's the Galway Runners!

FOGARTY: The Connemara Treadwells!

THE OLD MAN: The Donegal Lightfoots!

TIMULTY: And the fastest team of all is made up of Irishmen living in London.

THE OLD MAN *(reverently):* "The Queen's Own Evaders"!

FOGARTY: Fast, do you see, to flee from "God Save the Queen"?

> *All laugh, assent, pummel, gather about.* FINN *searches the writer's face.*

FINN: I see the details of the sport have bewildered you. Let me nail down the rules. Fogarty?!

FOGARTY: Here!

FINN: Door-listener supreme! Nolan! Kelly!

NOLAN and KELLY: Here!

FINN: Aisle-superintendent judges! Myself—*(Shows watch)* —Time-keeper. General spectators: Casey, Peevey, and Dillon. You've met Doone. O'Gavin's in the depths, there! So much for the participants. Now, the sports arena. *(Moves, pointing)* Much depends on the character of the theatre.

THE YOUNG MAN: The character?

THE OLD MAN *(hustling along):* Here's the exits, ya see? And inside—*(Opens a door, points)*—the lobby . . .

FINN *(cuts in):* Now, there be some liberal free-thinking theatres with grand aisles, grand lobbies, grand exits, and even grander, more spacious latrines . . .

NOLAN *(cutting in):* Some with so much porcelain, the echoes alone put you in shock . . .

TIMULTY *(cutting in):* And then again there's the parsimonious mousetrap cinemas with aisles that squeeze the breath from you, seats that knock your knees, and doors best sidled out of on your way to the men's lounge in the sweet-shop across the alley.

THE OLD MAN: Each theatre is carefully assessed before, during, and after a Sprint. A runner is judged by whether he had to fight through men and women en masse, mostly men, women with shopping bags which is terrible, or worst still, children at the flypaper matinees.

NOLAN *(illustrating):* The temptation with children, of course, is lay into them as you'd harvest hay, tossing them in windrows to left and right.

THE OLD MAN: So we've stopped that. Now it's nights only here at the ideal cinema of them all.

THE YOUNG MAN: Ideal? Why?

KELLY *(displays tape measure):* Its aisles, do you see, are neither too wide nor too narrow.

He and THE OLD MAN *pace off by the exit door. They illustrate with the tape.*

Its exits are well placed.

THE OLD MAN *(tests door):* The door hinges oiled.

They open the door and point in. THE YOUNG MAN *peers.*

TIMULTY: Its crowds, do you see? are a proper mixture of sporting bloods and folks who mind enough to leap aside should a Sprinter, squandering his energy, come dashing up the way.

THE YOUNG MAN *(suddenly thoughtful):* Do you . . . handicap your runners?

FINN: We do!

THE OLD MAN: Some nights, we put a summer coat on one, a winter coat on another of the racers.

TIMULTY: Or seat one chap in the fifth row, while the other takes the third.

FINN: And if a man turns terrible feverish swift, we add the sweetest known burden of all—

THE YOUNG MAN: Drink?

ALL: Ah . . . ah . . . ah . . .

All laugh, mumble, move in to clap and pat the dear, knowledgeable boy.

THE OLD MAN: What else! Nolan! Run this in! Make O'Gavin take two swigs, big ones! *(Aside)* He's a *two-handicap* man.

NOLAN *runs through the door.*

NOLAN: Two it is!

TIMULTY: While Doone here has already made his weight at Heeber Finn's.

DOONE *(drinking from the bottle):* Even all!

KELLY: Go on, Doone. Let our money be a light burden on you. Let's see you burst out that exit, five minutes from now, victorious and first.

FINN: Doone! Inside!

> DOONE *shakes hands all around. He waves to everyone as if going on a long voyage, opens the door. Sweet music flushes out about him—he basks in it a moment, then plunges through into darkness, gone. At which point* NOLAN *bursts back out.*

NOLAN *(waves flask)*: O'Gavin's handicapped!

THE OLD MAN: Fine! Kelly, now, go check the contestants, be sure they sit opposite each other in the fourth row, caps on, coats half buttoned, scarves properly furled.

KELLY *(running)*: It's already done!

> KELLY *vanishes back through in a surge of music of great romance.*

FINN *(checking his watch)*: In two more minutes—

THE YOUNG MAN *(innocently)*: *Post* Time?

TIMULTY *(with admiring affection)*: You're a dear lad.

KELLY *(bursting through door)*: All set! They're ready!

FOGARTY *(listening at the door)*: 'Tis almost over, you can tell, toward the end of any fillum, the music has a way of getting out of hand!

> *He opens the door wide and nods in. Sure enough, the music is in full heat now, surging all over the place. All listen and nod, eyes closed.*

TIMULTY: Full orchestra and chorus behind the singing maid. I must come tomorrow for the entirety.

FINN *(entranced)*: What's the tune?

THE OLD MAN: Ah, off with the tune! Lay the bets!

FINN *(recovering):* Right! Who's for Doone, who O'Gavin?

ALL *(hustling about, waving money and paper):* Doone! A shilling for O'Gavin. Doone! Two says it's Doone! Four on O'Gavin!

THE YOUNG MAN *(holding out money):* O'Gavin.

FINN *(shocked):* Without having *seen* him?

THE YOUNG MAN *(whispers):* A dark horse.

TIMULTY: A brave choice. Kelly, Nolan, inside as aisle judges. Watch sharp there's no jumping the *Finis.*

In go KELLY *and* NOLAN, *happy as boys.*

FINN: Make an aisle now. Yank, you over here with me!

All rush to form a double line, one on either side of the exit.

TIMULTY: Fogarty, lay your ear to the door!

FOGARTY *(does so):* The damn music is extra loud!

THE OLD MAN *(sotto voce to* THE YOUNG MAN*):* It will be over soon. Whoever's to die is dying this moment!

FOGARTY: Louder still! There!

He holds one door half wide. The last single chord of music blasts out.

FINN: The grand ta-ta! By God!

THE YOUNG MAN *(a quiet exclamation):* They're *off!*

FINN: Stand aside! Clear the door!

FOGARTY *(listens):* Here they come!

FINN: Listen to their feet!

THE OLD MAN: Like thunder it is!

We hear the feet rushing.

FINN: Come on, O'Gavin!

TIMULTY: Doone! Doone!

ALL: Doone! O'Gavin! Doone! O'Gavin!

The doors burst wide. DOONE, *breathless, plunges out alone.*

The winner!

DOONE *(surprised):* By God, so I *am!*

FINN: 'Tenshun! The National Anthem!

He holds the door wide. The men whip off their caps. The Anthem speeds swiftly to its end.

THE YOUNG MAN *(puzzled):* That was quick. Did they leave something out?

FINN: What *didn't* they!!

THE OLD MAN: Over the years, by some miracle or other, the Anthem has got shorter and shorter.

DOONE: Where's my competition?

All suddenly realize DOONE *stands alone, blinking back into the cinema dark, from which* NOLAN *and* KELLY *emerge, bewildered.*

THE OLD MAN: Jesus, you're right! Where's O'Gavin!

NOLAN: The idiot didn't run out the wrong exit, did he?

DOONE *(calling into the dark):* O'Gavin!?

KELLY: Could he've sprinted into the Men's?

FINN: Now what would he do there?

THE OLD MAN (*snorts*): There's a son of ignorant Ireland for you! *O'Gavin!*

FOGARTY: Good grief, maybe coming up the aisle he had a heart attack and is lying there in the dark gasping his—

ALL: That's *it!*

> *The men riot through the door,* THE YOUNG MAN *last.*

NOLAN: Maybe he broke his leg.

KELLY: Did you bring the gun?

THE OLD MAN: Ah, off with the gun! O'Gavin? Dear lad? How *is* it?

> *They mob around down, perhaps to the first row of the theatre, where they all peer at one man seated alone.*

NOLAN: O'Gavin!

FINN: You haven't *moved!*

THE OLD MAN: Why are you *sittin'* there?

FINN: What's that on his cheek?

FOGARTY (*bends close, peers*): A teardrop! A tear!

O'GAVIN (*moans*): Ah, God!

FINN: O'Gavin, are ya sick?

> *They all bend close.*

O'GAVIN: Ah, God . . .

> *He rises slowly and turns, brushing a tear from his eye. He shakes his head beatifically, eyes shut.*

She has the voice of an angel.

THE YOUNG MAN: Angel?

O'GAVIN *(nods back at the stage)*: That one up there, on the silver screen.

They all turn to stare at a silver screen that has come down behind them, where Finn's pub once was.

THE YOUNG MAN: Deanna Durbin, does he mean?

O'GAVIN *(blowing his nose)*: The dear dead voice of my grandmother—

TIMULTY: Your grandma's behind!

THE YOUNG MAN *(peering at the screen)*: Her singing? Just *that* made him forget to run?

O'GAVIN: Just! *Just!* It would be sacrilege to bound from a cinema after a recital such as that just heard! Might as well throw bombs at a wedding or—

TIMULTY: You could've at least *warned* us it was No Contest.

O'GAVIN: How? It crept over me in a divine sickness. That last bit she sang. "The Lovely Isle of Innisfree," was it not, Doone?

FOGARTY: What *else* did she sing?

THE OLD MAN *(exasperated)*: What *else?* He's just lost some of you a day's wages and you ask what else she sang!

O'GAVIN: Sure, it's money that runs the world. But it is music which holds down the friction.

PHIL *(a voice from the back of the theatre)*: Hey! What's going on down there!

TIMULTY *(aside to the Yank)*: It's the cinema projectionist—!

THE OLD MAN: Hello, Phil, darling! It's only the Team!

FINN: We've a bit of a problem here, Phil, in ethics, not to say esthetics.

THE OLD MAN *(smiling his grandest):* Yes, now, we wonder —could you run the Anthem over?

PHIL'S VOICE: Run it *over?!*

There is a rumble of protests from the winners, approval from the losers.

O'GAVIN: A *lovely* idea!

TIMULTY: It *is* not! Doone won fair and square!

THE OLD MAN: An Act of God incapacitated O'Gavin!

KELLY: A tenth-run flicker from the year nineteen hundred and thirty-seven caught him by the short hairs, you mean!

FOGARTY: We've never run a sprint over before——

O'GAVIN *(sweetly):* Phil, dear boy, is the *last* reel of the Deanna Durbin fillum still there?

PHIL'S VOICE: It ain't in the Ladies'.

O'GAVIN: What a wit the boy has. Now, Phil, do you think you could just thread the singing girl back through the infernal machine there and give us the *Finis* again?

PHIL: Is *that* what you *all* want?

There is a hard moment of indecision.

FOGARTY *(tempted):* Including, of course, all of the song "The Lovely Isle of Innisfree"?

PHIL: The whole damn island, sure!

Everybody beams. This has hit them where they live.

THE OLD MAN: Done! Places, everyone!

DOONE *and* O'GAVIN *race to sit down.*

THE YOUNG MAN: Hold on! There's no audience. Without them, there's no obstacles, no real contest.

FINN *(scowls, thinks):* Why, let's *all* of us be the audience!

ALL *(flinging themselves into seats):* Grand! Fine! Wonderful!

THE YOUNG MAN *is left alone, looking at his friends.*

THE YOUNG MAN: I beg pardon.

THE OLD MAN *(seated):* Yes, lad?

THE YOUNG MAN: There's no one outside by the exit, to judge who wins.

Everyone is shocked to hear this. They look around.

TIMULTY: Then, Yank, would you mind doing us the service?

THE YOUNG MAN *nods, backs off, then turns and runs back out to the exit door, onstage.*

PHIL'S VOICE: Are ya clods down there ready?

THE OLD MAN *(turning):* If Deanne Durbin and the Anthem is!

PHIL'S VOICE: Here goes!

The lights go out. The music surges. A voice sings. By the exit door, THE YOUNG MAN *tenses, waiting, checking his watch. He holds the door half open, listening.*

THE YOUNG MAN: Forty seconds . . . thirty . . . ten seconds . . . there's the Finale . . . ! They're—*Off!*

He flings himself back as if afraid a flood of men will mob out over him. We hear the grand Ta-Ta of cymbals, drums, brass. Then—silence.

THE YOUNG MAN *opens the door wide and peers into the dark, then stiffens to attention as*

The National Anthem plays. Even shorter this time, at double-quick speed.

When it is over, THE YOUNG MAN *steps in and peers down at the long row where the "audience" and the two competitors are seated. They all stand and look back and up at the projection room.*

Tears are streaming from their eyes. They are dabbing their cheeks.

THE OLD MAN *(calls):* Phil, darling . . . ?

FINN: . . . once more?

They all sit down. Only TIMULTY *remains standing, eyes wet. He gestures.*

TIMULTY: And this time . . . *without* the Anthem?

Blackout.

Music. A swift Irish reel, with blended overtones of the lilting "Innisfree," old Deanna Durbin songs, and at the very last, the Anthem, in its most truncated form.

The real *audience can, if it wishes, run for the exits, now, for our Play has come to*

THE END

The Queen's Own Evaders, an Afterword by Ray Bradbury

I had never wanted to go to Ireland in my life.

Yet here was John Huston on the telephone asking me to his hotel for a drink. Later that afternoon, drinks in hand, Huston eyed me carefully and said, "How would you like to live in Ireland and write *Moby Dick* for the screen?"

And suddenly we were off after the White Whale; myself, the wife, and two daughters.

It took me seven months to track, catch, and throw the Whale flukes out.

From October to April I lived in a country where I did not want to be.

I thought that I saw nothing, heard nothing, felt nothing of Ireland. The Church was deplorable. The weather was dreadful. The poverty was inadmissible. I would have none of it. Besides, there was this Big Fish . . .

I did not count on my subconscious tripping me up. In the middle of all the threadbare dampness, while trying to beach Leviathan with my typewriter, my antennae were noticing the people. Not that my wide-awake self, conscious and afoot, did not notice them, like and admire and have some for friends, and see them often, no. But the overall thing, pervasive, was the poorness and the rain and feeling sorry for myself in a sorry land.

With the Beast rendered down into oil and delivered to the cameras, I fled Ireland, positive I had learned naught save how to dread storms, fogs, and the penny-beggar streets of Dublin and Kilcock.

But the subliminal eye is shrewd. While I lamented my hard work and my inability, every other day, to feel as much like Herman Melville as I wished, my interior self kept alert, snuffed deep, listened long, watched close, and filed Ireland and its people for other times when I might relax and let them teem forth to my own surprise.

I came home via Sicily and Italy, where I had baked myself free of the Irish winter, assuring one and all, "I'll write nothing ever about the Connemora Lightfoots and the Donnybrook Gazelles."

I should have remembered my experience with Mexico, many years before, where I had encountered not rain and poverty, but sun and poverty, and come away panicked by a weather of mortality and the terrible sweet smell when the Mexicans exhaled death. I had at last written some fine nightmares out of that.

Even so, I insisted, Eire was dead, the wake over, her people would never haunt me.

Several years passed.

Then one rainy afternoon Mike (whose real name is Nick), the taxi-driver, came to sit just out of sight in my mind. He nudged me gently and dared to remind me of our journeys together across the bogs, along the Liffey, and him talking and wheeling his old iron car slow through the mist night after night, driving me home to the Royal Hibernian Hotel, the one man I knew best in all the wild green country, from dozens of scores of Dark Journeys.

"Tell the truth about me," Mike said. "Just put it down the way it was."

And suddenly I had a short story and a play. And the story is true and the play is true. It happened like that. It could have happened no other way.

Well, the story we understand, but why, after all these years, did I turn to the stage?

It was not a turn, but a return.

I acted on the amateur stage, and radio, as a boy. I wrote plays as a young man. These plays, unproduced, were so bad that I promised myself never to write again for the stage until late in life, after I'd learned to write all the other ways first and best. Simultaneously, I gave up acting because I dreaded the competitive politics actors must play in order to work.

Besides: the short story, the novel, called. I answered. I plunged into writing. Years passed. I went to hundreds of plays. I loved them. I read hundreds of plays. I loved them. But still I held off from ever writing Act I, Scene I, again. Then came *Moby Dick,* a while to brood over it, and suddenly here was Mike, my taxi-driver, rummaging my soul, lifting up tidbits of adventure from a few years before near the Hill of Tara or inland at the autumn changing of leaves in Killeshandra. My old love of the theater with a final shove pushed me over.

One other thing jolted me back toward the stage. In the last five years I have borrowed or bought a good many European and American Idea Plays to read; I have watched the Absurd and the More-Than-Absurd Theatre. In the aggregate I could not help but judge the plays as frail exercises, more often than not half-witted, but above all lacking in the prime requisites of imagination and ability.

It is only fair, given this flat opinion, I should now put my own head on the chopping-block. You may, if you wish, be my executioners.

This is not so unusual. Literary history is filled with writers who, rightly or wrongly, felt they could tidy up, improve upon, or revolutionize a given field. So, many of us plunge forward where angels leave no dustprint.

Having dared once, exuberant, I dared again. When Mike vaulted from my machine, others unbidden followed.

And the more that swarmed, the more jostled to fill the spaces.

I suddenly saw that I knew more of the minglings and commotions of the Irish than I could disentangle in a month or a year of writing and unraveling them forth. Inadvertently, I found myself blessing the secret mind, and winnowing a vast interior post-office, calling nights, towns, weathers, beasts, bicycles, churches, cinemas, and ritual marches and flights by name.

Mike had started me at an amble; I broke into a trot which was before long a Full Sprint pacing my dear friends, the Queen's Own Evaders.

The stories, the plays, were born in a yelping litter. I had but to get out of their way.

Now done, and busy with other plays about science-fiction machineries which will spin their cogs in yet another book—do I have an after-the-fact theory to fit play-writing?

Yes.

For only after, can one nail down, examine, explain.

To try to know beforehand is to freeze and kill.

Self-consciousness is the enemy of all art, be it acting, writing, painting, or living itself, which is the greatest art of all.

Here's how my theory goes. We writers are up to the following:

We build tensions toward laughter, then give permission, and laughter comes.

We build tensions toward sorrow, and at last say cry, and hope to see our audiences in tears.

We build tensions toward violence, light the fuse, and run.

We build the strange tensions of love, where so many of the other tensions mix to be modified and transcended, and allow that fruition in the mind of the audience.

We build tensions, especially today, toward sickness and then, if we are good enough, talented enough, observant enough, allow our audiences to be sick.

Each tension seeks its own proper end, release, and relaxation.

No tension, it follows, aesthetically as well as practically, must be built which remains unreleased. Without this, any art ends incomplete, halfway to its goal. And in real life, as we know, the failure to relax a particular tension can lead to madness.

There are seeming exceptions to this, in which novels or plays end at the height of tension, but the release is implied.

The audience is asked to go forth into the world and explode an idea. The final action is passed on from creator to reader-viewer whose job it is to finish off the laughter, the tears, the violence, the sexuality, or the sickness.

Not to know this is not to know the essence of creativity, which, at heart, is the essence of man's being.

If I were to advise new writers, if I were to advise the new writer in myself, going into the theatre of the Absurd, the almost-Absurd, the theatre of Ideas, the any-kind-of-theatre-at-all, I would advise like this:

Tell me no pointless jokes.

I will laugh at your refusal to allow me laughter.

Build me no tension toward tears and refuse me my lamentations.

I will go find me better wailing walls.

Do not clench my fists for me and hide the target.

I might strike you, instead.

Above all, sicken me not unless you show me the way to the ship's rail.

For, please understand, if you poison me, I must be sick. It seems to me that many people writing the sick film, the sick novel, the sick play, have forgotten that poison can destroy minds even as it can destroy flesh. Most poison bottles have emetic recipes stamped on the labels. Through neglect, ignorance, or inability, the new intellectual Borgias cram hairballs down our throats and refuse us the convulsion that could make us well. They have forgotten, if they ever knew, the ancient knowledge that only by being truly sick can one regain health. Even beasts know when it is good and proper to throw up. Teach me how to be sick then, in the right time and place, so that I may again walk in the fields and with the wise and smiling dogs know enough to chew sweet grass.

The art aesthetic is all encompassing, there is room in it for every horror, every delight, if the tensions representing these are carried to their furthest perimeters and released in action. I ask for no happy endings. I ask only for proper endings based on proper assessments of energy contained and given detonation.

Given all this, what are we to make of a book mainly composed of Irish comedies?

Well, the means whereby men "make do" with the world, which is more often than not by their wit and humor, is the good stuff of serious thought. We think long and much on the universe and the ways of God and man toward man, and then cry into our inkwells to service tragedies, or throw our heads way back and give one hell of a yell of laughter.

This time out, given poverty, given bicycle collisions in fogs that might turn deadly serious, given rank prejudice and raw bias, given suicidal cold and insufficient means against such cold, given Ireland that is, and all its priest-ridden and sleet-worn souls, I have chosen to lift my head from my hands, I have chosen not to weep but to laugh with them as they themselves must laugh, in order to survive, in the pubs, and on the roads of a lost and much-overpraised bog.

To take the plays more or less in the order of their veracity to life and my experience in Ireland, *The First Night of Lent,* as I have already noted, is a true portrayal of my adventures with Mike, the lone taxi-driver of Kilcock.

The Great Collision of Monday Last is based a bit more roughly on Truth, with a sidewise look at fancy and a backward glance at the lie which, once gone over, cannot be treaded again, for now it is booby-trapped. The fact is, collisions occur *all* the time in Ireland between hell-bent sinner bicyclists, with dread results. From the echoes of multiple collisions I harkened for further reverberations which became the play.

A Clear View of an Irish Mist can best be approached thiswise:

If Tintoretto, Michelangelo, Titian and others invented the wide-screen frozen cinema of the Renaissance, it was the

Irish first came full-blown with the Hi-Fi and the Long-Play Stereo.

Just open the doors of any pub, stand out of the blast, and you'll know what I mean.

I woke one night in Dublin, half-panicked by something, shook my wife and cried, I think, "The Troubles! They're on again!" or perhaps "There's a riot downstairs!"

"No such thing," my wife murmured, rolling over. "There was a dance up the street. It's just letting out." Or perhaps she protested, falling into a snooze, "They've just shut the pubs . . ."

No matter. A great river of Irish swept by below, all "tweeter," all "woofer," and playing on forever.

The flood took the better part of an hour to die away and empty into the Liffey; for little side-flurries swept into storefronts or whirlpooled at streetcorners with fearful arguments and ardent proclamations. Poets were striking blows for freedom, actors were pounding Yeats into the earth just to yank him out again. If women or girls were present, they were stormed to silence by the concussions.

In sum, if Guinness is the national stout, conversation is the royal republican wine, liberally manufactured and sold everywhere men so much as bump elbows in passing.

Irishmen inhale but never exhale: they *talk*.

And they surely regret the lost time it takes to draw breath, for during that split second some idiot with full lungs might dart in to seize the arguments and not give them back save by main force.

Given this overall and inescapable truth, I have fancied forth *A Clear View of an Irish Mist* to show what might happen to the National LP and the dear Hi-Fi should an irrational beast dare them to THINK.

Which leaves us at last with the Anthem Sprinters themselves.

Squashed betwixt wet sky and damp earth, sex has little

place to lie down in anywhere from Dublin to Galway. Women, strange creatures that they be, hesitate but a moment when offered a choice between a sodden tromp for love in the flooded fields or the dry cinema where one can squeeze out one's passions as well as can be under the circumstances by knocking knees, clubbing feet and squirming elbows. If the girl did not make this choice, the Church would make it for her. The growing and tumescent lad then has but two ports to put in at, the pub and the cinema. Both places overflow in all towns any night.

But the Church and State, synonymous, lurk everywhere.

The pubs close too early for Reason to have been completely defeated.

The American "fillums," which make clerical collars to jump up and down in apprehension, are censored.

And, Worst, at the end of each show, the damn Anthem is played.

It was while in Dublin, nightly attending old Wally Beery movies to get in out of the cold, I first noticed that my wife and I, like the rest, were on our feet and half up the aisle before FINIS hit the screen.

This observation put me within a hair of forming teams and scoring champs for their ability to make the MEN'S split seconds ahead of the infernal national ditty.

These plays have taught me much, but mostly about myself. I hope never, as a result, to doubt my subconscious again. I hope always to stay alert, to educate myself. But lacking this, in future I will turn back to my secret mind to see what it has observed at a time when I thought I was sitting this one out.

These then are a blind man's plays, suddenly seen. I am grateful that part of me paid attention and saved coins when I could have sworn I was poverty-stricken.

In addition, one can only hope that these plays have been taken in small doses, one at a time. One-act plays, short stories, shots of the best Irish whiskey, all should be savored separate and apart. Too, if one should sit down to read all these plays in one night, one would discover certain encounters or facts in one play not connecting up with encounters or facts in another. This results from all the plays being written separately, with no thought being given to plays future or plays past. The result is a series of one-acts meant to be done separately and read in the same fashion. Though, of course, with a few deletions and additions, the entirety could be staged of an evening. I have chosen, however, to let the plays stand as they are, separate and apart, for they are more enjoyable as creative units, and I insist you must look on them as such; that is my prerogative.

Call all of what you have read in this book mere frivolous calligraphy if you wish. But here, I believe, we find ways of making do with squalls of weather, melancholy drizzles of church rhetoric, the improbability if not the impossibility of sex, the inevitability of death, and the boring ritual of the same old pomp-and-drum corps washing, hanging out, and taking in the same tired old national linen.

The church has put her on her knees, the weather drowned, and politics all but buried her, but Ireland, dear God, with vim and gusto, still sprints for that far EXIT.

And, do you know? I think she'll make it.

Ray Bradbury
July 31st, 1962

THE WONDERFUL ICE CREAM SUIT

and Other
Plays

CONTENTS

INTRODUCTION
With Notes on Staging

First things first. This book is dedicated to Charles Rome Smith, who has directed all of my work for the theater so far, and who will, God allowing, direct more in the years ahead.

As for myself, I began with the theater and I shall probably end with it. I have not, up to now, made a penny, nickel or dime at it, but my love is constant and, in best cliché fashion, its own reward. It has to be. For no one stands about in the alleys after a show giving doughnut money to crazy playwrights.

My first dream in life was to become a magician. Blackstone summoned me up on stage when I was ten to help him with various illusions. I assisted in vanishing a bird in its cage, and helped stir a rabbit out of a strange omelet. Blackstone gave me the rabbit, which I carried home in happy hysterics. Named Tillie, the rabbit in short order produced six more rabbits and I was off and running as an illusionist.

At twelve I was singing leads in school operettas. At twelve and one-half, in Tucson, Arizona, I announced to my classmates that within two weeks I would be an actor broadcasting from local Radio Station KGAR. Self-propelled by my own infernal brass, I trotted over to the station, hung about emptying ashtrays, running for cokes, and being happily underfoot. Rather than drown me with a batch of kittens, the station gave up and hired me to read the Sunday comics to the kiddies every Saturday night. My pay was free tickets to the local theaters to see *The Mummy* and *King Kong*. I was undoubtedly overpaid.

In high school I wrote the Annual Student Talent Show. At nineteen I belonged to Laraine Day's Wilshire Players Guild in a Mormon Church only a block from my home in Los

Angeles. For Laraine, who was becoming a big star at MGM in those days in such films as *My Son, My Son,* I wrote a number of three-act plays that were so incredibly bad no one in the Guild dared tell me of my absolute lack of talent.

Nevertheless, I sensed my own mediocrity and quit playwriting. I vowed never to return to the theater for twenty years, until I had seen and read most of the plays of our time. I lived up to that vow. Only in my late thirties, with thousands of seen performances in my blood, did I dare to try my hand at theater work again.

Even then, licking my old wounds, I feared to let my plays fall into the hands of directors and actors. I seriously doubted my ability, and probably would have delayed additional years had not a friend, hearing of my one-act Irish plays, invited me over to his house one night for a reading. My work was read aloud by actors James Whitmore and Strother Martin. By the end of the evening, we were all on the floor, laughing. Suddenly I realized that the older Bradbury was at long last ready for the theater again.

The theater however, was not ready for me.

I could find no group, no director, no actor, no banker, prepared to put my plays on a stage.

Only in 1963, when Charles Rome Smith and I fell into each other's arms, did I begin to think of producing the plays, myself.

Now this, in itself, is extraordinary. In the entire history of the American theater, only a handful of playwrights have been brash enough, and dumb enough, to save their money and invest it in their own plays.

I talked it over with my wife, told her I thought the plays were more than good, that all the producers were wrong, as well as the bankers, and that I had to try, just once, to see whether or not I was the grandest fool of all.

We saved our money for a year, rented the Coronet Theatre in Los Angeles, finished three one-act plays, hired Charles Rome Smith to direct, and began casting.

The evening of one acts titled *The World of Ray Bradbury,* opened in October, 1964. The reviews were all, I repeat all, excellent. If I had written them myself, they couldn't have been better.

The World ran twenty weeks, after which we opened *The Wonderful Ice Cream Suit* for a run of twenty-four weeks, again to incredibly fine notices.

We took *The World of Ray Bradbury* to New York in 1965 where, with inferior casting and a dreary theater in a bad section of the Bowery, plus a newspaper strike which insured our nonexistence, we folded within three nights, to the tune of $40,000 and thirty-five belated and truly bad reviews, published after our closing, when the newspapers rushed back on the scene to give us a dark burial.

I took the slow train home, vowing to stay away from New York for another lifetime. So far, producers and directors in New York appear to feel the same way; I have not been invited East since.

What did I learn from these experiences?

That working with your own group, your own theater, your own director, your own actors, your own money, is best.

Working with an outside producer and outside money, one is constantly victimized by worries over losing their investment or toadying to their taste and will.

Working as your own producer, all the fun that *should* be in the theater comes to the surface. I have rarely had such a glorious time in my life. I dearly loved being with my actors and my director. I enjoyed the challenge of casting. I wrote most of the publicity for the theater myself, helped design the advertising, clean out the restrooms, and, finally, take the losses without a sigh or remorseful tear. Strange to report, losing one's own money doesn't hurt at all. Losing other people's money is, for me, anyway, a dreadful experience, one I hope to suffer rarely in a lifetime.

What else did I learn? To trust my own intuitive judgment and taste.

I guess what I'm saying here is, if you don't have taste, if you don't trust your intuition, if you don't believe in your plays and their ideas to start with, you shouldn't be in the theater. But if you do make the move, make it on your own, save up your money, it doesn't have to be a large amount, rent a warehouse, nail together a ramshackle stage, and do the damned play! I have spent as little as $49.50 producing one of my plays at a storefront theater in Los Angeles. At other times I have spent $200 and then again $20,000, which went into our final production of *The World of R.B.*

For what other reasons did I come back to the theater after almost twenty years away?

Because most of the plays I saw or read in those twenty years had no ideas in them.

Because most of the plays I saw or read had no language, no poetry in them.

I could not then, I cannot now, accept a theater that is devoid of ideas and poetry.

It seemed shocking to me that a country that has been built on ideas, both political and technological, a country that has influenced the entire world with its concepts and three-dimensional extrusions of those concepts in robot forms, would be so singularly lacking in the theater of ideas.

I have always thought that Bernard Shaw deserved to be the patron saint of the American theater. Yet I saw little of his influence here, a true playwright of ideas born to set the world right. Avant-garde in 1900, he remains light years ahead of our entire avant-garde today.

My other saint would be Shakespeare, of course; and I saw none of his best influence at work in our theater arts.

They say that novelists write the books they wish they could find in libraries.

I act out to write the plays I did not see on the American stage. Shaw? No. Shakespeare? Hardly. Yet if one's influences are not great and broad and wondrous, one has nowhere to start and nowhere to go. These fine ghosts were my instructors, my good company, my friends.

I rediscovered them through Charles Laughton.

In 1955, Charles Laughton and Paul Gregory asked me to adapt my novel *Fahrenheit 451* to the stage. I came up with a bad play. Laughton and Gregory gave me drinks one night at sunset and told me just how bad, but told me kindly. A few months later, Charlie had me up to his house. He stood on his hearth and began to talk about theater, about Molière, about the Restoration playwrights, but particularly about Shaw and then Shakespeare.

As he talked, his house filled with pageantry. The flagstones of his fireplace knew the print of horses and the cry of mobs. The theater of Shakespeare pulsed out of Charlie with great clarity and beauty. He taught me about language all over again.

In the following years I would often go over to swim on summer afternoons when Charlie was preparing to direct or appear in *Major Barbara, The Apple Cart,* or, at Stratford-on-Avon, *King Lear.* Charlie would float enormously about his pool, glad for my company, for I was silent, and he loved to talk theater and work out his ideas on character and style on anyone who had the good sense to listen.

It was the best school I ever had, and the best teacher.

I have not forgotten dear Charles Laughton's lessons.

Anything of mine you see on stage in the coming years will be touched by Charlie's presence. And, just at his elbow, Blackstone.

Their shared theater magic is very similar. What Laughton

accomplished with language, Blackstone accomplished with conniption-fit machineries and illusory contraptions.

The two come together and fuse in my science-fiction plays *The Veldt* and *To the Chicago Abyss.*

Science fiction is what happened to magic when it passed through the hands of the alchemists and became future history. Somewhere along the line we changed caps, labels, and became more practical, but the effect is the same. Television is no less magical for being capable of explanation. I still don't believe it works. Airplanes don't fly; the laws are all wrong.

Our modern technologies, then, are the equivalents of old astrological frauds, alchemical lies, and the nightmares of prehistory. We must build the old terrors up in metal forms and steam them to stranger destinations, first in our psyches, and very soon after in three dimensions, two of which are more often than not surprise and horror. The third is, of course, delight. We wouldn't build these immense toys if we didn't dearly love to wind them up and let them run to Doom's End or Eternal Life, sometimes one, sometimes t'other.

I wrote *The Veldt* because my subconscious knew more about children than has often been told. It began as a word-association test, the sort of thing I often do mornings when I go from bed to my typewriter and let anything jump out on the page that wishes to jump. I wrote the word "nursery" on a piece of paper. I thought to myself, Past? No, Present? No, Future? Yes! A nursery in the future, what would it be like? Two hours later the lions were feeding on the far veldt in the last light of day, the work was done, I wrote *Finis* and stopped.

To the Chicago Abyss was written because sociologists, amateur and professional psychologists, and grand intellectual thinkers bore, distract, or irritate me to madness. I do not believe, and never have believed, that mediocrities hurt people. I have loved all the mass media, looked down on by the intelligentsia, as I grew up. I wanted to do a play about a man who could not recall great quality but only quantity, and that of such dumb stuffs as to be beneath consideration. The boy in me remembered Clark Bars and their bright circus wrappings, and I was off!

To the Chicago Abyss was written long years before Pop Art came on the scene. The story and the play proved to be more than a little prophetic. Since that time, also, motion pictures, once disdained, have been discovered to be an art form. Where was everyone forty years ago? How come I knew it when I was ten? *To the Chicago Abyss* says: Enjoy! If we took all of the junk out of life, our juices would dry up, the sap would go dead in the trees, we would occupy an intellectual graveyard and read each other's headstones.

The Wonderful Ice Cream Suit came out of my experiences as a child and young man in Roswell, New Mexico, Tucson, Arizona, and Los Angeles. I grew up with many boys of mixed Mexican-American blood. My best friend at junior high school was a boy named Eddie Barrera. When I was twenty-one I lived in and around a tenement at the corner of Figueroa Street and Temple in L.A., where, for five years, I saw my friends coming and going from Mexico City, Laredo, and Juarez. Their poverty and mine were identical. I knew what a suit could mean to them. I saw them share clothes, as I did with my father and brother. I remembered graduating from Los Angeles High School wearing a hand-me-down suit in which one of my uncles had been killed by a holdup man. There was a bullet hole in the front and one going out the back of the suit. My family was on government relief when I graduated. What else, then, but wear the suit, bullet holes and all?

So much for the genesis of these plays. Now, how does one produce them?

As simply as possible.

Let the Shakespearean and Oriental theater teach you. Little scenery, few props, and an immense enthusiasm for myth, metaphor, language to win the day.

In a science-fiction play, the harder you try to create the world of the future, the worse your failure. Simplicity was the keynote for our sets and costumes. In *The Veldt,* the various living areas of the future house were defined by nothing more than complex geometric patterns of bright nylon and other synthetic threads. The house looked very much like a fragile tapestry works. You could easily see through all the walls. The main door leading into the playroom-nursery was a spider-web-like device which could expand or contract when pulled or released by other bright twines. Another minor psychological factor might be mentioned here; your average scrim, utilized in thousands of plays over the years, comes between your actors and the audience as an irritating obstruction. Our use of bright threads and twines was a good discovery. The audience never felt kept off, away, or obstructed, yet the feeling of a wall was there when we needed it.

When I first wrote *The Veldt* as a play, I had intended to project actual films of lions on a vast screen. This would have been an error of such immensity I can hardly believe I once entertained the idea.

Instead, I fell back on the lessons so amiably taught me by friend Laughton: stand in the center of the stage and create with words that world, these concepts, those carnivorous beasts.

The audience, then, was to become the veldt, and the sun-blazed lions. When in the playroom, my actors stared out and around in the wilderness that the audience became. This approach worked splendidly.

It worked also because we used sound tapes broadcast from the four corners of the auditorium. This allowed us to prowl the lion roars in circles around about and behind the audience, always keeping them a bit off-balance, never knowing where the sound of the lions might rise again in the long grass.

So I rediscovered an ancient fact. A well-written, well-spoken line creates more images than all the movies of the world. The Chinese were wrong. One word is worth a thousand pictures.

There are more than forty-two sound cues in *The Veldt*, and as many or more light cues.

This means you must find a stage manager, a lighting man, and a sound man of absolutely sterling quality, not liable to panics. The slightest error can throw *The Veldt* off-balance, drive the actors out of their minds, and send the director off to the nearest pub for the rest of the night.

Therefore, the technical rehearsals on *The Veldt* must be exhausting. This means staying up long after midnight in the final days before your opening to make sure that sound, light, and actors function as one whole. Your actors must sense each sound and light cue with hairline accuracy, so as to be able to relax and react truly to Africa "out beyond," hidden among the paying customers.

Every community has its hi-fi superconcussive sound nut. Find yours. Hire him. How? Lurk around your local woofer-tweeter outlet store. The guy with his hair standing on end, with a blind gaze and a bottle of ear medicine in his hand, is the expert at weird auditory hallucinations. Put up with him. Trust him. He will gladly run you up a sound tape of electronic moans, groans, and future musics as will fill the bill for *The Veldt*, and *To the Chicago Abyss!* Ignore the fact that he belongs to a motorcycle gang and is an astrology freak. You can't have everything. Right now, the world of the future can be juiced into existence by superkinks such as he. I have had three tapes invented by a variety of unwashed technicians. All have been amazing. All have been of fine good use in providing yet one more element for our future plays.

In putting together your sound tape for *The Veldt,* your technician should be the next thing to an electronic composer. The scene where George commands the playroom to build him Egypt, the Pyramids, the Sphinx, Paris at the blue hour, etc., must be electronically orchestrated so we *hear* those things being reared up out of the earth into the sky, surrounding the audience with the sounds of electric creation.

Of course, if you are in high school or junior high school, lacking the hi-fi freak in the student body, search for some faculty member whose wig is permanently frazzled from too many hi's and not enough bass. Every school has one. Flatter him by asking for his help. And when in doubt, simplicity is the answer here, also. A few bits of electronic sound and some really good lion roars will save *The Veldt.*

We have spoken at length about *The Veldt.* Now, let us move on to *To the Chicago Abyss* and *The Wonderful Ice Cream Suit.*

In both of these plays we used magic lantern projections, immense photographic cels tossed up on scrims behind the actors to indicate changes of scene.

My good friend Joe Mugnaini, who has illustrated many of my books during the last nineteen years, painted a series of futuristic sets which we projected in images roughly ten to fifteen feet tall, enabling us to shift scenes, change locales, in two or three seconds flat. The six young men pursuing life in their Ice Cream Suit were thus able to race from street to suit emporium to apartment to Red Rooster Cafe with no long mood-shattering pauses for set-movers to strike and rebuild.

Similarly, in *To the Chicago Abyss,* my Old Man who remembered mediocrities could amble from park to interior apartment to night train, crossing empty midnight country in the merest breath of time, because of our illustrated projections.

Joe Mugnaini painted us the whole interior apartment house in skeletal outline so one could x-ray up through floor levels at hundreds of rooms, empty of furniture, haunted by lonely people. At the play's finale, he painted a cel on which were lumped and crammed the crowds of sleeping shadow people surrounding the Old Man on the late-night passenger train.

I must add here that actors, God love 'em, are sometimes or often under-estimators of their own performances or the material at hand. Let me give you an example:

While *To the Chicago Abyss* was in rehearsal, my director Charles Rome Smith telephoned me. I could hear him tearing out his hair. "Get over here," he cried, "the cast is in revolution. They fear that your one-acts will not, in the end, work."

I called a taxi and arrived swiftly.

"Get up on the stage," I said. "Do *To the Chicago Abyss* for me, then we'll see if it's a beast of strength or a monstrous cripple."

I must add here also, I always stay away from rehearsal until weeks have passed. I don't like hanging about, pestering the actors and making the director pass kidney stones. I come in about two weeks before opening to stitch the seams and adjust the hems, as any good playwright should do.

The actors, including Harold Gould, who was at the start of a fine career, got up and did *To the Chicago Abyss*.

When they finished I jumped up on the stage and told everyone to go sit in the audience. I then looked them over quietly and said:

"You want to know what your problem is?"

"Yes," they said.

"The play is alive," I said, "but you're exhausted."

"We're *what?*" they said.

"Exhausted," I said. "You've been rehearsing the better part of four weeks, you're out on your feet, you can't tell what you're doing. But I can tell, for I've kept away to stay fresh so I could come in and be surprised at what I found. Well, let me tell you, this is the best play of the three we're doing. This play will get all the fine reviews and all of you will get great notices for your part, and you, Harold Gould, will get overwhelming reviews which will push you up the theater ladder. Trust me. All you are is tired. Take the afternoon off. Go swim. Go lie down. Bless you."

I never said I told you so until now. Our plays opened. Every one got fine reviews. But *To the Chicago Abyss* was the strawberry on top the celebratory cake. I went back to see Harold Gould three times a week for the next five months.

The inhabitants of the Ice Cream Suit live in a needed world of fantasy woven for them by the suit. The Old Man on his way to Chicago Abyss lives in his memories. Projected backgrounds, then, add yet another proper, right element to the people in these plays, immersed in dreams or half-dreams.

A minor but important detail. The scene in the Red Rooster Cafe where Toro grabs the Ice Cream Suit with Vamenos inside it must be played in SLOW MOTION, as indicated. This was an idea of Charles Rome Smith's, which came to him during rehearsals. It proved to be beautiful in execution, enabling the audience to savor every small part of this major encounter, the terror and despair of all the young men surrounding Toro, trying to get him to let go of the suit, the bravery of Gomez coming back again and again to say "Hit me, not him," and being clouted for his trouble. All, all in the slowest motion, so we can see and hear every special instant up to the beautiful moment when Toro, struck on the head, slowly debates whether to accept unconsciousness, then, like an avalanche, subsides to the floor.

You are not going to be able to find six actors all with the same "skeletons," as Gomez puts it. So I dread to tell you the news, but you must have three or four or perhaps even five suits made and ready for the members of your cast, for the proper fit, and for the quick changes demanded by the scenes. *We* had five suits, which had to be cleaned two or three times a week. Luckily, our cleaner liked the play, and gave us rates!

And now a really great remembrance. On the last night of *The Wonderful Ice Cream Suit* which had played from February through August, to only fine, I repeat fine, reviews, the cast of the play, knowing my jackdaw penchant for collecting bright things, signed all eighteen of their names inside one of the white suits, and gave it to me. I took it home and put it in the closet for twenty years.

Five years ago, when they were handing out the final Oscar for the performance by the Best Actor of the year at the Academy Awards, I said to my wife, "Wait, and watch!"

I went down to the closet, hauled out the Ice Cream Suit and ran it back up near the TV set as the last Oscar was handed over to the young actor. As he grabbed the Award, I opened the white Ice Cream Suit. Under the left armpit I read this pencilled signature:

F. Murray Abraham.

F. Murray Abraham! Who played Salieri, the man who may have caused Mozart's death, the prime role in the film *Amadeus.*

I sat by the TV set with the white Ice Cream Suit in my arms as F. Murray Abraham held the gold statue over his head. Then, I wept. My "son," as it were, had graduated from Harvard.

Well, here, then, are the first three plays I wrote for my Pandemonium Theatre Company. Why such a company name? Because it pleased and delighted me. Because it was an unexpected and frivolous name to give a company of glad fools. And because it meant when you came into our theater, you never knew what special kind of hell might break loose.

Now. . . .

Let the lions run.

Let the old man talk.

The Pandemonium Theatre Company, from here on, is yours.

Ray Bradbury
Los Angeles
August 22, 1971

The Wonderful
Ice Cream Suit

Production Note: The simpler the sets the better. The scrim that represents the "city" should give way easily to the poolroom, which is no more than a pool table, a chair, a light, and a scales. The clothing store could easily be nothing more nor less than a collection of men's dummies, with perhaps one small display case, a tie rack, and a mirror. The white suit itself could be enclosed in a curtained area to one side, and from it the "light" of the wonderful suit would emanate. The tenement room would be cots placed in a rough quadrangle. The bar would be a line of stools and some neon beer signs in the dark. The props should be everything: bright objects against dark backgrounds.

As the curtain rises, we see:

A lamppost in front of a café, a poolroom, a tenement. Three men lounge in various attitudes, enjoying the evening air. A jukebox is playing faintly somewhere. The three men seem to be waiting for something. They look here, they look there. Then:

A stranger walks briskly through. He drags on a cigarette, throws it over his shoulder as he exits.

The cigarette makes a lovely arc of fire in the air, lands on the sidewalk, but is there only a moment when it is retrieved by Villanazul, perhaps the oldest of the six men we will meet whose lives are joined in this summer evening. Villanazul is our dreamer-philosopher, but his movements are swiftly practical for all that.

He lifts the cigarette high and comes back, exhibiting it to the others.

VILLANAZUL: A meteor falls from space! It leaves a path of fire in the dark. It lands among us. It changes our lives.

161

He takes a deep puff, passes it to VAMENOS, *the dirty one, who sucks at it greedily. The third man,* MARTINEZ, *has to seize it away from him. He takes a leisurely puff, hands it back to* VILLANAZUL. *Then, together, the three men turn, look at the sky, the city, and exhale a soft breath of cigarette smoke.*

ALL: Ahhhhh . . .

MARTINEZ: It's a swell night, huh?

VAMENOS: Sure.

VILLANAZUL: Feel that silence. Ain't that a fine silence? A man can think now. A man can dream—

VAMENOS *(puzzled but impressed):* Hey . . . sure.

VILLANAZUL: In such weather as this—revolutions occur.

MARTINEZ: Nights like this you wish—lots of things.

VILLANAZUL: Thinking, I approve. Wishing, however, is the useless pastime of the unemployed.

VAMENOS *(snorts):* Unemployed, listen to him! We *got no jobs!*

MARTINEZ: So we got no money, no friends.

VILLANAZUL: You, Martinez, have us. The friendship of the poor is *real* friendship.

MARTINEZ: Yeah, but . . .

MARTINEZ *stops, stares. The others stare with him. A handsome young Mexican with a fine thin moustache strolls by, a woman on each careless arm, laughing. A guitar plays beautifully as they pass. When they are gone, the guitar goes, fading, with them.*

MARTINEZ *(slaps his brow): Madre mia,* no! Two! How does he rate *two* friends?!

VILLANAZUL: Such friendships are easily come by. Economics, *compadre.*

VAMENOS *(chews his black fingernail):* He means—that guy's got a nice brand-new summer suit. Looks sharp.

MARTINEZ *(watching the people go by):* Sure. And how am I dressed? Eh? Who looks at me? There! In the tenement. You see her? *(points)* In the fourth-floor window, the beautiful girl leaning out? The long dark hair. She's been there forever. That is to say, six weeks. I have nodded, I have smiled, I have blinked rapidly, I have even bowed to her, on the street, in the hall when visiting friends, in the park, downtown. Even now, look, I raise my hand, I move my fingers, I wave to her. And what happens—?

The others look, with MARTINEZ, *up and off in the air, waiting.* MARTINEZ *lets his hand fall at last. They all slump.*

VAMENOS: Nothing.

MARTINEZ: And more than nothing! *Madre mia!* If just I had one suit! One! I wouldn't need money, if I *looked* OK . . .

VILLANAZUL: I hesitate to suggest that you see Gomez. But he's been talking some crazy talk for a month now about clothes. I keep on saying I'll be in on it to make him go away. That Gomez.

Another man has arrived, quietly, behind them.

THE MAN: Someone calls my name?

ALL *(turning):* Gomez!

GOMEZ *(smiling):* That's me.

VILLANAZUL: Gomez, show Martinez what you got in your pocket!

GOMEZ: This?

Smiling, he pulls forth a long yellow ribbon which flutters in the air.

MARTINEZ *(blinking):* Hey, what you doing with a tape measure?

GOMEZ *(proudly):* Measuring people's skeletons.

MARTINEZ: Skeletons?

GOMEZ *squints at* MARTINEZ *and snaps his fingers.*

GOMEZ: *Caramba!* Where you been all my life? Let's try *you!*

He measures MARTINEZ'*s arm, his leg, his chest.* MARTINEZ, *uncomfortable, tries to fend him off.*

GOMEZ: Hold still! Chest—perfect! Arm length—*perfectamente!* The waist! Ah! Now—the height. Turn around! Hold still!

MARTINEZ *turns.* GOMEZ *measures him from foot to crown.*

GOMEZ: Five foot five! You're in. Shake hands!

MARTINEZ *(shaking hands, blankly):* What have I done?

GOMEZ: You fit the measurements! *(he stops)* You got ten bucks?

VAMENOS *(pulling out money):* I got ten bucks! I want a suit! Gomez, measure *me!*

GOMEZ *(shunning Vamenos): Andale! Andale!*

MARTINEZ *(in awe):* I got just nine dollars and 92 cents. That'll buy a new suit? How come? Why?

GOMEZ: Because you got the right skeleton.

MARTINEZ *(pulling back):* Mr. Gomez, I don't hardly know you—

GOMEZ: *Know* me? You are going to *live* with me! Come on!

> GOMEZ *rushes through the poolroom door. The poolroom lights flash on to show us no more than one pooltable, a hanging overhead light, one chair, perhaps, and a weight scales to one side. Reluctantly,* MARTINEZ *is pushed into the poolroom by a quietly competent* VILLANAZUL *and an eager and fawning* VAMENOS. *Two men,* MANULO *and* DOMINGUEZ, *look up from their game of pool as* GOMEZ *waves wildly at them.*

GOMEZ: Manulo! Dominguez! The long search has ended!

MANULO *(drinks from wine bottle):* Don't bother him. He has a most important shot.

> *All stare as* DOMINGUEZ *uses his cue; the balls roll. They click. Everyone is happy.* GOMEZ *leaps in.*

GOMEZ: Dominguez, we have our fifth volunteer!

> DOMINGUEZ *has tabled his cue and taken out a little book.*

DOMINGUEZ: The game is done. The game begins. In my little black book here I have a list of names of happy women who—*(he breaks off)* Caramba! Gomez! You mean—?

GOMEZ: Yes! Your money! Now! *Andale!*

> DOMINGUEZ *is torn between his little book and his news.* MANULO *is torn between his wine bottle and the news. Finally* DOMINGUEZ *puts the book down, takes some rumpled money from his pocket, looks at it, throws it on the*

green table. Reluctantly, MANULO *does the same.* VIL-
LANAZUL *imitates them, once cynical, but caught up at
last now, in the excitement.*

GOMEZ: Ten! Twenty! Thirty!

They look to MARTINEZ *who, disconcerted, nevertheless
counts out his bills and change. To which* GOMEZ *adds
his own money, lifting all the cash like a royal flush,
waving it.*

GOMEZ: Forty! Fifty bucks! The suit costs sixty! All we need
is ten bucks!

VILLANAZUL: And the sooner the better, Gomez. That wonderful ice-cream suit won't last forever. I seen people looking at it in the suit-store window. Only one of a kind! We
got to hurry.

MARTINEZ: Wait there, hey! *The* suit? *Uno? (holds up one
finger)*

GOMEZ *(does likewise): Uno.* One.

MARTINEZ: Ice cream . . . ?

GOMEZ: White. White as vanilla ice cream, white white like
the summer moon!

MARTINEZ: But who gets to own this one suit?

VILLANAZUL, MANULO, and DOMINGUEZ *(quickly, smiling, one
after another):* Me. Me. Me.

GOMEZ: Me. And *you!* OK, guys, line up!

VILLANAZUL, MANULO, DOMINGUEZ *rush to put their backs to
the poolroom wall.* GOMEZ *lines up with them, fourth in
line, and snaps a command at* MARTINEZ.

GOMEZ: Martinez, the other end!

MARTINEZ *takes his place at the other end of the line.*

GOMEZ: Vamenos, lay that billiard cue across the tops of our heads!

VAMENOS *(eagerly):* Sure, sure, sure!

> VAMENOS *places the cue across the tops of the five men's heads, moving along. The cue lies flat and without a rise or fall.* MARTINEZ *leans out to see what is happening and is stunned with revelation.*

MARTINEZ: Ah! Ah!

> GOMEZ *turns his head to smile down the line at* MARTINEZ.

GOMEZ: You see!

> *The men are laughing now, happy with this trick.*

MARTINEZ: We're *all* the same *height!*

ALL *(laughing almost drunkenly):* Sure! Sure! The same!

> GOMEZ *runs down the line with his tape measure, rustling it about the men so they laugh even more.*

GOMEZ: Sure! It took a month, four weeks, to find four guys the same size and shape as me, a month of running around, measuring. Sometimes I found guys with five-foot-five skeletons, sure, but all the meat on their bones was too much or not enough. Sometimes their bones were too long in the legs or too short in the arms. Boy, all the bones! But now, five of us, same shoulders, chests, waists, arms, and as for the *weight?* Men! *(points)*

> *The men march onto the weight scales, one after another.* VAMENOS, *eager to be of service to his gods, puts in a penny for each. The machine grinds and lets drop for each a tiny card which he holds up to peer at, to read aloud, to announce proudly.*

MANULO: 144 pounds!

He steps down, DOMINGUEZ *steps up. The penny drops. The machine grinds. The new card falls out into his hands.*

DOMINGUEZ: 146!

VILLANAZUL *is next, and reads out:*

VILLANAZUL *(quietly proud):* 142.

GOMEZ *weighs himself.*

GOMEZ: 145!

He waves MARTINEZ *aboard.* MARTINEZ *shouts the result.*

MARTINEZ: 144! A miracle!!

VILLANAZUL *(simply):* No . . . Gomez.

They all smile upon GOMEZ, *the saint, who puts his arms about them, circling them in.* VAMENOS *hovers in the background, pretending to be part of all this.*

GOMEZ: Are we not fine? All the same size. All the same dream: the suit. So each of us will look beautiful, eh, at least one night every week!

MARTINEZ: I haven't looked beautiful in years. The girls run away.

GOMEZ: They will run no more, they will freeze, when they see you in the cool white summer ice-cream suit.

VILLANAZUL: Gomez, just tell me one thing.

GOMEZ: Of course, *compadre.*

VILLANAZUL: When we get this nice new white ice-cream summer suit, some night you won't put it on and walk down to the Greyhound bus in it and go live in El Paso for a year in it, will you?

GOMEZ: Villanazul, how can you *say* that?

VILLANAZUL: My eye sees and my tongue moves. How about the EVERYBODY WINS! punchboard lotteries you ran and kept running when nobody won? How about the United Chili con Carne and Frijole Company you were going to organize and all that ever happened was the rent ran out on a two-by-four office?

GOMEZ: The errors of a child, now grown! Enough! In this hot weather, someone may buy the special suit that is made just for us that stands waiting in the window of Shumway's Sunshine Suits! We have fifty dollars. Now we need just one more skeleton!

Everyone tries not to notice VAMENOS, *twitching nearby.*

VAMENOS: Me! My skeleton! Measure it! It's great! Sure, my hands are big, and my arms, from digging ditches—but—

As he talks, he grabs the tape and measures himself. His plea is falling on dull ears until, outside, we hear the guitar, the man and his two women passing, laughing. At this, anguish moves over the faces of the five men in the poolroom, like the shadow of a summer cloud. It is too much for them. They wish to weep. They turn again, in agony, to examine VAMENOS. *Not daring to speak,* VAMENOS *runs over to the penny scale and nervously drops in a penny. The machine grinds. The white card flips into the slot below.* VAMENOS, *eyes closed, breathes a prayer.*

VAMENOS: *Madre mia . . . Please.*

He opens his eyes and looks at the card.

VAMENOS: 145 pounds! Another miracle! *Isn't* it? Eh? *(pauses)* Eh . . . ?

He turns and holds out the card for them in one hand, his ten-dollar bill in the other.

The men look at him, for a long time, sweating.

GOMEZ *breaks, snatches the ten-dollar bill.*

GOMEZ: The clothing store! *Andale!* The suit! The suit!

VAMENOS *lets out a battle yell of delight. All rush out.* MARTINEZ *hesitates, shaking his head.*

MARTINEZ: Santos, what a dream. White as the summer moon, he said. Six men. One suit. What will come of this? Madness? Debauchery? Murder? But then—I go with God. He will protect me.

MARTINEZ, *seeing that the others are gone, runs, but stops, sees something on the table, grabs it.*

MARTINEZ: Hey, Dominguez! You left your black book with the kind ladies' names! Dominguez! Hey! Hey! *(exits)*

Blackout.

In the darkness, the guitar music is very loud and fast. To it, we hear the sound of their running feet. At last, it all fades away as . . . the lights come up again and we see . . .

A neon light flashes: SHUMWAY'S SUNSHINE SUIT SHOP.

Here and there are male mannequins displaying the very niftiest men's fashions. These, and a few racks of shoes and ties, are the furniture of Shumway's. To one side is a green curtained booth, the curtains pulled.

MR. SHUMWAY *and his assistant,* LEO, *enter, bringing a new shipment of ties.*

MR. SHUMWAY: Bring the ties, Leo.

LEO: A pleasure, Mr. Shumway. Such fine ties. Look.

MR. SHUMWAY: I looked, Leo.

LEO: Feel. I . . .

LEO *stops, surprised, because* GOMEZ *has just popped in through the front door, popped out again, casually, hands in pockets.*

MR. SHUMWAY *has not seen this.*

MR. SHUMWAY: Something wrong, Leo?

LEO: Nothing, Mr. Shumway. *(turns away)*

MR. SHUMWAY: Like I said—

Now, MR. SHUMWAY *has caught a fleeting glimpse.* VILLANAZUL *this time, strolling in from the dark, peers around, worried, strolls out.*

LEO: Something wrong, Mr. Shumway?

MR. SHUMWAY: It's too early to tell, Leo.

They go on racking the ties. Next time, both MR. SHUMWAY *and* LEO *turn just as* MARTINEZ *and* MANULO *dart by.*

LEO *(stunned):* Two this time.

MR. SHUMWAY *(getting suspicious):* It couldn't be—a gang is planning to rob my store . . . ?

LEO: Rob . . . ?

At which point, VAMENOS, *alone, appears in the doorway, exhaling smoke, puffing on his villainous cigar, looking thoroughly disreputable, unshaven, and fly-specked.*

LEO *and* MR. SHUMWAY *are riven by the image, which after inspecting the shop casually, wanders off, dropping ashes, into the night.* SHUMWAY *panics, shoving an object at* LEO.

MR. SHUMWAY: Leo, hide this in the suit on the dummy!

LEO: Your *wallet!*

LEO *does not move—so, panicking,* MR. SHUMWAY *thrusts the wallet into the dummy's inside pocket, just in time, for all six of the men have drifted into the doorway.*

Feeling their presence, MR. SHUMWAY *pretends to fix the dummy's tie.*

SHUMWAY: The telephone, Leo. Pretend you're making just a call . . . the police . . .

LEO *edges toward the phone. As he picks it up,* GOMEZ *cries out.*

GOMEZ: It's gone!

SHUMWAY: Quick, Leo! The police!

VILLANAZUL: The police? Hey, wait!

All six men rush forward.

GOMEZ: Where is it? Where!?

SHUMWAY *(points):* The money!? The inside pocket!

GOMEZ: Money?

VAMENOS: No, no! The *suit!*

SHUMWAY: The suit . . . ?

All the men freeze like statues, waiting for GOMEZ *to give tongue to their fear.*

GOMEZ: You . . . didn't . . . *sell* it?

SHUMWAY *(puzzled):* I didn't?

LEO: What didn't Mr. Shumway sell?

VAMENOS: The only suit in the world!

MANULO: The ice-cream white!

GOMEZ: Size thirty-four!

MARTINEZ: Was in your window just an hour ago!

LEO *(exhaling): That* suit?

SHUMWAY *(in disbelief): That's* what you want? *(almost hysterical with relief)* Leo . . . ?

LEO: The booth?

SHUMWAY *(eyes closed):* The booth.

> *Everyone watches as* SHUMWAY, *like a pontiff, leads the way.* LEO *is ahead of him and takes hold of the green curtains on the front of the booth.* SHUMWAY *turns, totally relaxed at last, and glances eagerly about.*

SHUMWAY: For which gentleman?

GOMEZ: All of us.

SHUMWAY *(dismayed again):* All?

MARTINEZ: All for one! One for all!

> *The phrase proves felicitous. The crowd mills about happily, pounding* MARTINEZ *on the back, proud of his creative rhetoric.*

THE CROWD: Sure! Hey! Great! All! All!

SHUMWAY, *undaunted, pontifically accepting this freshly batted shuttlecock of fate, nods to them, then briskly to* LEO. LEO *sweeps back the curtain.* SHUMWAY *seizes a light cord, jerks it, points in.*

SHUMWAY: Gents. There she is. The 59-dollar, 59-cent pure white vanilla ice-cream summer suit!

The men stare, riven. We cannot see into the booth. We only see the reflected pure white, holy light of the suit shimmering out like illumination from some far Arctic floe. The men's faces are washed in snowy color. They peer in as at a shrine.

ALL: Ahhhhhhh . . .

LEO *(sotto voce)*: Mr. Shumway . . . *one* suit? Ain't that a dangerous precedent to set? What if *everyone* bought suits this way?

ALL *(murmuring)*: Ah . . . ah . . .

SHUMWAY *puts his hand on* LEO's *shoulder like a father. He nods to the wondrous crowd of men.*

SHUMWAY: Listen. You ever *hear* one 59-dollar suit make so many people happy at one time?

The six men, their faces glowing with the suit's reflection, still peer, smiling, into the booth.

VAMENOS: White . . . so white it puts out my eyes! *(he squints)*

MARTINEZ: White as angel's wings . . .

MR. SHUMWAY *and* LEO *peer over the six men's backs and nod, proudly.*

SHUMWAY: You know something, Leo? That's a *suit!*

Blackout.

Music.

We hear the six men's voices yelling, singing, shouting. They reenter and pass before the drawn curtain or dark scrim on their way to the tenement.

GOMEZ *(points ahead):* There's my place! You all move in with me. Save money on rent as well as clothes. Martinez, you got the suit?

Enter MARTINEZ, *surrounded by helpers, a white gift box among them.*

MARTINEZ: Have I! From *us* to *us!* Aye-yah!

GOMEZ: Who's got the dummy?

VAMENOS, *chewing his cigar, waltzes in, scattering sparks, clutching a headless clothes dummy.*

VAMENOS: Who else! Watch *us!*

At which point, VAMENOS *slips. The dummy falls. Pandemonium. Everyone yells.* VAMENOS *retrieves the dummy, sheepishly.*

VAMENOS *(to himself):* Vamenos, you clumsy! Idiot!

They seize the dummy from him. To retrieve himself, VAMENOS *snaps his fingers.*

VAMENOS: Hey, we got to celebrate! I'll go borrow some wine!

He almost falls, scattering sparks, as he runs. The others peer after him.

GOMEZ *(unhappily):* All right, guys, inside. Break out the suit!

The others hurry off, leaving MARTINEZ *with* GOMEZ.

MARTINEZ: Hey, Gomez, you look sick.

GOMEZ: I am. What have I *done?*

He waves toward the others.

GOMEZ: I pick Manulo, a great man with the guitar. I pick Dominguez, a fiend, a devil with the women, but who sings sweet, eh? So far so good. I pick Villanazul who reads books.

MARTINEZ: I like to hear him talk.

GOMEZ: I pick you, you wash behind your ears. But *then* what do I do? Can I wait? No! I got to buy that suit! So the last man I pick is a clumsy slob who has the right to wear my suit—*our* suit—one night a week! Maybe to fall downstairs in it, burn it—Why, why did I *do* it!

MARTINEZ *starts to speak when* VILLANAZUL *calls from off right, softly, lovingly.*

VILLANAZUL: Gomez, the suit is ready!

MARTINEZ: Let's go see if it looks as good in *your* apartment with *your* light bulb.

They run off.

Blackout.

When the lights rise again we find ourselves in the tenement apartment with three of the men clustered around an unseen object. GOMEZ *and* MARTINEZ *enter from a door to the right rear.* GOMEZ *only half-looks at the working men.*

GOMEZ: Ready?

VILLANAZUL: Almost!

GOMEZ *turns away, eyes shut.*

GOMEZ: Is it on the dummy?

MANULO: Almost!

They make half-hidden adjustments.

GOMEZ: Just the one light, overhead!

MARTINEZ *scurries to shut off various lamps.*

VILLANAZUL: There!

MANULO: You can look now.

VILLANAZUL *(softly)*: Gomez . . .

GOMEZ *turns. They stand aside.* MARTINEZ *turns on the overhead light. There, as* GOMEZ *opens his eyes, is the phosphorescent, the miraculous white suit, shimmering like a ghost among them. None dare touch, but move in awe around it.*

GOMEZ *(exhales)*: Madre mia . . . !

MARTINEZ *(whispering)*: It's even *better!*

MANULO: . . . White . . . as clouds . . . on a summer night . . .

GOMEZ: . . . Like the milk in the bottles in the halls at dawn . . .

VILLANAZUL, *his face reflecting the whiteness of the suit, speaks.*

VILLANAZUL: White . . . white as the snow on the mountain near our town in Mexico called the Sleeping Lady . . .

The others nod.

GOMEZ *(quietly)*: Say that again, please.

VILLANAZUL, *proud yet humble, is glad to repeat his tribute.*

VILLANAZUL: . . . White as the snow on the mountain called . . .

Smoke is exhaled about all their faces from one side. Slowly, all of them turn to see who is there. VAMENOS, *smiling, is behind them, smoking, holding a wine bottle up.*

VAMENOS: I'm back! A party! The wine! Eh, who gets to wear the suit first tonight! Me?

GOMEZ *(panicky; peers at watch):* It's too late. Nine o'clock!

VAMENOS *(shocked): Late!*

ALL: Late?!!

DOMINGUEZ *goes to the window to look, to point down.*

DOMINGUEZ *(to music):* Late? It is a fine Saturday night in a summer month. The air is sweet. Hear the far music? While women drift through the warm darkness like flowers on a quiet stream . . .

The men make a mournful, trapped sound. The far guitar dies.

VILLANAZUL *(wielding pad and pencil):* Gomez, I ask the favor. You wear the suit tonight from nine-thirty to ten. Manulo till ten-thirty, Dominguez till eleven, myself till eleven-thirty, Martinez till midnight—

VAMENOS *(indignant; removing cigar from mouth):* Hey! Why me *last?*

MARTINEZ *(thinking quickly): After* midnight is the best time of all!

VAMENOS *(thinks)*: Sure. That's *right!*

(smiles) OK.

GOMEZ: OK. And from tonight on, we each wear the suit one night a week, eh? On the extra night, Sunday, we draw straws to see who wears the suit then.

VAMENOS: Me, *every* time! I'm *lucky!*

Every face falls at this news.

MANULO: Can the talk! Gomez, you thought of this. You wear the suit first!

GOMEZ *manages to tear his eyes away from the disreputable* VAMENOS. *He accepts fate and shrugs. Then, impulsively, like a snake shedding his skin in one great movement, he shucks off his old coat and shirt, almost in one motion, yelling.*

GOMEZ: Aye-hah! Aye-yeeeeeeee!

Blackout.

Fast guitar.

In the dark, more happy cries: "The clean shirt!" "Here!" "The pants!" "Here!" "Now the new socks!" "The socks!" "Who ties the best tie?" "Me!" "The shoes!" "All polished!" "Now, now—at last—The coat if you please!"

The lights come up. The men are gathered, we think, to the dummy, as before, fussing with it. Then they stand back.

GOMEZ *stands alone in the center of their excitement.*

VILLANAZUL: Ah!

MANULO: Gomez, you look like a saint! *(looks up)* Forgive me, God, for saying that!

GOMEZ *is like a bullfighter posed there, imperturbably proud, waiting for the last investment with his "suit of lights." He gestures.* VILLANAZUL *and* MARTINEZ *together lift the coat behind him.*

VILLANAZUL and MARTINEZ: The coat! Here!

GOMEZ *(breathes in):* Oh, it even smells good!

VILLANAZUL: How clean it sounds! Listen! How easily it whispers, going on!

They all listen as GOMEZ *assumes the sleeves. He poses like a matador! Far away, a loving crowd sighs: "Ole!"*

GOMEZ *(after the beat):* We got no mirror!

VILLANAZUL: Sure you got a mirror! Here. All of us! Stand close.

VILLANAZUL *arranges the others close-packed with himself.* GOMEZ *falls in with this kindness, and preens himself before them. They look where he walks, turns, adjusts his tie, fixes his cuff. Their gaze is bright.*

GOMEZ: Ah, God, I can see myself in your eyes, your faces! Put me in a store window, I don't deserve to go out!

VILLANAZUL *(softly):* Out, Gomez . . . out . . .

He smiles into that "mirror" and goes to the door, where he places his ears, eyes shut.

GOMEZ: Listen to all those women out there . . . waiting.

They listen. They nod. GOMEZ *turns about once and goes out left. As the door slams,*

Blackout.

Guitar music.

Then, almost immediately, GOMEZ *reenters far stage left.*

The tenement room is, of course, gone. A spotlight fixes GOMEZ *as he adjusts his tie and checks the button on his coat and lovingly touches the snowy sleeves of the suit. Then he looks up and out.*

A voice speaks from the darkness!

THE VOICE: Gomez! Is that you?!

He looks left.

In a spotlight, hanging upon the air is a long, semitransparent scarf hung floating, provocative, light, soft, beautiful.

GOMEZ: Rosita!

Another voice speaks from further over.

THE SECOND VOICE: Gomez! I didn't know you!

A second spot flicks on. In it drifts a second long and diaphanous scarf, a different color. GOMEZ *bows to it.*

GOMEZ: Marguerita, it is me!

Other voices call. Other scarves appear in a double line across the darkness.

THE VOICES: Gomez! Gomez! Gomez! *Que hermosa!* Where are you going?

GOMEZ: This way!

He runs. On the way, he "reaps" the scarves, a half dozen over his right arm, a half dozen over his left.

Blackout.

Music.

The lights come on again almost immediately to find the owners of the suit waiting on each side of the apartment door.

VAMENOS: Half hour's up!

MARTINEZ: Where's Gomez?

VILLANAZUL: Wait! Listen! He's outside the door.

They listen.

VAMENOS: *Someone's* out there, OK.

MARTINEZ: Why don't he come in?!

VILLANAZUL *opens the door.* GOMEZ *stands there, entranced with his experience with the suit, arms out away from his body as if a half dozen "women" were draped over each.*

VILLANAZUL: Gomez! Come in! How was it?

GOMEZ *wanders in. His arms are, of course, empty, but the memory of his encounters lingers. He dreams. He floats.*

MARTINEZ: Gomez! *Say* something!

GOMEZ *takes a deep breath, sighs, and says at last:*

GOMEZ: Who's next?

MANULO: Me!

MANULO *darts in from off right, stripped to his shorts. Everyone shouts.*

Blackout.

Music.

When the light comes up, the music slows. Now who do we find but MANULO *playing the guitar, a little louder, a little faster, luring from the shadows, with the whiteness of his suit and the playing of his music, the shapes of women, perhaps the two women whom we saw earlier passing on the arms of the stranger. The two women reach* MANULO, *who pretends not to see them drawn to him. At the last moment he strikes a chord, tosses the guitar aside, embraces them both. Blackout.*

ALL *(in darkness):* Who's next? Dominguez!

*Fast music. And the spotlight again. And dancing to the music, in the spotlight—in the white suit—*DOMINGUEZ! *He whirls about, he poses. Blackout.*

ALL *(in darkness):* Who's next? Villanazul!

The music is very slow and thoughtful. VILLANAZUL *comes out of the darkness, looking here and there, all about. He is wearing the suit now and looks warmly happy. A single sign is posted: THE PLAZA. There is a vast muttering, murmuring, as of many people in a good argument.* VILLANAZUL *moves like a fish in his proper element, bathed in the free flow of words. We can hear a few snatches of the discussions being carried on.*

ONE VOICE: —there is only one way to stop the gold from flowing out of the country—

A SECOND VOICE: —in the next election, as an individual, I say to you people in the Plaza—we can only look—

VILLANAZUL *has reached a small soapbox. He ascends it.*

Almost immediately there is a hush, a different kind of murmur.

With a single proud but benevolent nod, VILLANAZUL *tunes down the murmur another decibel. With one smile he brings absolute cutoff silence. He waits a heartbeat and then:*

VILLANAZUL: Friends. Do you know Thomas Carlyle's book *Sartor Resartus?* In that book we find *his* Philosophy of *Suits . . . !!*

The audience gasps in admiration.

The spot on VILLANAZUL *grows intensely bright.*

The audience lets out its admiration in a great "Ah!" as if watching a bright fireworks come down amongst them.

And as the "Ah" fades, so does the light.

Darkness.

And we hear a single chord of the guitar.

And then another.

And at last from a door on the far stage right, MARTINEZ *ventures with great trepidation out, and moves through the darkness to stand under a window to the far left.*

MARTINEZ: This is where she lives. That is her window. She *must* feel the suit burning even through those walls. Come on, suit! Bring her to the window.

He shuts his eyes. He leans on the night, eagerly, thinking. A small light comes on in the window above.

MARTINEZ *opens his eyes at this.*

MARTINEZ: Yes!

A brighter light comes on.

MARTINEZ: Yes!

A shadow moves at the window.

MARTINEZ: Yes!

The window opens, the beautiful young woman is there.

MARTINEZ *(softly):* Yes.

The young woman looks around, as if she had been hearing her name called for some minutes and that is why she has come to the window.

MARTINEZ *(whispers):* This way.

The young woman looks off into the distance, a strange expression in her eyes.

MARTINEZ *(as above):* Here . . . !

But still she looks all around.

MARTINEZ: What's wrong?!! Ah, God, even the *blind* can see this suit!

The girl looks down, squints.

MARTINEZ: Ah . . .

He starts to speak. The girl turns, vanishes.

MARTINEZ *(stunned):* No! No . . .

But now she returns. She lifts her hand. A pair of horn-rimmed glasses appear in that hand.

MARTINEZ: *Madre mia,* speak of the lovely blind . . .

She peers about, then sees something.

THE YOUNG WOMAN *(to herself):* What is that whiteness down there?

MARTINEZ *(half aloud, an anxious whisper):* The suit! The suit!

THE YOUNG WOMAN: What is that *other* whiteness down there?

MARTINEZ beams up, all teeth.

At last she puts on her glasses.

THE YOUNG WOMAN: A smile!

MARTINEZ *(waves politely once, nods):* Manuel Martinez.

Shyly she looks down at him through her horn-rims.

THE YOUNG WOMAN *(quietly):* Celia Obregon.

MARTINEZ *(remembering it):* Celia Obregon.

THE YOUNG WOMAN *(likewise):* Manuel Martinez.

MARTINEZ: Next Wednesday night, may I visit your family?

THE YOUNG WOMAN: Yes.

MARTINEZ: You will not forget?

She takes off her glasses.

THE YOUNG WOMAN: No. I see you clearly, even now. The two whitenesses. The suit. The smile.

MARTINEZ: I will bring them both! Celia Obregon.

THE YOUNG WOMAN: Manuel Martinez.

She shuts the window. The light goes out.

MARTINEZ crows like a rooster, happily turning in circles.

MARTINEZ: Aye-hah! Heeee! Oh, friends! Gomez! Villanazul! Manulo!! Dominguez! *To* you! *For* you! *With* you!

He makes one fine pool shot as he names GOMEZ. *He rrr-rolls the name of* VILLANAZUL. *Shouting "Manulo!" and "Dominguez!" he strums a guitar once, twice, throws it into darkness, and furiously dances as the lights black out and the music continues in a fine frenzy.*

As soon as possible the lights come on in the tenement room. The men are waiting by the door. MANULO *is listening, his ear to the keyhole.*

MANULO: *Atencion!* Here comes someone! Martinez! He's singing!

We hear the singing.

MANULO: He's dancing!

We hear the dancing, as do the coowners of the suit.

MANULO: He's drunk!

There is a knock on the door, one, two!

VILLANAZUL *opens the door.* MARTINEZ *looks in, smiling.*

MARTINEZ: I am looking for Manuel Martinez!

Everyone gasps, bemused, puzzled.

VILLANAZUL: Manuel, *you* are Martinez!

MARTINEZ: No, no! Martinez is gone! In his place—who knows?

MANULO: He's drunk!

MARTINEZ: With the *suit!* With *life!* Us all together! The store, here, and laughing, and feeling more drunk, eh, without drinking, and everyone in and out of the coat, the pants, grabbing hold, falling, eh? And one walking out and coming back, and another, and another, and now *me!* Here *I* am! So tall! So pure! Like one who gives orders and the world grows quiet and moves aside . . . Martinez, who is he? Who am I?

DOMINGUEZ: *Here! Look!* We borrowed this while you were out!

GOMEZ: Three mirrors, count them!

MANULO and DOMINGUEZ run forward carrying a three-way mirror, which they set up.

MARTINEZ *(with delight):* Ah! Ah! Look! Three men! Who are they? There's Manulo! Inside the suit! And Dominguez!

MANULO: Hey, what?

DOMINGUEZ: Let *me* see!

They crowd around. MANULO *puts his head on* MARTINEZ's *left shoulder, posing.* DOMINGUEZ *puts his head on the right shoulder.* MARTINEZ *now has three heads.*

MANULO and DOMINGUEZ: Ah! Ah!

MARTINEZ: And Gomez and Villanazul!

They crowd in, too, with general elation. Only VAMENOS *stands back, uneasily.*

GOMEZ: There we *all* are!

VILLANAZUL: Don't we look good? Ah. Touch the mirrors this way, that. See? In the glass! A thousand, a million Gomezes, Manulos, Dominguezes, Martinezes, march off in white armor, away down the line, reflected, re-reflected again and again, indomitable, forever!

MANULO *(quietly):* Don't he speak pretty? Villanazul, you speak pretty.

MARTINEZ *takes off the coat. He holds it out on the air. In a trance, the others stand back as a dirty hand reaches to take the coat.*

GOMEZ: Vamenos!

MARTINEZ *freezes.* VAMENOS *pulls back his hand.*

VAMENOS *(blows smoke)*: What did *I* do?

GOMEZ: Fire eater! Pig! You didn't wash. Or even shave!

ALL *(seizing him)*: The bath! The bath!

VAMENOS: No, mercy! The night air! My death and burial! No!

They hustle him as the lights go out. There is a furious sound of thundering water, splashes, groans, the sound of a body heaved in, VAMENOS *protesting. From darkness we hear:*

VAMENOS: I'm drowned!

GOMEZ: No! No! Just clean!

DOMINGUEZ: Where's the razor?

MANULO: Here!

VAMENOS: Cut my throat, it's quicker!

More water, more thunder, more shouts, and then at last the plug pulled and the great suction away down in the night. All fades to silence. The lights now come slowly up. Five men are standing in a circle on one side of the room, working over some unseen statue like careful and exceptionally neat sculptors.

VILLANAZUL: There.

MANULO: I can't believe it.

DOMINGUEZ: It's him, all right.

MARTINEZ *(in awe)*: Vamenos . . .

They move back, away, to reveal VAMENOS, *unbelievable indeed in the white suit, his beard shaved, hair combed, hands clean.*

He goes to look in the mirror.

VAMENOS: Is that *me?!*

VILLANAZUL: That's Vamenos all right. Of whom it is said that when Vamenos walks by, avalanches itch on mountaintops, flea-maddened dogs dance about on their muddy paws, and locomotives belch forth their blackest soots to be lifted in flags to salute him. Ah, Vamenos, Vamenos, suddenly the world *sizzles* with flies. And here you are, a huge, fresh-frosted cake.

MANULO *(sadly)*: You sure look keen in that suit, Vamenos.

VAMENOS: Thanks.

He twitches uneasily under their stare, trying to make his skeleton comfortable where all their skeletons have so recently been. There is a long pause.

VAMENOS *(faintly)*: Can I go now?

Another pause, in which GOMEZ *suddenly cries:*

GOMEZ: Villanazul! A pencil! Paper!

VILLANAZUL *(whipping them out)*: Okay!

GOMEZ: Copy down these rules for Vamenos.

VILLANAZUL: Ready.

GOMEZ: Rule number one.

VAMENOS *(listening close)*: One, yes.

GOMEZ: Don't fall down in that suit.

VAMENOS: I won't.

GOMEZ: Two: don't lean against buildings in that suit.

VAMENOS: No buildings.

GOMEZ: Don't walk under trees with birds in them in that suit.

VILLANAZUL *(writing):* . . . birds . . .

VAMENOS *(eager to please):* . . . trees, no, no trees.

MARTINEZ *(chiming in):* Don't smoke!

DOMINGUEZ: Don't drink!

GOMEZ: Good, no smokes, no drinks—

VAMENOS *(cuts in):* Please. Can I *sit down* in this suit?

VILLANAZUL: When in doubt—take the pants off, fold them over a chair.

Everyone looks at the philosopher, pleased. VILLANAZUL *goes on, writing, pleased with himself.*

VAMENOS *mops his brows with his handkerchief. He edges toward the door, gingerly.*

VAMENOS: Well . . . wish me luck.

GOMEZ *(a real prayer):* Go with God, Vamenos.

ALL: Aye . . . aye . . .

He waves a little wave. He opens the door. He goes out quickly. He shuts it.

There is a ripping sound!

GOMEZ: *Madre de dios!*

All stand, riven by the terrible sound.

VILLANAZUL: Vamenos!

He whips the door open.

There stands VAMENOS, *two halves of a torn handkerchief in his hands.*

VAMENOS: Rrrrip! Look at those faces! *(He tears the cloth again)* Rrrrip! Oh, oh, your faces! Ha!

Laughing, VAMENOS *slams the door, leaving them stunned.* GOMEZ *sinks slowly into a chair.*

GOMEZ: Stone me! Kill me! I have sold our souls to a demon!

VILLANAZUL *digs in his pockets, takes out a coin.*

VILLANAZUL: Here is my last 50 cents. Who else will help me buy back Vamenos' share of the suit?

MANULO *(displaying a dime)*: It's no use. We got only enough to buy the lapels and buttonholes.

At the window, DOMINGUEZ *reports, looking down.*

DOMINGUEZ: There goes Vamenos. He's in the street. Hey! Vamenos! *(leans out)* No!

GOMEZ *leaps up.*

GOMEZ: What's he doing?

DOMINGUEZ: Picking up a cigar butt and lighting it . . .

GOMEZ *tears to the window.*

GOMEZ: Vamenos! Pig! No cigars! Away!

DOMINGUEZ: There. Ah. *(relaxes)* Now he is making a very strange gesture to us with his hand. *(waves)* The same to you, friend. There he goes.

GOMEZ: There goes our suit, you mean.

Everyone has drifted or hurried to the window now. They are crushed together, worriedly, looking out and down.

MANULO: I bet he eats a hamburger in that suit.

VILLANAZUL: I'm thinking of the mustard.

GOMEZ *(turns away; pained):* Don't! No, no.

MANULO: I need a drink, bad.

MARTINEZ: Manulo, there's wine here, this bottle—

But MANULO *is out the door. It shuts.*

GOMEZ *stands alone with his thoughts. The others fidget. After a moment,* VILLANAZUL, *with a great pretense of being casual, stretches, yawns, strolls toward the door.*

VILLANAZUL: I think I'll just walk down to the plaza, friends.

VILLANAZUL *exits. The others look at the door, the window, the door, the window.*

GOMEZ: Can you still see it?

DOMINGUEZ *(at the window):* Who?

GOMEZ: The suit! And the monster in it!

DOMINGUEZ: He's a long way off there. He's turning down Hill Avenue. That's a dark street, ain't it?

GOMEZ *(twitching):* How should I know!

DOMINGUEZ *ambles toward the door.* GOMEZ, *his back turned, feels the motion.*

GOMEZ: Dominguez?

DOMINGUEZ *(guiltily takes his hands off the door):* Eh?

GOMEZ: If you just happen—

DOMINGUEZ: Eh?

GOMEZ: Hell, if you should bump into, run into Vamenos, by accident, I mean, warn him away from Mickey Murillo's Red Rooster Café. They got fights not only *on* but *out front* of the TV, too, there.

MARTINEZ: Mickey Murillo's Red Rooster Café. That's on Hill Avenue, right?

DOMINGUEZ *(nervously):* He wouldn't go into Murillo's. That suit means too much to Vamenos.

MARTINEZ: Sure.

DOMINGUEZ: He wouldn't do anything to hurt it.

GOMEZ: Sure.

DOMINGUEZ: He'd shoot his mother, first.

MARTINEZ: Any day.

DOMINGUEZ: Well . . .

GOMEZ and MARTINEZ: Well?

DOMINGUEZ *takes the cue. He exits, fast.*

MARTINEZ *and* GOMEZ, *alone, listen to* DOMINGUEZ's *footsteps hurry away downstairs. Now they circle the undressed window dummy.* GOMEZ *returns at last to the window, where he stands biting his lip and at last, unhappily, begins to search through his clothes until at last from a pocket he draws forth a piece of pink folded paper.*

GOMEZ: Martinez, take this.

MARTINEZ: What is it? Names. Numbers. *(reads)* Hey! A ticket on the bus to El Paso a week from now!

GOMEZ *(nods):* Turn it in. Get the money.

MARTINEZ: You were going to El Paso, alone?

GOMEZ: No. With the suit. *(a beat)* But now, after tonight, I don't know. Hell, I'm crazy. Turn it in. We may need the money to buy back Vamenos' share. With what's left over, we buy a nice new white Panama hat to go with the white ice-cream suit, eh?

MARTINEZ: Gomez—

GOMEZ: Boy, is it hot in here! I need air.

MARTINEZ: Gomez. I am touched.

GOMEZ: Shut up. Maybe the white suit don't even *exist* anymore. *Andale!*

GOMEZ *runs out.* MARTINEZ *starts to follow, comes back, pats the dummy for luck, reaches up, jerks the light string—blackout. We hear the door slam as he leaves.*

Fast guitar music.

In the darkness after a time, as the guitar confines itself to single chords, a neon sign blinks on and off to the music: MICKEY MURILLO'S RED ROOSTER CAFÉ.

Out of the night, VILLANAZUL *strolls as nonchalantly as possible. Angled across stage right is the front of the café with swinging doors and a great flake-painted glass window through which one can peer through those places where the paint has snowed away.*

VILLANAZUL *pretends not to be interested in the café or anything inside it, but at least he is drawn to peer in the door at the darkness from which voices murmur. He then puts his eye to a flaked place on the window and stands thus until:*

MANULO *enters, looking back, wondering if he is being followed. He ducks into a setback near the café and peers out, at which point* DOMINGUEZ *comes mysteriously on.* MANULO *snorts and steps out.*

MANULO: *Caramba,* it's you!

DOMINGUEZ: Manulo! What you doing here?

MANULO *(lying badly):* I was looking for a good place to have a drink.

DOMINGUEZ: I was just walking, myself. *There's* a good place. *(points)*

MANULO *(amazed):* Sure! The Red Rooster Café. Why didn't *I* think of that!

DOMINGUEZ: So many places, they're crowded. Let's look before we go.

They line up with VILLANAZUL, *one on each side, peering through the flaked glass. Once they are half-bent,* VILLANAZUL *becomes sentient, he feels them on the other side, but does not look yet.*

MANULO: What do you see?

DOMINGUEZ: Nothing.

VILLANAZUL: He's in there, OK.

MANULO *(looks up): Who* is?

DOMINGUEZ *(the same):* Where!

BOTH *(turning):* Villanazul!

VILLANAZUL: Manulo! Dominguez! What *you* doing here?

BOTH: What! What?! Ha!

As if well rehearsed, all three turn back to the window and search for the best peepholes. Now GOMEZ *and* MAR-TINEZ *hurry on, do a double take, and line up with them. This time there are no greetings, no rationalizations.*

GOMEZ: Is our white suit in there?

MARTINEZ: Wait! Sure! Way back in the dark there!

MANULO *(in awe):* Hey, yeah . . . there's the suit, and, praise God, Vamenos is still *in* it!

VILLANAZUL: It's moving! It's coming this way!

Off in the café we see a whiteness drifting.

MANULO: He's got money! He's going to play the jukebox!

The whiteness moves. We hear a fearful clangor of machinery as the money drops in and is digested. There is a vast hiss. Then, in one blast of light and sound, a huge behemoth of a jukebox explodes into color and brilliance, at the same time emitting such concussive brass and tympani that the five men are jarred from the window. Now, in full rainbow light, we see the suit, and VAMENOS. *He stands delightfully drenched with music, like a child out in the welcome rains of summer.*

VAMENOS *lifts his hand. A glass is in it.*

MANULO: He's drinking!

The men gasp. Inside, VAMENOS *sips wine.*

VILLANAZUL: He's smoking.

Inside, VAMENOS *scatters sparks, blows smoke.*

MARTINEZ: He's—eating!

It isn't easy, but juggling the items around in his hands, VAMENOS *shifts his cigar, his glass, and raises food to his mouth.*

DOMINGUEZ: A taco!

GOMEZ *(turns away)*: No!

MANULO: A *juicy* taco!

That's what it is. A very juicy taco that VAMENOS *has to lean in at, arching his body so it won't drop on the clothes.*

VILLANAZUL: *Ay, caramba!*

GOMEZ: What's he doing now?

MARTINEZ: Dancing!

GOMEZ: Dancing!!???

VILLANAZUL: With the cigar, the wine, and the taco!

MANULO *(moving his feet and hips)*: The Enchilada Cha-Cha-Cha. That's a good tune.

GOMEZ *(enraged)*: Good *tune*? It's our funeral march!

MARTINEZ: Hold everything! Someone's coming to dance with him!

GOMEZ *(eyes closed)*: Wait! Don't tell me! The big one . . . weighs two hundred pounds on the hoof? Ruby Escuadrillo?

A woman who is as big, colorful and impressive as the jukebox dances out of the shadows and circles VAMENOS.

ALL *(gasping)*: Ruby Escuadrillo!

GOMEZ *must turn back now and look in.*

GOMEZ: That ox! That hippo!

MARTINEZ: She's crushing the shoulder pads!

It's true. She has hold of one of the shoulders of the white suit with her huge hand.

DOMINGUEZ: They've stopped dancing.

MARTINEZ: They're going to sit down. She's going to sit in his lap!

VILLANAZUL: No, not with all that powder and lipstick!

GOMEZ: Manulo! Inside! Grab that drink! Villanazul, the cigar! Dominguez, the taco! Martinez, dance Ruby Escuadrillo away!

ALL: Aye! Check! Right! Done!

They start to move, but freeze when:

A great two-ton truck of a man lumbers into sight from the street beyond, and pushes them out of the way, going into the café.

MARTINEZ: Toro!

VILLANAZUL: Hi, Toro!

GOMEZ: Toro? Was that Toro Ruiz? Ruby Escuadrillo's boyfriend?

MANULO: Sure!

MARTINEZ: If he finds her with Vamenos!

MANULO: The white suit!

VILLANAZUL: It'll be covered with blood!

GOMEZ: Don't make me nervous! Quick! As before; taco, drink, cigar, Ruby. Me! I'm for Toro Ruiz!

MANULO: What a brave one, you, Gomez!

GOMEZ: *Andale!*

They all rush in and collide to a halt for they see:

TORO RUIZ, *who has discovered* VAMENOS *and* RUBY, *just as* RUBY, *laughing, sits down on* VAMENOS'*s lap.*

Bellowing, TORO *runs forward.* RUBY *jumps up.*

GOMEZ: Wait!

TORO, *his hand out, freezes.* VILLANAZUL *runs, grabs the cigar out of* VAMENOS'*s mouth, smokes it. From here on, everyone moves in slow motion. They also speak in slow motion.*

VILLANAZUL *(puffs):* I need a smoke!

VAMENOS *(surprised):* Hey!

MANULO *grabs the glass, slowly.*

MANULO *(gulps):* I need a drink!

VAMENOS *(upset):* Hey!

DOMINGUEZ *seizes the taco, in slow motion.*

DOMINGUEZ *(chewing):* I'm hungry!

VAMENOS *(irritated):* Hey!

MARTINEZ *grabs* RUBY, *slowly.*

MARTINEZ: Ruby! Ruby!

He dances her off, slowly.

VAMENOS and TORO *(angrily):* Hey!

VAMENOS *jumps up.* TORO *thinks he is being attacked and catches* VAMENOS. *He grabs several yards of lapel and squashes it, but all with beautiful slow motion precision.*

TORO: You! You!

At which all six owners of the suit yell, slowly.

GOMEZ: Let go!

MARTINEZ: Let go of Vamenos!

VILLANAZUL: No, let go the *suit!*

TORO: You dance, hah?

VAMENOS: No!

TORO: You tired, hah? I help you!

He dangles VAMENOS *like a marionette, so* VAMENOS *tap-dances in spite of himself.* TORO *cocks a fist, slowly.*

GOMEZ *thinks quickly and steps in, slowly.*

GOMEZ *(smiles):* Don't hit *him.* Hit *me.*

TORO *hits him smack on the nose.*

GOMEZ *holds his nose and wanders off, tears stinging his eyes.*

GOMEZ: *Chi-hua-hua* . . .

VILLANAZUL *grabs one of* TORO's *arms,* MANULO *the other.*

MANULO: You're wrinkling the lapels!

VILLANAZUL: You're ripping the buttons!

VAMENOS: You're killing *me!*

DOMINGUEZ: Peon! Drop him! Let go!

MANULO: *Cabron! Coyote! Vaca!*

TORO wrenches the suit. All the men twist, wrench, in pantomime, with the agonized torture of the suit.

VILLANAZUL: Vamenos, go with the motion! Don't fight. Where the suit goes, go! Otherwise—

TORO cocks his fist again, and in doing so, shakes MANULO free, as easily as knocking a poker chip from his elbow.

TORO: Now!

GOMEZ wanders back, just in time.

GOMEZ *(smiling bravely, holding his nose):* Don't hit him. Hit *me.*

TORO beams. TORO hits GOMEZ on both the nose and the hand holding the nose. GOMEZ puts the damaged hand under his other arm and puts a new hand up to his freshly mangled nose, wandering off.

GOMEZ: *Chee-wah-wah* . . .

At which point a chair, beautifully uplifted by MARTINEZ, comes down on TORO's head.

ALL: Aiiieeeeee!

They all stand back, waiting.

TORO shakes his head and carefully thinks over the facts: he has been hit; maybe, maybe he will not fall down. He cannot quite make up his mind. He sways. The men sway. He turns, dragging VAMENOS, by the suit, with him. The men turn.

Now, slowly, TORO starts to sink down, down. But he still has hold of the lapels.

The men shout in at him, as if he were a long way off, and needs urgent instruction.

MANULO: Toro!

VILLANAZUL: The suit! The lapels!

GOMEZ: Let *go!*

TORO *seems to hear their faint far calling. His glazed eyes flicker. But still he sinks.*

ALL: Let . . . go!

And at the last moment, TORO *blessedly opens his huge banana fingers.*

VAMENOS *falls into the arms of his* compadres.

TORO, *like a poled ox, topples over, kicks, and lies, smiling foolishly. Instantly, the slow motion stops. From here on, everything returns to normal motion.*

VAMENOS *(blinks):* Hey . . . what's going on?

GOMEZ: What?! *Compadres!* Out!

VAMENOS *is helped, lifted, carried around the ruin.*

VAMENOS: Wait a minute! My drink! My taco! Ruby!

The doors slam shut. As they do so, the lights flash off. The jukebox goes off. The interior of the café vanishes from view, RUBY *and* TORO *with it.*

Outside, the men hold VAMENOS.

VAMENOS: Put me down!

GOMEZ *nods. They put him down. The picture of outraged dignity,* VAMENOS *brushes the suit, fixes his tie, shakes away their hands which try to adjust the lapels and button the buttons.*

VAMENOS: OK, OK. My time ain't up!

ALL *(incredulous at his temerity)*: What!

    VAMENOS *takes* GOMEZ's *wrist to peer at the watch.*

VAMENOS: I still got two minutes and—let's see—ten seconds—

GOMEZ: Ten sec—you! You dance with a Guadalajara cow! You smoke, you drink, you eat tacos, you pick fights, and now you got the nerve to say you got two minutes and ten seconds—

VAMENOS *(nervously)*: Two minutes flat, now!

    A woman's voice from off, away somewhere.

THE VOICE: Hey, Vamenos!

VAMENOS: Who's that?

THE VOICE *(calling)*: Vamenos! Here! Ramona!

VAMENOS: It's Ramona. Hey, Ramona!

THE VOICE: Vamenos, you sure look sharp!

    All the men have turned to look off across the street.

VAMENOS: Ramona, wait! I'm coming over!

GOMEZ: Vamenos, come back! The street!

MANULO: What can you do in one minute and—*(checks watch)*—forty seconds?

VAMENOS *(winks)*: Watch! Ramona, here I come!

    He runs off into darkness.

GOMEZ: Vamenos! Watch out!

MARTINEZ: That car!

MANULO: Jump!

We hear the car, the brakes, the horn. Out of sight, we hear VAMENOS *cry out.*

ALL: Aaiiieeee . . . no!

A light flashes across the stage. The men all hold onto each other in fright, looking off, gabbling, no, no. Their heads move up over and along.

VAMENOS *is hurled backward out of darkness, falls on his back, rolls over and lies on his face, still.*

The car guns its motor and races off. GOMEZ *looks at the silent figure of* VAMENOS. *Then suddenly it hits him what has happened and he runs a few steps after the car.*

GOMEZ: Fiends! Fools! Murderers! Come back, come back! *(He stops and sways)* Kill me, someone. I don't want to live.

But the car is gone.

Now all the men stand breathing hard, unable to move. They hold to each other a moment longer. Then the smallest motion from VAMENOS *sets them walking, shambling, then running to surround him. They stand looking down.*

GOMEZ: Vamenos! You're . . . alive!

VAMENOS *has his eyes shut, his hands clenched at his sides, his whole body stiff. He moans, he cries out.*

VAMENOS: Tell me, tell me, oh, tell me, tell me.

MANULO: Tell you what, Vamenos?

VAMENOS: Tell me . . .

He stops to grind his teeth, to moan.

The men crouch lower.

VAMENOS: What have I done . . . to the suit, the suit, oh, the suit . . . ?

The men touch him.

VILLANAZUL: Vamenos . . . why.

MARTINEZ: It's OK . . . !

VAMENOS *(eyes still shut):* You lie! It's torn, it must be, and around, underneath . . . ?

They touch him further, they handle him gently, they turn him over.

GOMEZ: No. Vamenos, all around, underneath, on top, it's OK!

VAMENOS *(opens his eyes):* A miracle! Praise the saints! Oh, good, good!

Distantly a siren wails. The men look up.

DOMINGUEZ: Someone must've phoned for an ambulance!

VAMENOS *(stricken):* An ambulance! Quick! Set me up! Take off our coat!

MANULO: Vamenos, you—

GOMEZ: Don't worry, we—

VAMENOS *(rolling his eyes, gibbering):* Idiots! The coat! The coat! Get it off me!

They humor him, lift him, start to take it off. The siren is louder.

VAMENOS: Yes, yes, that's it! Quick! There!

They have the coat off.

VAMENOS: Now, *andale,* the pants!

ALL: The pants?!

VAMENOS: The pants, the pants, fools! Lost ones! Quick, *pe-ones!* Those doctors!

GOMEZ: Doctors?

VAMENOS: You seen the movies!

MARTINEZ: Movies?

VAMENOS: In the movies they rip the pants with razors to get them off! They don't care! They're maniacs!

ALL: Maniacs!

> *They fly to work. Zip, zip, the pants are coming off now in a frenzy.*

VAMENOS: Ah, God, careful! Ah, ah! Jesus, come after me, there, quick! The siren!

GOMEZ: Here it comes! The ambulance!

> *Everyone handles* VAMENOS *at once.*

VAMENOS: Right leg, easy, hurry, cows! Left leg, now, left, Ow, God . . . Martinez, now, your pants!

MARTINEZ: Mine?

VAMENOS: Take them off!

MARTINEZ: What?

ALL: Off! Fool! All is lost!

> GOMEZ *flips at* MARTINEZ'*s belt buckle swiftly.* MARTINEZ *falls to and, hopping about, starts to get his pants off.*

VAMENOS: Give me! Give!

GOMEZ: Form a circle! In! In! Close in!

The men circle MARTINEZ. *We see his pants flourished on the air. We see the white pants fly upward on the air.*

VAMENOS: Quick, here come the maniacs with the razors. Right leg, right! Yes! Ah! Left leg, easy, ah-ow!

The men bend, leaving MARTINEZ *to hop around getting into the white pants. The siren pulls up offstage and dies. A light from the ambulance has flushed the stage.*

VAMENOS: The zipper, cows! Zip my zipper! Ow!

The ambulance men run onstage with a portable carrier. VAMENOS *lies back down, exhaling.*

VAMENOS: *Madre mia,* just in time. *Gracias, compadres, gracias.*

MARTINEZ *strolls off away, casually buckling the belt on the white trousers. The ambulance men bend and examine* VAMENOS.

ONE INTERN: Broken leg. What happened?

GOMEZ: He—

VAMENOS *(quickly):* I fell down . . . running after a woman.

The interns look from VAMENOS *to the others, expectantly. At last,* GOMEZ *nods.*

GOMEZ *(quietly):* He fell down . . . running after a woman.

They are all proud of VAMENOS *and his fine lie, in this moment. Now he is placed on the canvas carrier gently by the men.* MARTINEZ *has put on the white coat.*

VAMENOS: *Compadres . . . ?* Don't be mad with me.

VILLANAZUL: Who's mad?

Now the carrier is lifted and the men stand around VAMENOS *as he speaks, faltering.*

VAMENOS: *Compadres,* when . . . when I come from the hospital . . . am I still in the bunch?

There is a long silence.

VAMENOS: You won't kick me out? Look, I'll give up smoking, keep away from Murillo's, swear off women—

MARTINEZ *(gently):* Vamenos. Don't promise nothing.

VAMENOS *looks at* MARTINEZ, *his eyes brimming.*

VAMENOS: Oh, Martinez, you sure look great in our suit. *Compadres,* don't he look beautiful?

They carry VAMENOS *out.*

VILLANAZUL: Vamenos, I'll go with you!

VILLANAZUL *waves to the others and hurries out.*

MANULO: I'll go with you, Vamenos!

GOMEZ: Me, we'll *all* go with you, Vamenos!

The siren brays. The guitar music plays. The men run out. Darkness.

When the light comes on again it is the raw overhead bulb in the tenement room under which stands DOMINGUEZ *ironing the white coat on a board.* MARTINEZ *stands nearby with the pants over his arm. Now* DOMINGUEZ *finishes and holds up the coat.*

DOMINGUEZ: There! Clean, pressed! White as a gardenia! Sharp as a razor!

They place the suit on the dummy and stand back.

GOMEZ: So . . . it's late. Two o'clock. Friends, the room is yours. Sleep.

He nods, he waves about. The men move to collapsible cots. Some lie on the floor. But they make a circle, enclosing the suit on the dummy. They all lie, looking at its whiteness. MARTINEZ *alone remains standing by the suit, fixing its lapels.*

MARTINEZ: *Ay, caramba,* what a night. Seems ten years since seven o'clock, when it all started and I had no friends. Two in the morning I got all *kinds* of friends. Even Celia Obregon, the girl in the window. All kinds of friends. I got a room. I got clothes. You tell *me.* Hey! *(softly)* Funny. When I wear this suit, I know I will win at pool like Gomez. I will sing and play the guitar like Manulo. I will dance like Dominguez. I will talk fine talk like Villanazul. Be strong in the arms like Vamenos . . . So . . . so, tonight I am Gomez, Manulo, Dominguez, Villanazul, Vamenos. Everyone . . . *Ay . . . ay . . .*

There is a moment of silence. Outside, flushing in through the windows, we see the light of various neon signs flashing on and off. MARTINEZ *stands musing.*

GOMEZ *(quietly):* Martinez? You going to sleep?

MARTINEZ: Sure. I'm just—thinking.

MANULO: What?

MARTINEZ *(softly):* If we ever get rich, it'll be kind of sad. Then we'll all have suits. And there won't be no more nights like tonight. It'll break up the old gang. It'll never be the same after that.

The men lie thinking of it for a moment.

GOMEZ *nods at last, a sudden sadness in his voice.*

GOMEZ: Yeah . . . it'll never be the same . . . after that.

MARTINEZ pulls the light cord. The light goes out. From outside the neon lights flash on and off, on and off.

MARTINEZ strokes the white suit a last time, then lies down near it.

The men look at the suit in the flashing on-and-off light. It stands in the middle of the room, in the middle of their lives, white in darkness, now seen, now vanishing, now seen, now vanishing, as the neon lights flash, flash, and again flash, flash, and the guitar plays slow, slow, a chord, another sweet, sad chord and

the curtain slowly, slowly descends.

THE END

The Veldt

The curtain rises to find a completely empty room with no furniture of any kind in it. This room encompasses the entire front half of the stage. Its walls are scrim which appear when lighted from the front, vanish when lighted from the rear. In the center of the room is a door which leads to the living quarters of a house circa 1991. The living quarters dominate the entire rear half of the stage. There we see armchairs, lamps, a dining table and chairs, some abstract paintings. When the characters in the play are moving about the living area, the lights in the "empty" room, the playroom, will be out, and we will be able to see through into the back quarters of the house. Similarly, when the characters enter the empty playroom, the lights will vanish in the living room and come on, in varying degrees, as commanded, in the play area.

At rise of curtain, the playroom is dimly lit. An electrician, bent to the floor, is working by flashlight, fingering and testing electrical equipment set under a trapdoor. From above and all around come ultrahigh-frequency hummings and squealings, as volume and tone are adjusted.

George Hadley, about thirty-six, enters and moves through the living area to look through the playroom door. He is fascinated, delighted in fact, by the sounds and the flicker of shadows in the playroom. He looks out through the fourth wall, as he will do often in the play, and treats the audience area, on all sides, as if it were the larger part of the playroom. Much lighting, and vast quantities of sound, will come from the sides and back of the theater itself.

At last, excited, George turns and calls.

GEORGE: Lydia! Lydia, come here!

> *She appears, a woman about thirty-two, very clean and fresh, dressed simply but expensively for a housewife.*

GEORGE *(waving):* Come on! It's almost ready!

She joins him at the door as the humming, squealing dies. The ELECTRICIAN *slams the trapdoor, rises, and comes toward them with his kit.*

THE ELECTRICIAN: It's all yours, Mr. Hadley.

GEORGE: Thanks, Tom.

The ELECTRICIAN *turns to point a screwdriver into the room.*

ELECTRICIAN: There's your new—how does the advertisement read?—Happylife Electrodynamic Playroom! And *what* a room!

LYDIA *(ruefully):* It ought to be. It cost thirty thousand dollars.

GEORGE *(taking her arm):* You'll forget the cost when you see what the room can do.

ELECTRICIAN: You sure you know how to work it?

GEORGE: You taught me well!

ELECTRICIAN: I'll run on, then. Wear it in health! *(exits)*

GEORGE: Good-bye, Tom.

GEORGE *turns to find* LYDIA *staring into the room.*

GEORGE: Well!

LYDIA: Well . . .

GEORGE: Let me call the children!

He steps back to call down a hall.

GEORGE: Peter! Wendy! *(winks at his wife)* They wouldn't want to miss this.

*The boy and the girl, twelve and thirteen, respectively,
appear after a moment. Both are rather pale and look as
if they slept poorly.* PETER *is engrossed in putting a point
to his sister as they enter.*

PETER: Sure, I know, I know, you don't like fish. OK. But fish
is one thing and fishing is something else! *(turning)* Dad
and I'll catch whoppers, won't we, dad?

GEORGE *(blinking)*: What, what?

PETER *(apprehensively)*: Fishing. Loon Lake. You remember
. . . *today* . . . you promised . . .

GEORGE: Of course. Yes.

*A buzzer and bell cut in. A TV screen, built into one
wall at an angle so we cannot see it, flashes on and off.*
GEORGE *jabs a button. We see the flickering shadows on
his face as the screen glows.*

GEORGE: Yes?

SECRETARY'S RADIO VOICE: Mr. Hadley . . .

GEORGE *(aware of his son's eyes)*: Yes? yes . . .

SECRETARY'S VOICE: A special board meeting is called for 11.
A helicopter is on its way to pick you up.

GEORGE: I . . . thanks.

GEORGE *snaps the screen off, but cannot turn to face his
son.*

GEORGE: I'm sorry, Peter. They own me, don't they?

PETER *nods mutely.*

LYDIA *(helpfully)*: Well, now, it isn't all bad. Here's the new
playroom finished and ready.

GEORGE *(hearing):* Sure, sure . . . you children don't know how lucky you are.

The children stare silently into the room, as GEORGE *opens the door very wide so we get a good view.*

WENDY: Is that all there is to it?

PETER: But—it's *empty.*

GEORGE: It only *looks* empty. It's a machine, but more than a machine!

He has fallen into the salesman's cadence as he tries to lead the children through the door. They will not move. Perturbed, he reaches in past them and touches a switch. Immediately the room begins to hum. Slowly, GEORGE HADLEY *steps gingerly into the room.*

GEORGE: Here, now. Watch me. If you please.

GEORGE *has addressed this last to the ceiling, in a pompous tone.*

The humming becomes louder.

The children wait, unimpressed.

GEORGE *glances at them and then says, quickly:*

GEORGE: Let there be light.

The dull ceiling dissolves into very bright light as if the sun had come from a cloud! Electronic music begins to build edifices of sound.

The children, startled, shield their eyes, looking in at their father.

GEORGE: Paris. The blue hour of twilight. The gold hour of sunset. An Eiffel Tower, please, of bronze! An Arc de Triomphe of shining brass! Let fountains toss forth fiery lava. Let the Seine be a torrent of gold!

The light becomes golden within the room, bathing him.

GEORGE: Egypt now! Shape pyramids of white-hot stone. Carve Sphinx from ancient sand! There! There! Do you see, children? Come in! Don't stand out there!

The children, standing on either side of the door, do not move. GEORGE *pretends not to notice.*

GEORGE: Enough! Begone!

The lights go out, leaving only a dim light spotted on GEORGE'*s face. The electronic music dies.*

GEORGE: There! What do you think, eh?

WENDY: It's great.

GEORGE: Great? It's a miracle, that's what it is. There's a giant's eye, a giant's ear, a giant's brain in each of those walls, that remembers every city, town, hill, mountain, ocean, every birdsong, every language, all the music of the world. In three dimensions, by God. Name anything. The room will hear and obey.

PETER *(looking steadily at him):* You sound like a salesman.

GEORGE *(off balance):* Do I? Well, no harm. We all have some melodrama in us needs bleeding out on occasion. Tones the system. Go in, kids, go on.

WENDY *creeps in a toe.* PETER *does not move.*

GEORGE: Peter, you heard me!

Helicopter thunder floods the house. All look up. Huge shadows flutter in a side window. GEORGE, *relieved, breaks, moves from the room.*

GEORGE: There's my helicopter. Lydia, will you see me to the door?

LYDIA *(hesitating)*: George . . . ?

GEORGE *(still moving)*: Have fun, kids! *(stops, suddenly, thinking)* Peter? Wendy? Not even "Thanks"?

WENDY *(calmly)*: Thanks a lot, dad.

She nudges PETER, *who does not even look at his father.*

PETER *(quietly)*: Thanks . . .

The children, left behind, turn slowly to face the door of the playroom. WENDY *puts one hand into the room. The room hums, strangely, now, at her approach. It is a different sound from the one we heard when* GEORGE *entered the place. The hum now has an* atonal *quality.*

WENDY *moves out into the empty space, turns, and waits for* PETER *to follow, reluctantly. The humming grows.*

WENDY: I don't know what to ask it for. You. Go ahead. Please. Ask it to show us something.

PETER *relents, shuts his eyes, thinks, then whispers.*

WENDY: What? I didn't hear you.

PETER: The room did. Look.

He nods. Shadows stir on the walls, colors dilate. The children look about, obviously fascinated at what is only suggested to the audience.

WENDY: That's a lake. *Loon* Lake!

PETER: Yes.

WENDY: Oh, it's so blue! It's like the sky turned upside down. And there's a boat, white as snow, on the water! It's moving toward us.

We hear the sound of water lapping, the sound of oars at a distance.

WENDY: Someone's rowing the boat.

PETER: A boy.

WENDY: Someone's behind the boy.

PETER: A man.

WENDY: Why, it's you, and dad!

PETER: Is it? Yes. Now we've stopped, the lines are out, fishing. *(suddenly excited)* There. I've caught a big one! A big one!

We hear a distant splash of water.

WENDY: It's beautiful. It's all silver coins!

PETER: It's a beaut, all right. Boy! Boy!

WENDY: Oh, it slipped off the line! It's gone!

PETER: That isn't—

WENDY *(disappointed):* The boat . . . it's going away. The fog's coming up. I can hardly see the boat . . . or you or dad.

PETER: Neither can I . . .

WENDY *(forlorn):* The boat's gone. Bring it back, Peter.

PETER: Come back!

An echo, way off, repeats his words. The playroom grows dimmer.

PETER: It's no use. The room's broken.

WENDY: You're not trying. Come back! Come back!

PETER: Come back!

LYDIA *enters on this last, slightly concerned.*

LYDIA: Peter, Wendy? Is everything all right?

PETER: Sure, swell . . .

LYDIA *(checks her watch)*: Have you tried Mexico yet? The instructions book said the most wonderful things about the Aztec ruins there. Well! I'll be downtown at 10:45, at Mrs. Morgan's at 11:30, at Mrs. Harrison's at noon, if you should want me. The automatic lunch timer will go off at 12:15, eat, both of you! At one o'clock do your musical tapes with the violin and piano. I've written the schedule on the electric board—

PETER: Sure, mom, sure—

LYDIA: Have fun, and don't forget Bombay, India, while you're at it!

She exits and is hardly gone when: a thunderous roar ensues. PETER, *throwing out one hand, pointing at the walls, has given a shout.*

PETER: All right! Now! Now! Now!

An unseen avalanche thunders down a vast mountain in torrents of destruction. WENDY *seizes* PETER's *arm.*

WENDY: Peter!

PETER: Now! More! More!

WENDY: Peter, stop it!

The avalanche filters away to dust and silence.

WENDY: What are you doing? What was that?

PETER *(looks at her strangely):* Why, an avalanche, of course. I made an avalanche come down a mountain, a hundred thousand tons of stone and rocks. An avalanche.

WENDY *(looking about):* You filled the lake. It's gone. The boat's gone. You and dad are gone.

PETER: Did I? Is it? Are they? *(awed):* Yeah . . . sure . . . that's right. Hey, this is . . . *fun* . . . *(he accents this last word oddly) You* try something now, Wendy.

WENDY: I—London Bridge. Let me see—London Bridge.

The shadows spin slowly. PETER *and* WENDY *stand, watching.*

PETER: You're stupid. That's no fun. Think, girl, think! Now! Let's see. *(a beat)* Let there be darkness! Let there be —night!

Blackout.

The lights come up. We hear a helicopter come down, fly away. GEORGE *enters, stage left.*

GEORGE: Hi! I'm home!

In a small alcove, which represents only a section of the kitchen, far stage right, LYDIA *is seated staring at a machine that is mixing something for her.*

GEORGE *advances across the stage.*

GEORGE: Hi! How goes it?

LYDIA *(looking up):* Oh, hello. Fine.

GEORGE: Perfect, you mean. Flying home just now I thought, Good Lord, what a house! We've lived in it since the kids were born, never lacked for a thing. A great life. Incredible.

LYDIA: It's incredible, all right, but—

GEORGE: But what?

LYDIA: This kitchen. I don't know. It's—*selfish*. Sometimes I think it'd be happy if I just stayed out, stayed away completely, and let it work. *(she tries to smile)* Aren't I silly?

GEORGE: You are indeed. All these time-saving devices; no one on the block has half as many.

LYDIA *(unconvinced)*: You're right, of course. *(she pauses)* George . . . I want you to look at the playroom.

GEORGE: Look at it? Is it broken? Good Lord, we've only had it eight weeks.

LYDIA: No, not broken, exactly. Well, see it first, then you tell *me*.

She starts leading him across the stage.

GEORGE: Fair enough. Lead on, Macduff.

LYDIA: I first noticed this "thing" I'm going to show you about four weeks ago. Then it kept reoccurring. I didn't want to worry you, but now, with the thing happening all the time—well—*here*.

She opens the playroom door. GEORGE *steps in and looks as across a great distance, silently.*

GEORGE: Lord, but it's quiet.

LYDIA: Too quiet, yes.

GEORGE: Don't tell me. I know right off. This is—Africa.

LYDIA: Africa.

GEORGE: Good Lord, is there a child in the world hasn't wanted to go to Africa? Is there one exists who can't close his eyes and paint the whole thing on his inner lids? High blue deep warm sky. Horizons a billion miles off in the dust that smells like pulverized honeybees and old manuscripts and cloves and cinnamons. Boma-trees, veldtland. And a lush smell. Smell it?

LYDIA: Yes.

GEORGE: That must mean a water hole nearby, bwana. *(laughs)* Oh, Lydia, it's perfect, perfect! But—the sun—damn hot. Look, a perfect necklace of sweat right off the brow! *(shows her)* But I've lost the point. You brought me here because you were worried. Well—I see nothing to worry about.

LYDIA: Wait a moment. Let it sink in.

GEORGE: Let *what* sink in? I—

Shadows flick over their faces. He looks quizzically up. She does, too, with distaste. We hear a dry rustling leathery sound from above; distant strange bird cries.

LYDIA: Filthy things.

GEORGE *(looking up, following the circling birds)*: What? Vultures? Yes, God made his ugliest kites on the day he sent those things sailing. Is *that* what worries you?

LYDIA: That's only part of it. Look around.

GEORGE *turns slowly. There is a heavy, rich purring rumble from off to the right.* GEORGE *blinks and smiles.*

GEORGE: It couldn't be—the lions?

LYDIA: I think so, yes. I don't like—having lions in the house.

GEORGE *(amused):* Well, they're not exactly *in* the house, dear. There! Look at that big male. Face like a blast furnace at high noon, and a mane like a field of wheat. Burns your eyes to look at him. There's another—a female—*and* another, a whole pride—isn't that a fine word? A pride—a regular tapestry of lions woven of gold thread and sunlight. *(an afterthought)* What are they up to?

He turns to LYDIA, *who is watching the unseen beasts, disquieted.*

LYDIA: I think they're—feeding.

GEORGE: On what? *(squints)* Zebra or baby giraffe, I imagine.

LYDIA: Are you certain?

GEORGE *(shielding his eyes):* Well, it's a bit late to be certain of anything. They've been lunching quite some time. No— lunch is over. There they go toward the water hole! *(he follows with his eyes)*

LYDIA: George? On our way down the hall just now . . . did you . . . hear a scream from in here?

GEORGE *(glances at her):* A scream? No. For God's sake—

LYDIA: All right. Forget it. It's just, the lions won't go away.

GEORGE: What do you mean? Won't go?

LYDIA: Nor will Africa, either. George, the fact is the room has stayed that way for thirty-one days. Every day that same yellow sun in the sky. Every day the lions with teeth like daggers dusting their pelts out there, killing, slavering on the red-hot meat, printing their bloody tracks through the trees, killing, gorging, over and over, no day different, no hour any change. Doesn't it strike you as odd that the children never ask for a different locale?

GEORGE: No! They must love Africa as all kids do. The smell of violence. Life stark, raw, visceral. Here, you, hey! Hey!

He snaps his fingers, points, snaps his fingers again. He turns smiling to LYDIA.

GEORGE: You see, they come to pay their respects.

LYDIA *(nervously; gasps):* Oh, George, not so close!

The rumbling of the lions is very loud now, to the right, we feel the approach of the beasts. The light from the right side of the room becomes more brightly yellow.

GEORGE: Lydia, you're not afraid?

LYDIA: No, no, it's just—don't you *feel* it? It's almost as if they can see us!

GEORGE: Yes, the illusion *is* three-dimensional. Pure fire, isn't he? There. There. *(holds out his hands)* You can warm yourself at a hearth like that. Listen to him breathe, it's like a beehive swarming with yellow.

He stretches one hand further out.

GEORGE: You feel you could just—reach—and run your hand over the bronze, the gold—

LYDIA *(screams):* Look out!

There is a fearful snarling roar. The shadows race in the room. LYDIA *falls back, runs,* GEORGE, *startled, cannot stop her, so follows. She slams the door and falls against it. He is laughing. She is almost in tears.*

GEORGE: Lydia, dear Lydia!

LYDIA: George, they almost—

GEORGE: Almost what? It's machinery, electronics, sonics, visuals!

LYDIA: No, *more!* Much more! Now listen to me, I insist, I insist, do you hear, that you warn the children this playing in Africa must cease!

GEORGE *(comforting, kissing her):* OK, I'll talk to them.

LYDIA: Talk to them, no; lay down the law. Every day for a month I've tried to get their attention. But they just stroll off under that damned hot African sky! Do you remember that night three weeks ago when you switched the whole room off for twenty-four hours to punish the children?

GEORGE *(laughing quietly):* Oh, how they hated me for that. It's a great threat. If they misbehave, I'll shut it off again.

LYDIA: And they'll hate you again.

GEORGE: Let them. It's perfectly natural to hate your father when he punishes you.

LYDIA: Yes, but they don't say a word. They just look at you. And day by day, the playroom gets hotter, the veldtland wider and more desolate, and the lions grow big as the sun.

There is an awkward moment. Then a buzzer rings, loudly. GEORGE *presses a panel in the wall. A loudspeaker bell sounds, there is a faint crackle and:*

PETER'S VOICE: Mom, we won't be home for supper.

WENDY'S VOICE: We're at the automation show across town, OK?

GEORGE: I think that—

PETER'S VOICE: Swell!

WENDY'S VOICE: Keen!

Buzz ding! Silence. LYDIA *stares at the ceiling from which the voices came.*

LYDIA: No hellos, no good-byes, no pleases, no thank-yous.

GEORGE *takes her hand.*

GEORGE: Lydia, you've been working too hard.

LYDIA: Have I really? Then why is something wrong with the room, and the house and the four people who live in the house?

She touches the playroom door.

LYDIA: Feel? It trembles as if a huge bake oven were breathing against it.

She takes her hands off, burnt.

LYDIA: The lions—they can't come out, can they? They can't?

GEORGE *smiles, shakes his head. She hurries off.*

GEORGE: Where are you going?

She pauses near the door.

LYDIA: Just to press the button . . . that will make us our dinner.

She touches the wall panel. The lights go out. End of scene.

In the dark, music. As the light comes up dimly again we find GEORGE *in his easy chair, smoking his pipe, glancing at his watch, listening to the hi-fi system. After a moment, impatiently, he gets up and switches off the music. He moves next to the radio, switches it on, listens to a moment of news:*

WEATHER VOICE: Weather in the city tomorrow will be 66 in the morning, 70 in the afternoon, with some chance of rain.

He cuts this off, too, checking his watch. Next he switches on a TV screen to one side, its face away from us. For a moment, the ghostly pallor of the screen fills the room. He winces, shuts it off. He lights his pipe. There is a bell sound.

LYDIA'S VOICE: George, are you in the living room?

GEORGE: I couldn't sleep.

LYDIA: The children *are* home, aren't they?

GEORGE: I waited up for them—*(finishes lamely)* Not yet.

LYDIA: But it's midnight! I'll be down in a minute—

GEORGE: Don't bother—

But the bell has rung. LYDIA *has cut off.* GEORGE *paces the floor, taps out his pipe, starts to reload it, looks at the playroom door, decides against it, looks again, and finally approaches it. He turns the knob and lets it drift open.*

Inside the room it is darker. GEORGE *is surprised.*

GEORGE: Hello, what? Is the veldt gone? Wait—no. The sun's gone down. The vultures have flown into the trees far over there. Twilight. Bird cries. Stars coming out. There's the crescent moon. But where—? So you're *still* there, are you?

There is a faint purring.

GEORGE: What are you waiting for, eh? Why don't you want to go away? Paris, Cairo, Stockholm, London, they and all their millions of people swarmed out of this room when told to leave. So why not you? *(snaps his fingers)* Go!

The purring continues.

GEORGE: A new scene, new place, new animals, people! Let's have Ali Baba and the Forty Thieves! The Leaning Tower of Pisa! I demand it, room! *Now!*

A jackal laughs off in the darkness.

GEORGE: Shut up, shut up, shut up! Change, change, now! *(his voice fades)* . . . now . . .

The lions rumble. Monkeys gibber from distant trees. An elephant trumpets in the dusk. GEORGE *backs off out the door. Slowly he shuts the door, as* LYDIA *enters stage left.*

GEORGE: You're right . . . the fool room's out of order. It won't obey.

LYDIA: Won't, or *can't?*

She lights a candle on a table to one side.

GEORGE: Turn on the light. Why do you fuss with candles like that?

She looks at the flame as she lights a second and a third candle.

LYDIA: I rather like candles. There's always the chance they will blow out and then I can light them again. Gives me something to do. Anything else in the house goes wrong, electronic doors don't slide or the garbage disposal clogs, I'm helpless and must call an engineer or a photoelectric brain surgeon to put it right. So, as I think I said, I like candles.

GEORGE *has seated himself.* LYDIA *turns to come to him now.*

LYDIA: George, is it possible that since the children have thought and thought about Africa and lions and those terrible vultures day after day, the room has developed a psychological "set"?

GEORGE: I'll call a repair man in the morning.

LYDIA: No. Call our psychiatrist.

GEORGE *looks at her in amazement.*

GEORGE: David Maclean?

LYDIA *(steadily):* Yes, David Maclean.

The front door springs open, PETER *and* WENDY *run in laughing.*

PETER: Last one there's an old maid in a clock factory!

WENDY: Not me, not me!

GEORGE: Children!

The children freeze.

GEORGE: Do you know what time it is?

PETER: Why, it's midnight, of course.

GEORGE: Of course? Are you in the habit of coming in this late?

PETER: Sometimes, yes. Just last month, remember, you had some friends over, drinking, and we came in and you didn't kick up a fuss, so—

GEORGE: Enough of that! We'll go into this late-hour business again. Right now I want to talk about Africa! The playroom . . .

The children blink . . .

PETER: The playroom . . . ?

LYDIA *tries to do this lightly.*

LYDIA: Your father and I were just traveling through African veldtland; lion grass, water holes, vultures, all that.

PETER: I don't remember any Africa in the playroom. Do you, Wendy?

WENDY: No . . .

They look at each other earnestly.

PETER: Run see and come tell.

WENDY *bolts.* GEORGE *thrusts out his hand.*

GEORGE: Wendy!

But she is gone through the door of the playroom. GEORGE *leaps up.* PETER *faces him calmly.*

PETER: It's all right, George. She'll look and give us a report.

GEORGE: I don't want a report. I've seen! And stop calling me George!

PETER *(serenely):* All right—father.

GEORGE: Now get out of the way! Wendy!

WENDY *runs back out.*

WENDY: It's not Africa at *all!*

GEORGE *stares, astonished at her nerve.*

GEORGE: We'll see about that!

He thrusts the playroom door wide and steps through, startled.

Lush green garden colors surround him in the play-room. Robins, orioles, bluebirds sing in choirs, tree shadows blow on a bright wind over shimmering banks of flower colors.

Butterfly shadows tatter the air about GEORGE's *face which, surprised, grows dark as he turns to:*

The smiling children; they stop smiling.

GEORGE: You—

LYDIA: George!

GEORGE: She changed it from Africa to *this!*

He jerks his hand at the tranquil, beautiful scene.

WENDY: Father, it's only Apple Valley in April—

GEORGE: Don't lie to me! You changed it! Go to bed!

PETER *takes* WENDY's *hand and backs out of the room. Their parents watch them go, then turn to be surrounded again by green leaf colors, butterfly shadows, and the singing of the birds.*

LYDIA: George, are you sure you didn't change the scene yourself, accidentally?

GEORGE: It wouldn't change for me or you. The children have spent so much time here, it only obeys them.

LYDIA: Oh, God, I'm sorry, sorry, sorry you had this room built!

He gazes around at the green shadows, the lovely flecks of spring light.

GEORGE: No. No, I see now, that in the long run, it may help us in a roundabout way, to see our children clearly. I'll call our psychiatrist first thing tomorrow.

LYDIA *(relieved):* Good, oh good . . .

They start to move from the room. LYDIA *stops and bends to pick something from the floor.*

LYDIA: Wait a moment.

GEORGE: What is it?

LYDIA: I don't know. What does it look like, to you?

GEORGE *(touches it):* Leather. Why, it must be—my old wallet!

LYDIA: What's happened to it?

GEORGE: Looks like it's been run through a machine.

LYDIA: Or else—it's been chewed. Look, all the teethmarks!

GEORGE: Teethmarks, hell! The marks of cogs and wheels.

LYDIA: And this?

They turn the wallet between them.

GEORGE: The dark stuff? Chocolate, I think.

LYDIA: Do you?

He sniffs the leather, touches it, sniffs again.

GEORGE: Blood.

The room is green spring around and behind them. The birds sing louder now, in the silence that follows the one word he has pronounced. GEORGE *and* LYDIA *look around at the innocent colors, at the simple and lovely view.*

Far away, after a moment, we hear the faint trailing off of one scream, or perhaps two. We are not quite certain. GEORGE *quickens.*

LYDIA: There! You heard it! This time, you *did!*

GEORGE: No.

LYDIA: You did. I know you did!

GEORGE: I heard nothing, nothing at all! Good Lord, it's late, let's get to bed!

He throws the wallet down, and hurries out.

After he is gone, LYDIA *picks up the shapeless wallet, turns it in her hands, and looks through the door of the playroom.*

There the birds sing, the green-yellow shadows stir in leaf patterns everywhere, softly whispering. She describes it to herself.

LYDIA: . . . flowering apple tree . . . peach blossoms . . . so white . . .

Behind her, in the living room, GEORGE *blows out one candle.*

LYDIA: . . . so lovely . . .

He blows out the other candle. Darkness.

The scene is ended.

After a moment of silence and darkness, we hear a helicopter thunder down outside the house. A door opens. When it shuts, the lights come on, and GEORGE *is leading* DAVID MACLEAN *on.*

GEORGE: Awfully nice of you to come by so early, David.

DAVID: No bother, really, if you'll give me my breakfast.

GEORGE: I'll fix it myself—or—rather—almost fix it myself. The room's there. I'm sure you'll want to examine it alone, anyway.

DAVID: I would.

GEORGE: It's nothing, of course. In the light of day, I see that. But—go ahead. I'll be right back.

> GEORGE *exits.* MACLEAN, *who is carrying what looks like a medical kit, puts it down and takes out some tools. Small, delicate tools of the sort used to repair TV sets, unorthodox equipment for a psychiatrist. He opens a panel in the wall. We see intricate film spools, lights, lenses there, revealed for the first time.* MACLEAN *is checking it when the playroom door opens and* PETER *comes out. The boy stops when he sees* MACLEAN.

PETER: Hello, who are you?

DAVID: David Maclean.

PETER: Electronics repair?

DAVID: Not exactly.

PETER: David Maclean. I know. You read the bumps on people's heads.

DAVID: I wish it were that simple. Right now I've come to see what you and your sister have written on the walls of this room.

PETER: We haven't written—oh, I see what you mean. Are you always this honest?

DAVID: People know when you lie.

PETER: But they don't! And you know why? They're not listening. They're turned to themselves. So you might as well lie, since, in the end, you're the only one awake.

DAVID: Do you really believe that?

PETER *(truly amazed):* I thought everyone did!

He grabs the playroom door as if to go back in.

DAVID: Please.

PETER: I must clean the room.

DAVID *steps between him and the door.*

DAVID: If you don't mind, I'd *prefer* it untidy.

PETER *hesitates. They stare each other down.*

PETER: All right. It doesn't matter. Go ahead.

PETER *walks off, circling once, then runs, gone.*

MACLEAN *looks after the boy, then turns to the door of the playroom, and slowly opens it. From the color of the light inside the room we can sense that it is Africa again. We hear faint lion sounds, far off, and the distant leather flapping of wings.* MACLEAN *looks around for only a moment, then kneels on the floor of the room where he opens a trapdoor and looks down at intricate flickering machineries where firefly lights wink and glow and where there is oiled secretive motion. He touches this button, that switch, that bit of film, this sprocket, that dial.*

In obedience to this, the light within the room gets fierce, oven-white, blinding as an atomic explosion, the screams get a bit louder, the roaring of the lions louder.

MACLEAN *touches into the paneling again.*

The roars get very loud, the screams very high and shrill, over and over, over and over as if repeated on a broken phonograph record. MACLEAN *stands riven. There is a tremendous rustling of wings. The lion rumble fades. And as silence falls, the color of the walls of the room is stained by crimson flowing red until all is redness within the room, all is bleeding sunset light upon which, slowly, slowly, with grim thoughtfulness,* DAVID MACLEAN *closes the trapdoor and backs out into the living room area.*

LYDIA *enters with a tray on which is breakfast coffee and toast.*

When she sees that MACLEAN *is deep in thought, she says nothing, puts down the tray, pours coffee for three, at which point* GEORGE *enters and frowns when he sees* MACLEAN's *deep concern. The husband and wife look at each other, and wait.* MACLEAN *at last comes over, picks up his coffee, sips it thoughtfully, and at last speaks.*

MACLEAN: George . . . Lydia . . .

He hesitates a moment, drinks more coffee, prepares himself.

MACLEAN: When I gave my approval of your building that playroom it was because the record in the past with such playrooms has been exceptionally good. They not only provide imaginative atmospheres wherein children can implement their desires and dreams, they also give us, if we wish, as parents, teachers, psychiatrists, the opportunity to study the patterns left on the walls by the children's minds. Road maps, as it were, which we can look at in our leisure time to see where our children are going and how we can help them on their way. We humans are mostly inarticulate, there is so much we wish to say we cannot say, so the rooms, and the walls of such rooms, offered a way of speaking out with the silent tongue of the mind. In ninety-nine cases out of a hundred, it works. Children use the rooms, parents observe the blueprints marked on the walls of the rooms, and everyone is happy. But in this case—*(he stops)*

LYDIA: This case?

MACLEAN: I'm afraid the room has become a channel *toward* destructive thoughts rather than a release away from them. George . . . Lydia . . . why do your children hate you so much?

LYDIA *(surprised):* Hate us? They don't hate us!

GEORGE: We're their parents!

MACLEAN: Are you really? Let's see.

> MACLEAN *paces the room, pointing out this door, indicating that machine panel, or another here or there.*

MACLEAN: What kind of life do you lead? Machines make your bed, shine your shoes, blow your noses for you. Machines listen for you, learn for you, speak for you. Machines ventilate your house, drive you down the street at ninety miles an hour, or lift you straight up into the sky, always away and away from your home. I call on the phone and another machine answers, pre-recorded, and says you're not here. How long has it been since you got out of your car and walked with your children to find your *own* air, which means air no one else has breathed, outside of town? How long since you flew a kite or picked do-it-yourself wild strawberries? How long? How long? How long?

> MACLEAN *sits. The parents are silent. Unnoticed,* PETER *and* WENDY *have come into the door at the far side of the room.* MACLEAN *drinks his coffee and finishes, as quietly as possible, thus:*

MACLEAN: You haven't been around. And since you haven't been around, this house and its machines, that playroom has become the only available garden where your children can take root. But when you force-grow flowers in a mechanical greenhouse, don't be surprised if you wind up

with exotic orchids, strange tiger-lilies or Venus's fly-
traps.

GEORGE: What must we do?

MACLEAN: Now, very late, after playing an idiot Father
Christmas for years, I'm going to ask you to play what
will seem like Ebenezer Scrooge to your children.

GEORGE *rises up and turns toward the playroom door.*

GEORGE: You want me to switch off the room?

MACLEAN: The room, the house, the damned "sprinklers" in
the lawn! Get out, stay out, get away; send the kids to me
for treatment, but better yet, treat them yourselves. Look
at them with your eyes, show them your faces, talk to
them not on the intercom, but let them feel your warm
breath in their ears, comb their hair with your fingers,
wash their backs with your hands, sing to them, run with
them a little way before they run so far ahead they run out
of your lives.

GEORGE *moves toward the door.*

GEORGE: But if I switch off the room, the shock—

MACLEAN: Better a clean, hard shock now than letting the
kids get any further from reality.

GEORGE: Yes . . . yes . . .

*He opens the door of the room. Crimson light pours
out. The walls inside bleed with running color. Reacting
to this,* GEORGE *kneels to the panel in the floor and tears
at it.*

Suddenly, PETER *stands out from the door.*

PETER: George! No!

MACLEAN *and* LYDIA *are on their feet at this.*

MACLEAN: Hold on, George. Not with the children here.

GEORGE *whips the panel open.* PETER *leaps forward and slams it shut.*

PETER: No, George, no, no!

MACLEAN: Listen to me—wait!

GEORGE: Get out of the way.

PETER: George!

GEORGE *(evenly):* Don't call me George.

He thrusts the boy aside, gets the panel open, but the boy is scrabbling now. Screams well out the walls of the scarlet room in a tidal blast. MACLEAN *and* LYDIA *freeze as the boy and* GEORGE *fight over the switches. Heat shimmers, animal heartbeats ricochet from walls, avalanches of zebras panic away with okapi, gazelle, and wildebeest, thundering, shrieking.*

GEORGE *knocks* PETER's *hands off, twists and shoves him, and hits all the switches at once.*

There are great elephant trumpetings, a final cry from many creatures now struck by electronic death, dying . . . The sounds run down like a phonograph record. In a flush of red light, all the colors of the room dissolve like oil down the walls into the floor as blood might be let from a flask. Silence. The room shadows into darkness. GEORGE *slams the trap and locks it with his key and stands on it. The only sound is* PETER's *sobbing and crying, slumped by* GEORGE.

PETER: You! You!

GEORGE *(to himself):* Yes . . . me . . . me!

PETER *(rising):* You killed them! You killed them! I hate you! I wish you were dead! I wish you were dead!

GEORGE *slaps his face.*

PETER *holds his cheek, startled, then jumps and runs from the room.* WENDY, *bewildered, at the door, follows.*

GEORGE *holds out a key to no one in particular.*

GEORGE *(barely audible):* Lock the door.

LYDIA *does so.* GEORGE *holds out other keys.*

GEORGE: Now . . . turn off the stoves, the voice clocks, the talking books, the TVs, the telephones, the body scrubbers, the bedmakers, turn off everything!

LYDIA *takes the keys, looks at* GEORGE's *face, and hurries away.* MACLEAN *looks after her.*

MACLEAN: No, George. That was badly handled. Brutal . . . brutal!

MACLEAN *hurries off after* LYDIA.

GEORGE, *alone, rests his head against the playroom door, listening, eyes closed.*

GEORGE *(to himself):* Brutal? Yes, but dead! Are you dead in there?! Good. *(tiredly)* Good . . .

He moves away across the room, exhausted, and at the door turns to look back at the door.

GEORGE: I wonder . . . does the room hate me, too? Yes . . . it must. Nothing ever likes to die. Even a machine.

He exits.

Blackout.

Music in darkness.

A small bedlight comes slowly up after half a minute. We see LYDIA *in bed at the front of the stage. A dark scrim has come down between the bed and the set in back, so we do this scene in-one.* LYDIA *rouses.*

LYDIA: George?

She sees him to stage left now, back turned, in his dressing robe, looking out an imaginary window, smoking.

LYDIA: Can't sleep?

GEORGE: Who can?

LYDIA: Not me, anyway.

GEORGE: It's after midnight.

LYDIA: Yes. Listen. The house is so still. *(she sits up, listening)* It used to hum all the time, under its breath . . . I never quite guessed the tune . . . though I listened for years and tried to hum the same way, I never learned. . . .

GEORGE: Thank God for small favors. Good Lord, it was strange, walking around, shutting off all the heaters and scrubbers and polishers, and washers. For an hour there, the house felt like a cemetery, and me its keeper. That's past now. I'm adjusting.

LYDIA: The children will, too. They cried themselves to sleep, but they will forgive us.

She sits up listening as if she had heard something.

LYDIA: There's no way for them to—tamper—with the room, is there?

GEORGE: Tamper?

LYDIA: I just don't want them doing anything down there, messing about, rearranging things—they couldn't do anything to the room, could they?

GEORGE: *To* the room? What would they want to do *to* the room? Anyway, there's a lot of electricity in those walls with all the machinery. They know better than to mess, and get a nasty shock.

She listens again, and breaks up her own mood by trying to be jocular.

LYDIA: Oh, I'm glad we're leaving tomorrow, mountains, fishing, everything out in the open again after years.

GEORGE: Dave said he'd bring his helicopter round after breakfast and take us to the lake himself. Good old Dave!

GEORGE *comes back to sit on the edge of his wife's bed.*

GEORGE: Lydia?

LYDIA: Yes?

He takes her hand. He kisses her on the cheek. She jerks away suddenly.

GEORGE: What is it?

LYDIA: Oh, listen, listen!

Far away, the sound of running antelope, the roar of lions.

WENDY and PETER *(very remote)*: Help! Mother! Father! Help! Help!

LYDIA: The children!

GEORGE: The playroom! They must have broken into it!

PETER and WENDY *(remote)*: Mother! Father, help, oh, help!

LYDIA: Peter! Wendy!

GEORGE: Kids! Kids! We're coming! We're coming!

The parents rush off into darkness, as the lights go off over the bed.

In the dark the voices continue.

PETER: Father, father, quick! Quick!

GEORGE: Peter, Wendy!

LYDIA: Children, where are you?

WENDY: Here, oh, here!

The lights flash on; GEORGE *and* LYDIA *rush in through the playroom door.*

GEORGE: They're in the playroom!

LYDIA: Peter! Wendy!

Once inside the door they peer around.

LYDIA: That's strange . . .

GEORGE: I'd have sworn—

They look about to left and right and straight ahead through the fourth wall, at the audience.

LYDIA: George, it's—Africa again, the sun, the veldt, the vultures . . .

She backs off. GEORGE *half turns and as he does so, the door slams shut behind them.* GEORGE *leaps toward it.*

GEORGE: Damn door. A draft must have—

Locks click outside.

GEORGE *tries the lock, beats at the door.*

GEORGE: It's locked!

LYDIA: It can't be! There's no way for it to lock itself!

GEORGE *(thinking)*: No. . . . no . . . Peter? Wendy?

LYDIA: George, over there, under the trees . . .

GEORGE: Kids, open up . . . I know you're out there.

LYDIA: The lions . . . they're walking out into the sun . . .

GEORGE *(shaking the door)*: Peter, Wendy, now don't be ridiculous. Unlock this door!

> *The light is getting brighter in the room, the sun is blazing from above. The sound of the rustling vulture wings grows louder. Shadows flash across the faces of* GEORGE *and* LYDIA. *The rumbling of the lions is nearer.*

LYDIA: George, the lions, they're running toward us!

> GEORGE *looks out through the fourth wall, grows uneasy, somewhat panicky, and bangs at the door.*

GEORGE: It's all right, Lydia. Children, damn you, you're frightening your mother, open up! You hear?

LYDIA: Running! Running! Near! Near!

GEORGE: Peter!

LYDIA: Oh, George, the screams, the screams. I know now what I never said . . . the screams were familiar . . . the voices . . . because the voices, the screams were us, you and me, George, you and me . . .

GEORGE: No! Kids! Hear me!

> *He bangs the door, turns, freezes, horrified.*

LYDIA: George, stop them running, stop them, stop, stop!

She throws up her hands to guard her face, sinks to her knees.

LYDIA: They're going to jump! Stop, stop!

GEORGE: No, they can't, they can't! No! no!

The light blazes, the lions roar! A great shadow rushes from the audience, as if the lions, in a solid pack, were engulfing the stage in darkness!

Swallowing blackness takes all light away.

In the darkness, LYDIA *and* GEORGE *scream and scream. Then abrupt silence, the roar, the bumbling purr of the yellow beasts fading away.*

After a long while of silence, a helicopter lands nearby. We hear DAVID MACLEAN *calling in the darkness.*

MACLEAN *(easily):* George! Lydia! I'm here! George? Lydia?

The lights come slowly up. We are still inside the playroom. Seated facing the audience on two corduroy pillows are PETER *and* WENDY, *their faces impassive, as if they had gone through all that life might ever do to them and were beyond hearing, seeing, feeling. On a pillow between them are small cups and saucers, a sugar and creamer set, and a porcelain pot.* WENDY *holds one cup and saucer in her frozen hands, as does* PETER.

The door to the playroom opens. MACLEAN *peers in, does not see the children immediately.*

MACLEAN: George—

He stops, peering off into the distance, as across a veldt. We hear the faint roar of lions. He hears the flap of vulture wings sailing down the sky, and looks up into the burning sun, protecting his eyes. Then at last he looks over at the children, sees them, and in his face is the beginning of realization, of horror, of insight into what they have done.

MACLEAN *(slowly):* Peter? . . . Wendy . . . ?

PETER *turns his head slowly to look beyond the man.*

PETER: Mr. Maclean.

WENDY *turns more slowly, in shock, to hold out before her the small cup, her eyes blind to any sight, her voice toneless.*

WENDY: A cup of tea?

Blackout.

THE END

To the
Chicago Abyss

The curtain rises.

The empty stage represents a park. There is a bench at far-stage left and another at far-stage right. On the left sits a middle-aged woman who is busy taking a knitted sweater apart, unweaving the yarn, and rolling it into an unclean ball. She carries knitting needles with her and it is obvious she intends to reknit the yarn into a new garment once she finishes the destruction of the original sweater.

On the right bench a young man leans over, drawing in the dust with a stick, very intent, very much to himself.

The old man enters now, gazing all about as if he wanted to see everything, looking ahead, looking behind, looking up, looking down. On his way perhaps he finds an old gum or candy wrapper, peers at it with admiration and puts it in his pocket for later reference. He is dressed poorly, his clothes are stiff and ancient with dirt, his feet are not so much in shoes as they are repaired, tacked together, and bandaged in leather and black friction tape.

As the old man moves, he seems alert for something, as if he had been searching for years, and might have to search many more years. His mouth and eyes are almost apprehensive. His eyes dart. His mouth trembles, as he talks to himself, as if there was much he wished to say, but could not bring it out.

Now, in the middle of the stage, he looks around. Though he does not speak yet, we read the desolation of the city in his face. He turns in a slow circle, as if surveying the city and his eyes tell us that the place is dead. He cannot bear to look at it. He glances now, instead, with vitality renewed, at either bench. He must decide where to sit. He chooses the bench with the woman on it and very quietly, with a slight bow, which she does not acknowledge, approaches, and sits at the far end away from her. She goes on taking the sweater apart.

The old man waits, not looking at her. He shuts his eyes. His mouth works for a long while. His head moves as if his nose were printing a single word on the air, invisible, before him. When he is done printing the word, he mouths it, silently. Then, eyes still shut, sitting up straight, in a loud clear voice he makes his announcement:

THE OLD MAN: Coffee!

> *The woman gasps and stiffens, she ceases work, but does not look at him. Eyes still shut, he goes on.*

THE OLD MAN: Twist the key! Hissss! Bright red, yellow-letter can! Compressed air. Sssssst! Like a snake, a snake! Psssss!

> *The woman snaps her head about as if slapped, to stare in dreadful fascination at* THE OLD MAN's *moving tongue, his hands tumbling in pantomime on his lap.*

THE OLD MAN: The odor, the scent, the smell, the aroma of rich dark wondrous Brazilian beans, fresh ground!

> *The woman leaps up, reeling as if gun-shot, steadying herself on the back of the bench. Her yarn ball falls to the ground.* THE OLD MAN, *feeling her leap, opens his eyes. Perhaps he hopes to make her sit back now, just by talking her down.*

THE OLD MAN *(sniffs):* The first sniff. Ah, like the warm air rising off the dusky earth in hot summer twilight. Coffee. Coffee . . .

> *That does it. She breaks to run, remembers her yarn, turns, is afraid to reach for it.*

THE OLD MAN: No, don't . . . please . . .

She scrabbles for it. He hands it to her. She grabs it and bolts off.

THE OLD MAN: Please, I didn't mean. You needn't—*(resigned)* Gone.

Which indeed she is, clutching her goods, looking back at him as if he were insane.

THE OLD MAN *watches her out of sight, half-risen from the bench, his hand out to plead after her. Now, weighted with her desertion, he sinks to the bench again and remains, giving one great silent exhalation. Then, from the corner of his eyes, he sees the other bench. He sits up. He straightens his shoulders. He rises and with great unconcern, picking up pieces of paper and pocketing them or throwing them away as he chooses, approaches the other bench where the* THE YOUNG MAN, *not seeing him, has stopped drawing in the dust and has taken out some dried grass which he is rolling into a thin piece of old newsprint or toilet paper, making himself a poor imitation of a cigarette.*

THE OLD MAN *watches, intrigued, standing just beyond the bench, until* THE YOUNG MAN *finally finds a match on his person and lights the cigarette, leans back, squinting deliciously, blowing smoke. As the smoke dissolves in the air,* THE OLD MAN *watches the patterns and says, as if this touched his memory unbeknownst:*

THE OLD MAN: Chesterfields.

THE YOUNG MAN, *the cigarette clenched in his mouth, grips his knees with his hands.*

THE OLD MAN: Raleighs. Lucky Strikes.

THE OLD MAN, *not really talking to anyone but himself, not putting on a performance for anyone, but just living in another day, another time, continues, sitting down now as if* THE YOUNG MAN *weren't really there, even though* THE YOUNG MAN *is staring at him.*

THE OLD MAN: Kents. Kools, Marlboros. Those were the names. Pall Malls. Old Golds. White, red, amber packs, grass green, sky blue, pure gold with the red slick small ribbon that ran around the top you pulled to zip away the crinkly cellophane like soft glass, and then the blue government tax stamp, and the tin-foil you saved in a big bright silver ball and sold to the junkman and—

THE YOUNG MAN *(coldly)*: Shut up.

THE OLD MAN *(hasn't heard)*: . . . buy them in drugstores, fountains, subways . . .

THE YOUNG MAN: Quiet!

THE OLD MAN *opens his eyes, surprised that someone has called. He looks to see* THE YOUNG MAN's *expression, his open and irritable mouth. He sizes up the situation.*

THE OLD MAN: Gently . . .

THE YOUNG MAN: Gently, he says. Gently. He doesn't even know where he is and gently . . .

THE OLD MAN: I'm in the park, in the city.

THE YOUNG MAN: What park? What city? Look *up* for a change instead of running around like a damn hound dog, your nose on the ground.

THE OLD MAN: I'm *looking* up.

THE YOUNG MAN: Whatta you see out there?

THE OLD MAN: Buildings . . .

THE YOUNG MAN: No, ruins!

THE OLD MAN: Streets . . .

THE YOUNG MAN: No, bomb craters.

THE OLD MAN: I'm sorry. It was such a nice friendly day—

THE YOUNG MAN: I'm no friend.

THE OLD MAN: We're all friends now, or why live?

THE YOUNG MAN: Some friend. Look what you made me do. Ruined my smoke. *(he brushes the cigarette "makings" off his pants, angrily)* Who knows friends? Who *had* one? Back in 1970, maybe, sure—

THE OLD MAN: 1970. You must have been a baby then. Why, they still had Butterfingers that year in bright yellow wrappers. Baby Ruths. Clark Bars in orange paper. Milky Ways . . . swallow a universe of stars, comets, meteors . . . *(he unwraps an imaginary bar, bites it, chews)* Nice . . .

THE YOUNG MAN: It was never nice. What's wrong with you?

THE OLD MAN: I remember limes and lemons, that's what's wrong with me. Do you remember oranges? *(picks one off the air)*

THE YOUNG MAN: Damn right. Oranges. Hell. You calling me liar? You want me to feel bad? You nuts? Don't you know the law? You know I could turn you in, don't you?

THE OLD MAN: I know, I know. The weather fooled me. It made me want to compare—

THE YOUNG MAN: Compare rumors, that's what the police'd say, huh, eh? The special cops'd say "rumors," you troublemaking bastard, you—

He seizes THE OLD MAN'*s lapels, which rip so* THE YOUNG MAN *has to grab a second handful, yelling down into his face.*

THE YOUNG MAN: Why don't I just blast the living Jesus out of you? I ain't hurt no one in *so long . . .*

He shoves THE OLD MAN, *which gives him the idea to pummel, which in turn gives him the idea to punch and then rain blows upon* THE OLD MAN'*s shoulders, arms, chest.* THE OLD MAN *tries to fend off this rain of assault.*

THE YOUNG MAN: Candies, damn it, smokes, damn you! Kents! Kools! Baby Ruths, Butterfingers! Kents Kools Butterfingers! Butterfingers!

THE OLD MAN *slips and falls to roll over, balling himself up, for* THE YOUNG MAN *is starting to kick but stops now, for he is sobbing.* THE OLD MAN *looks up, surprised, and takes his hands away from his face.*

THE OLD MAN: Please . . .

THE YOUNG MAN *weeps louder, turning away.*

THE OLD MAN: It's my fault. I apologize. I didn't want to make anyone cry. Don't. We won't be hungry forever.

THE OLD MAN *is sitting up as he talks.*

THE OLD MAN: We'll rebuild the cities. Listen. No crying. I just wanted people to think where are we going, what are we doing, what've we done? You weren't hitting me, anyway. You meant to hit something else, the Time, huh, the way things are? But who can hit Time, hit the way things are? I was handy. But look, I'm sitting up fine . . . I . . .

THE YOUNG MAN *has stopped crying during this and now breaks in.*

THE YOUNG MAN: You . . . you can't go around making people unhappy. I'll find someone to fix you. I'll find . . . someone! *(exits)* Someone!

THE OLD MAN: Wait, no, no!

But, still on his knees, he cannot pursue. THE YOUNG MAN *has run off, shouting. His shouting fades.*

THE STRANGER *(nearby; quietly):* Fool.

THE OLD MAN, *feeling his bones, looks around. The* STRANGER, *about forty, having entered during the brawl, has stood behind the farthest bench, in shadow, watching.*

THE OLD MAN: Beg pardon?

STRANGER: I said: Fool.

THE OLD MAN: You were there, all the time, you saw, and did *nothing?*

STRANGER: What, fight one fool to save another? No.

He walks forward to help THE OLD MAN *to his feet, and brush him off.*

STRANGER: No, I save my fighting for where it pays. Come on. You're going with me.

THE OLD MAN: Where? Why?

STRANGER: Where? Home. Why? That scum'll be back with the police any minute. I don't want you stolen away, you're a very precious commodity. I've heard of you for months, searched for you for days. Then just when I find you, good grief, you're up to your famous tricks. What did you say made that boy mad?

THE OLD MAN: I said about oranges and lemons, candy, cigarettes. I was just getting ready to recollect wind-up toys, briar pipes and back scratchers, when he dropped the sky on me.

STRANGER *(handing over a handkerchief):* I almost don't blame him. I almost wanted to hit you, myself. There's a siren! Double-time. Out of the park!

THE OLD MAN, *the bloodied handkerchief to his ruined mouth, allows himself to be led, but stops and bends.*

THE OLD MAN: Wait! I can't leave this behind. Very precious stone, very precious!

They both stare at it.

THE OLD MAN *(proudly):* My tooth!

He tosses it in the air, grabs it in a tight fist, and together they hurry from the park, as the siren rises.

Blackout . . . or swirling shadows as a door, or several doors come down out of darkness, a table and some chairs slide in, and suddenly a seedy and ill-kempt apartment has swarmed to steady itself and fall into focus about THE OLD MAN. He stands looking at the table and chair as if not knowing what to do with them. The STRANGER gives him a hint.

STRANGER: Sit down.

THE OLD MAN: Yes. Thank you.

STRANGER: There's food.

THE OLD MAN: Food? I don't know. My mouth—

STRANGER: Wine, then, until your mouth feels better. Dear?

His WIFE, *standing near, remembers the wine bottle and the single glass in her hand, pours, hands it to* THE OLD MAN.

THE OLD MAN: Wine? I can't believe it. Aren't you having any?

STRANGER *(laughing):* We have only one glass. We'll have to share our toast. No, you first.

THE OLD MAN *sips, eyes shut.*

THE OLD MAN: Wine. Wine. Incredible. To you, kind lady, kind sir.

He sips, and passes the glass to the woman, who drinks timidly and passes it to her husband, who also drinks.

STRANGER: To all of us. To other years. To old men who talk too much. To pummelings, beatings, and lost teeth.

The WIFE *drops a plate on the table, at this.*

STRANGER: Relax. No one followed us. Set the table, put out the food.

She brings dishes and food to the table. THE OLD MAN *watches her, fascinated.*

STRANGER: Old man, the beating, how did it happen? Why do you behave like a saint panting after martyrdom? You're famous, you know. Everyone's heard of you. Many would like to meet you. Myself, first, I want to know what makes you tick. Well?

But THE OLD MAN *is counting as the woman puts the food out on the plate with a fork.*

THE OLD MAN: 17, 18, 19 strands of spaghetti. 25, 26, 27, 28, 29 green peas. *(glances up)* Forgive me. But I shall pray over these like a fine rosary! 19 strings of spaghetti,

29 peas, and—no—one meat ball! What a still life. How fine!

The others pull up their chairs.

THE OLD MAN: But, madame, you have only 28 peas, and you, sir, 27! It's not fair I have 29.

THE WIFE: You are the guest.

THE OLD MAN: So I am, and most grateful.

He touches the peas with a fork, gingerly, reminiscently.

THE OLD MAN: 29 peas. Remember, remember. A motion picture I saw as a child. A comedian in the film—do you know the word "comedian"? A funny man to make you laugh—this comedian met a lunatic in a midnight haunted house in this film and—

The STRANGER and his WIFE have laughed, tentatively, quietly.

THE OLD MAN *(abashed)*: I'm sorry, that's not the joke yet. *(clears his throat, squints to remember)* The lunatic sat the comedian down to an empty table, no knives, no forks, no food! "Dinner is served!" he cried. Afraid of murder, the comedian fell in with the make-believe. "Great!" he cried, pretending to chew steak, vegetables, dessert. He bit into nothings. "Fine!" He swallowed air. "Wonderful!" *(pause)* You may laugh now. Eh . . .

But the husband and WIFE, grown still, only look at their sparsely strewn plates. THE OLD MAN, disquieted at what he has done with the tale, tries to carry it on, cheer them up.

THE OLD MAN: The comedian, thinking to impress the madman, exclaimed, "And these spiced peaches! Superb!" "Peaches?" screamed the madman, and drew a pistol. "I

served no peaches. You must be nuts!" And shot the comedian in the behind.

THE OLD MAN *laughs in a kind of half-gasped quiet laughter, at the same time picking up and weighing one pea
on his fork. He is about to put it in his mouth when—*

*Bam! a terrible ramming knock once, pause, once twice,
on the slatty door!*

POLICEMAN *(outside):* Special police!

*In one flowing motion the lights shift, and move toward
dusk.* THE OLD MAN *rises, automatically taking his plate
and fork with him, the* WIFE *moves toward the spotlighted door on stage right, the husband steers* THE OLD
MAN *toward a wall at midstage and as the* WIFE *touches
the front door, a panel opens in the wall and* THE OLD
MAN *steps through as the* WIFE *opens the front door and
the panel slides shut, hiding* THE OLD MAN. *The panel is
scrim, and, illumined from behind, we can see* THE OLD
MAN *standing abandoned, the plate in one hand, the fork
in the other.*

As the special POLICEMAN *steps through the door, the
lighting changes even more, getting darker, except
where he stands. The husband and* WIFE, *moving off,
stand far over on stage left, as if not wishing to be anywhere near the* POLICEMAN. *They move into dark, as it
were, so he cannot search their faces too carefully as
they talk. The* POLICEMAN *probes about with a flashlight.*

POLICEMAN: Special police.

STRANGER: You said that.

POLICEMAN: I'll say it again, and you'll listen. Special police.
And I'm looking for a criminal fugitive.

THE OLD MAN (to himself, listening): Isn't this world full of criminal fugitives?

> As the POLICEMAN talks and the STRANGER and his WIFE listen, THE OLD MAN, hidden between, behind the scrim panel wall, turns now this way, now that, cupping an ear on occasion, listening, responding. We can hear his response, but know that the POLICEMAN and the couple cannot.

POLICEMAN: A man in patched and dirty clothes—

THE OLD MAN (to himself): I thought everyone's clothes were patched and dirty!

POLICEMAN: —an old old man—

THE OLD MAN: But isn't everyone old?

POLICEMAN: If you turn him in, there's a week's rations as reward.

> THE OLD MAN quickens at this, as do the STRANGER and his WIFE.

THE WIFE: A week's rations!!?

STRANGER (cutting across her): He—he must be Much Wanted.

POLICEMAN (consulting his dossier): Much.

THE WIFE (musing): A week's rations.

THE OLD MAN (amazed himself): A whole week!

POLICEMAN (sensing his line is good): Plus!!

THE OLD MAN: Plus?

POLICEMAN: A bonus of ten cans of vegetable soup and five cans of beans!

STRANGER *(in spite of himself):* Soup?

THE WIFE: Beans?

THE OLD MAN: Real tin cans, it must be, real cans with bright red labels. Cans that flash like silver meteors, oh I can see them even in the dark. What a fine reward. Not $10,000 for the old talking man, no, no, not $20,000, but . . . something that *counts,* that really *means* something . . . ten incredible cans of real not imitation soup, and five, count them, five brilliant circus-colored cans of exotic beans. *Think* of it. *Think!*

> *There is a long silence in which the husband and* WIFE *lean all unawares toward the* POLICEMAN.

POLICEMAN: Think of it! Think!

THE OLD MAN: I *am.* They *are.* Listen. The faint murmurs of stomachs turning all uneasy. Too many years the world has fed them hairballs of nightmare and politics gone sour, a thin gruel. Now, their lips work, their saliva runs like Niagara!

> *The* POLICEMAN *listens as if he can hear their appetites at work, then turns and with his back to them, hand on the door, says,*

POLICEMAN: Beans. Soup. Fifteen solid-pack cans!

> *Slam, he is out the door, gone. Bang, he knocks on other far doors, bang, bang.*

POLICEMAN *(fading away):* Special police . . . special police . . .

> *They listen to the fading sound until it is absolutely gone. Then they relax their knotted fists, and unlean their bodies. The secret panel whispers up. The husband and* WIFE *cannot bring themselves to look at* THE OLD

MAN, *who stands there looking at them and then at the pitiful plate of food and the fork in his two hands. He does not move for a long time.*

THE OLD MAN *(gently, in awe):* Even I . . . even *I* was tempted to turn myself in, claim the reward, eat the soup . . .

He moves out to touch at their elbows, each in turn.

THE OLD MAN: Why? Why didn't you hand me over?

The husband breaks away, impulsively, as if he must. He rushes to the table in a terrible hunger and crams all the food in his mouth as if to stave off his awful fear, need, and appetite.

STRANGER: Eat! Eat! You'll find out. Wife, go on, you know what to do, get!

THE WIFE *hesitates and goes out.*

THE OLD MAN *(worried):* Where is she—?

STRANGER: Eat, old man, eat!

THE OLD MAN *brings his plate forward and, nonplussed, picks at the food.*

THE OLD MAN: Your wife—?

STRANGER: She's gone to get the Others.

THE OLD MAN *(half-rising):* Others!?

STRANGER: Everyone in the apartment house.

THE OLD MAN *(really on his feet now):* Everyone!!??

STRANGER: Old man, look, if you're going to run risks, shoot off your mouth, why not do it in the aggregate, one fell blow? Why waste your breath on one or two people if—

There are noises of people now approaching, murmuring, a shuffling of feet, and many shadows. THE OLD MAN *looks around as if the room were filling.*

THE OLD MAN: Yes, but what shall I *tell* them?

STRANGER: What *won't* you tell them! Isn't this better than taking a chance in the open?

The crowd is coming in, unseen, with murmurs, shadows. THE OLD MAN *is still bewildered, uncertain.*

THE OLD MAN *(half-nods):* Yes. Strange. I hate pain. I hate being hit and chased. But my tongue moves . . .

STRANGER *(encouraging him):* Yes, that's it . . .

THE OLD MAN: . . . I must hear what it has to say . . .

STRANGER *(egging him on):* That's it!

THE OLD MAN *looks around as the shadows move and the crowd begins to quiet. He pecks at his food, uncertainly.*

STRANGER *(still trying to distract him):* That's no way to eat! *Shovel* it in!

As if needing this sustenance and to break the spell, THE OLD MAN *loads his fork.*

THE OLD MAN: One shovel and it's gone. *(shrugs)* So . . . one shovel. *(eats)*

And as he swallows, the weight of the food, it almost seems, sinks him down into the chair and gives him strength at the same time, and the crowd is there now, all about we see their shadows, and THE WIFE *enters and nods.*

At her nod, the crowd goes to complete waiting silence. Surrounded by their breathing, THE OLD MAN *is uneasy somewhat, still.*

The STRANGER, *sensing this, half-attacks.*

THE STRANGER: Now tell me, why are you such a damn fool you make *us* damn fools seek you out and risk our necks to bring you here, eh? Well . . . ?

THE OLD MAN, *looking around, recalls something, his eyes half-light, he shakes his head with recollection.*

THE OLD MAN: Why . . . it's almost like the theater . . . motion-picture houses . . .

THE STRANGER *(urging this on):* Drive-in movies, too, yes, yes . . .

THE OLD MAN *gazes about, half-pleased, half-afraid, both in and out of other years now. He rises, steps forward.*

THE OLD MAN: But . . . the show . . . the entertainment . . . why . . . it's . . . *me!*

The crowd murmurs a bit in response, eager, and THE OLD MAN *puts down his empty plate as if gathering his resources. He nods sadly, going back in his mind. He half-squints his eyes.*

THE OLD MAN: Yes, yes. The hour grows late in the day, the sun is down the sky, and soon, in the evening hours, with the lights dim, the entertainment begins, the show starts, the wonders commence, things will be said, people will hold hands and listen like the old days with the balconies and the dark, or the cars and the dark . . . And in the midst of the smell of popcorn and spearmint gum and orange crush . . . the show begins . . .

Now, thoroughly oriented, THE OLD MAN *looks up out of his own depths and is ready for the performance. Slowly he looks at his audience, to the left, to the right and straight ahead. He glances at the* STRANGER, *then forgets him and talks.*

THE OLD MAN: Fool. That's what you called me. I accept the name. Well then, how did I *start* my foolishness? Years ago, I looked at the ruined world, the dictatorships, the dead states, the empty nations, and said, "What can I do? Me, a tired old man, what? Rebuild a devastation? Ha!" But lying half asleep one night I remembered a phonograph record I once owned . . .

He lifts THE WIFE'*s hand like a phonograph-arm and her fingertip the needle. He cranks the air. He puts her "needle" finger down.*

THE OLD MAN: The phonograph, the record. What a phonograph, what a song! An ancient vaudeville team, the Duncan Sisters!

The record hisses and we hear the Duncan Sisters, singing.

THE SONG: "Remembering, is all I do, dear, Remembering" . . . etc.

THE OLD MAN: You hear that? Hear some *more!*

They listen, THE OLD MAN *sways, almost dances.*

THE OLD MAN: Remembering? Remembering. I sang the song. Remembering. And suddenly it wasn't a song, it was a *way of life!*

STRANGER: A way of life?

THE OLD MAN: What did I have to offer a world that was forgetting? My memory! How could my memory help? By offering comparisons! By telling the young what *once* was. By *considering our losses!* I found the more I remembered, the more I *could* remember! Millions of things.

STRANGER: Like what?

The music has faded, but remains as a ghost echo all through the following:

THE OLD MAN: Like . . . imitation flowers.

Suddenly he has some in his hand.

THE OLD MAN: Kazoos. You ever *play* a kazoo?

He produces one and plays "Remembering" for a few notes.

THE OLD MAN: Jew's harps . . . ! Harmonicas!

He produces both.

THE OLD MAN: Thimbles! How long since you saw, if you *ever did see,* a thimble!

Like a sorcerer he produces one, two, three, four, five thimbles, one for each finger and thumb of his left hand.

THE OLD MAN: Bicycle clips, not bicycles, no, but *first* bicycle *clips!*

These he clips onto his pants.

THE OLD MAN: Antimacassars. Do you *know* them??? Giant snowflakes for the furniture! And . . . ! Once a man asked me to remember just the dashboard dials on a Cadillac. I remembered. I told him in detail. He listened. He cried great tears down his face. Happy tears or sad? I can't say. I only remember. Not literature, no. I never had a head for plays or poems, they slip away, they die. All I am, really, is a trash-heap of the mediocre, the third-rate-hand-me-down, useless and chromed-over slush and junk of a racetrack civilization that ran "last" over a precipice and still hasn't struck bottom. So all I can offer really is scintillant junk, the clamored-after chronometers and absurd machineries of a never-ending river of robots and robot-mad owners. Yet, one way or another, civilization must get back on the road. Those who can offer fine butterfly poetry, let them remember, let them offer. Those who can weave and build butterfly nets, let them weave, let them build. My gift is smaller than both, and perhaps contemptible in the long hoist, climb, jump, toward the old and amiably silly peak. But I *must* dream myself worthy. For the things, silly or not, that people remember are the things they will search for again. I will then ulcerate the people's half-dead desires with vinegar-gnat memory. So perhaps they'll rattle-bang the Big Clock together again, which is the City, the State, and then the World. Let one man want wine, another lounge chairs, a third a batwing glider to soar the March winds on and so you build even greater electropterodactyls to scour even greater winds with even greater peoples—Someone wants moron Christmas trees and some wise man goes to cut them. Pack this all together, wheel in wheel, want in want, and I'm there to oil and keep it running. Ho, once I would have raved, "Only the *best* is best, only *quality* is true!" But roses grow from blood manure. Mediocre must be, so most-excellent fine can bloom. And I shall be the Best Mediocre there is and fight all who say, "Slide under, sink back, dust-wallow, let brambles scurry over your living grave!" I shall protest the roving apeman tribes, the sheep-people munching the far fields preyed on by the feudal land-baron wolves who rarefy themselves in the few skyscraper summits and hoard unremembered foods. And these villains I will kill with can opener and corkscrew, I shall run down with ghosts of Buick, Kissel-Car, and Moon, thrash them with licorice whips until they cry "Mercy!" Can one *do* this?

He surveys the full panoply of memories hung upon his inner eye. He finishes:

THE OLD MAN: . . . one can only try.

THE OLD MAN *stands among his memories in a moment of silence.*

Someone clears his throat.

THE OLD MAN *starts out of his spell. The crowd murmurs.*

THE OLD MAN *and the* STRANGER *look around as if not guessing the reaction of the audience, which murmurs louder now, half like a disturbed or perhaps wounded but perhaps placated and petted Beast, not knowing whether to applaud the poetry or damn the sad upheaval of old memory!*

THE STRANGER: Old man . . .

THE OLD MAN (*looking around*): What did I *say?*

THE STRANGER: You'd better go now—

THE OLD MAN: Did they *hear* me?

THE STRANGER: They—

THE OLD MAN: Did they *understand?* What—?

The STRANGER *takes his elbow and thrusts a folded red ticket, very long and bright, upon him.*

THE STRANGER: To be on the safe side—

THE OLD MAN: Safe side . . . ?

THE STRANGER: Here's a ticket from a friend of mine in Transportation. One train crosses the country each week.

Each week I get a free pass for some idiot I want to help. *This* week, it's *you.*

THE OLD MAN *(taking the paper):* Me? Ticket? . . . *(reads)* "One-way to Chicago Abyss." *(glances up)* Is the Abyss still *there?*

THE STRANGER *(trying to move him, glancing around uneasily at the audience now himself, which still murmurs)* Yes, yes. This time next year, Lake Michigan may break through the last crust and make a new lake in the bomb crater where the city once was. There's life of sorts around the crater rim, and a branch train runs west once a month. After you leave here, keep moving . . .

THE OLD MAN: Moving . . . ?

THE STRANGER: Forget you met or know us.

THE OLD MAN: Forget?! *(almost laughs at the suggestion)* Me?!

THE STRANGER: And for God's sake, for the next year in the open, alone, declare a moratorium. Keep your fine mouth shut. *(hands over a second, yellow card)* And here. This is a dentist I know near Kansas Trace. Tell him to make you a new set of teeth that will only open at mealtimes.

> THE OLD MAN *has been pushed and urged toward the door, but cannot resist looking back, out and around.*

THE OLD MAN: Oh, God. *Did* they hear? Do they *know?*

> *The crowd becomes dreadfully still, cuts off. Silence. A beat.* THE OLD MAN *stares as if to fathom them. He looks at the red ticket. Then, seizing the* STRANGER's *hand and arm, he shakes, he wrings it in terrible friendship, and . . .*

> *Bolts! Runs off as if wildly pursued.*

Swift running darkness!

A locomotive whistle, the sound of a train rushing on tracks.

Somehow, we find a train, or the echo of a train, the phantom semblance of a train, is under and around THE OLD MAN. *He sways. The night sweeps by, running in a blizzard of snowflakes and sound.*

Standing, swaying amidst all this, among crumpled masses of clothing which must be people crammed into a narrow room, and on benches, THE OLD MAN *speaks to the night and the running train, peering first, in awe, at the ticket in his hand, reading the words to believe them, then looking around at his swift, strange environment . . .*

THE OLD MAN *(to himself):* . . . Chicago Abyss . . . night . . . time . . . snow . . . a blizzard of cold snow falling on the earth . . . ancient train . . . old cars . . . crammed with unwashed people . . . hundreds, thousands . . . sleeping in the aisles, jammed in the rest rooms, fighting to sleep, hoping not to dream . . .

He looks around, as if suddenly reminded of something, as he finds a place for himself jammed among the ragbags which must be sleeping humans.

THE OLD MAN *(to himself as he sits):* Remember, quiet, shut up, no, don't speak, nothing, stay still, think, careful . . . cease . . .

The train roars its whistle, flashes over a viaduct with new disturbs of thunder, fades, THE OLD MAN *sways.*

THE OLD MAN *(to himself):* Wait . . . wait . . .

For now a light has come slowly on to show us a BOY *of some ten or eleven years, who is sitting near* THE OLD MAN, *watching him with a steady gaze. He has been watching during all the above, but only now does his gaze, like a beacon, pick out* THE OLD MAN *and cause him to cease communing with himself. Now the light is very bright upon* THE BOY; *he becomes the most important thing on the train. The rest of the lights, showing us the crowded humanity on the floors and benches, begin to fade now. The sound of the train is a muted humming dream.*

Fascinated, THE OLD MAN *looks at* THE BOY *who looks back, unblinking, his eyes wide, his face pale, his ticket clenched in his hand, a look of great lost loneliness and traveling by himself in his gaze.*

THE OLD MAN *turns away, shuts his eyes.* THE BOY *looks at him.* THE OLD MAN *turns back, looks at* THE BOY, *and again turns away.*
THE BOY *watches him.*

THE OLD MAN *opens his eyes, argues with himself, moving his lips . . . but we cannot hear what he says . . . we only see him shrug, almost hit at his own arms, and firmly resolve not to look at* THE BOY. *Again he glances over at* THE BOY *but more swiftly now turns away, for* THE BOY *has not blinked and still fixes him with a clear pale look.*

At last, looking around, to see if all are asleep, and no one is listening, THE OLD MAN *looks at* THE BOY *again, swallows, wets his lips, revs up his courage, and speaks.*

THE OLD MAN *(leaning forward):* Shh, boy. Your *name?*

The train roars up a bit, fades. THE BOY *waits and speaks.*

THE BOY: Joseph.

The train sways and creaks, snow light falls down in a silent blizzard of Time around them.

THE OLD MAN: Joseph . . . ? *(he nods)* Ah . . .

He looks around one last time and leans further forward toward that pale face, those great round bright waiting eyes.

THE OLD MAN: Well, Joseph . . .

THE OLD MAN *lifts his fingers softly on the air.*

THE OLD MAN: . . . once upon a time . . .

All freezes in tableau. The lights dim.

In the dark, the train runs away and away, fading, with a last cry of its lost whistle.

By which time the curtain has come down and we are at

THE END

PILLAR OF FIRE
and Other
Plays

for today,
tomorrow,
and beyond
tomorrow

CONTENTS

Introduction

This book is dedicated to Kirk Mee, the first director to produce *Pillar of Fire*. His imagination brought the play to life with incredible intensity. His theatrical knowledge enabled me to cut and revise the play for its own benefit.

Kirk Mee is a proper way to start, for he taught me some of the old truths all over again. The best one being: simplicity is the soul of drama production. I have seen too many plays founder and roll on their sides when overproduced, overdressed, overstaged. When in doubt, strip away, lower your voice, stand in center stage with one light, and do the play. Better no sets than too many. Better one candle than a battery of glare. Better a whisper than all the fake sounds of all the fake rock artists in modern times.

There are exceptions to this, of course, but so rare as to have little bearing on my preface here.

Let me give an example of the sort of trouble you get into if you try to overproduce the plays in this book.

Some years back I put my two-act comedy *The Anthem Sprinters* in rehearsal here in Los Angeles, with my commendable director Charles Rome Smith, and as fine a cast of Irish/Scotch/Welsh actors as ever fell into a pub and poured out the other side. Since we had no money with which to put on the play, they gave me their lives three or four nights a week for a year. We celebrated our first anniversary as a "family" long before we got enough money to stage the comedy. During that year I wrote and rewrote yet again the long play, and, on occasion, we staged it at small drama societies around town. We liked what we saw. We liked what we felt about the play.

Then we made a dire mistake. We found some money. Some was in my pockets. Some was in the pockets of a man who haplessly wandered into our rehearsal one night. We rented the Coronet Theatre and first off built us a bog. Now why I ever let my producer convince me that we could *use* a bog, I cannot say. It is all lost in fog and mist back there in time. I went along with it, anyway, for the producer said we needed the blamed thing for my army of Sprinters to trudge through, philosophising about the dearth of sex and the squander of rain.

No sooner was the bog built than the play sank. Which is to say every time our actors climbed up and down around the rear of the stage where the bog was waiting for them, their voices were swallowed by space and went down without a trace.

"Speak up!" I yelled, on occasion, breaking a vow of silence I have kept pretty faithfully in connection with my actors and my director.

Speak up they did, but to little effect. The bog was too far back and their yelling spoiled what their philosophy was about.

"My God," I said to my director and producer, "let's get them out of that bog. March them down into the audience and around in front of the stage apron. Let the area just in front of the audience be the bog. *That* way we can at least hear the lines."

"That bog cost us five thousand dollars, we *got* to use it!" cried my producer.

"It may have cost us five thousand dollars, but right now it is costing us the entire play. If you can't hear the lines, you don't stay awake. And I'll be blasted if I'll stage a comedy for a company of sleepers. To hell with the bog, to hell with the five thousand dollars. Get those actors out of stage rear and up stage front! Try it!"

We tried it. It worked.

The actors marched around in the audience and the bog

was there, by magic, simply because it didn't exist, but *did* exist in the language spoken.

So when the curtain went up on opening night, we still had that five thousand dollar bog waiting at stage rear. Everyone could see it. But no one ever used it, save for a fast exit or a nice quick entrance.

I should have seen the problem before we spent the money.

I give you the same advice about the plays you hold here in your hands. Don't spend money, spend imagination. There is no reason to overdress or overproduce these texts. All three plays can be done without sets, with rear-projection, on occasion, if you wish, but don't let it worry you. Build me no bogs; when you sink out of sight, I won't be able to help you.

How did these plays *happen* to me?

The Foghorn resulted from an encounter I had one night with the tumbled ruins of the Venice Pier and the gigantic roller-coaster tracks and ties lying in the sand. Looking at them, I said, "What's this dinosaur doing lying on the shore, why did it come here?" Two nights later I awoke hearing the foghorn blowing and blowing far down the coast. "Of course!" I thought. "The foghorn! It sounds like an animal. *It* called that dinosaur in to the shore!"

I jumped out of bed and wrote *The Foghorn* in a few hours.

Pillar of Fire was caused by the quasi-intellectuals who mob through our society bullying us about our tastes, telling us that comic-strip cartoon books are bad for our digestion, worse for our imagination, and so should be burned. I would gladly Gunpowder Plot these ignorant social reformers out of existence, at least in my stories, and so set out in a fine rage to erase them with a large India rubber eraser.

Kaleidoscope was a word-association test I tried twenty-five years ago to see how terrified I might be if I threw myself down an elevator shaft.

If I were to further describe the essence of these three plays, how would I describe them?

Well, *The Foghorn* is a poetic dialogue, really, isn't it, about Loneliness and Time and strangely unrequited love? I didn't know this at the time I wrote it, but that's how it turned out. A fine lovely sad Surprise.

Pillar of Fire? One can best explain it as the drama of a sympathetic madman enveloped and finally destroyed by his obsession. This story, this character, this play, I see now, were rehearsals for my later novel and film *Fahrenheit 451*. If Montag is a burner of books who wakens to reading and becomes obsessed with saving mind-as-printed-upon-matter, then Lantry is the books themselves, he is the thing to be saved. In an ideal world, he and Montag would have met, set up shop and lived happily ever after: library and saver of libraries, book and reader, idea and flesh to preserve the idea.

So you play Lantry as pure paranoia. You play him like a whole library run amok because it knows, and we know, that unless it runs fast with Lantry's legs, it will be put to the torch and carried off in smoke. Lantry's family is all of the dark/bright lovely/horrible books ever written. If he had any childhood at all, he was Quasimodo aged three. If he had middle years, they were Jekyll and Hyde. If ever he loved, it was behind the mask of the Phantom of the Opera in Paris.

You play the obsessions then, and whatever image and metaphor come to hand. You play the passion to survive. Lantry is every library that we ever loved and hated to leave when someone whispered "closing time" and the green-shaded lamps dimmed and we had to shut our books and creep on mouse-feet home. That love, turned to despair at saving the love, inhabits *Pillar of Fire*.

And what inhabits *Kaleidoscope?* Panic and terror and

sadness, with a touch of beauty. One day twenty-five years ago I turned a bunch of men out, upside down, into space, to see what horrors and delights I might find with men so abandoned and so turned. What if, I asked myself, one night you fell downstairs into your basement but the stairs never ended, the basement had no bottom, and you kept falling forever?

In this last play then, what you enact is panic and exhilaration, terror and self-revelation; that moment when each man, alone, falling, dredges up what pitiful ounce of philosophy he has in the bin to help him through a night that, no matter what he does, will never end.

What you have in most of my stories and plays, then, is rarely a highly individualized character (I blunder into these on occasion), but Ideas grown super outsized; Ideas that sieze people and change them forever. So, I should imagine, in order to do my plays at all, you must become the Idea, the Idea that destroys, or the Idea that prevails.

Whether or not you can cram a dinosaur into a theatre, I do not know. You must try. And one of the ways of trying, of course, along with the aid of a good sound track and fine lighting, is to let the Idea of Loneliness itself invade your very bones so that you become Loneliness, the Night, the horn crying out, and the Beast come searching to see, find, know, and turn away to go lose himself in another billion years of loveless sleep.

So it follows that the actors in my plays, instead of playing character in the old fashioned or accepted sense, must become, if you wish, a purer, or at least a different thing: an Idea in motion, a passion on its way to destruction or survival, a love lost or kept, a panic continuing until death shuts it off.

Costumes for the plays must be, and are, simple.

The two characters in *The Foghorn* can be dressed in

ordinary work shirts and pants, with a seaman's cap, perhaps, for the older man.

The merest skeleton of a set will do. Build a slight, circular rise in mid-stage down front, with a rail to hold onto, as the two men pace and speak, looking out at the audience as if the audience were the night-sea itself. The rest is darkness, spot-lighting, and the sounds of sea, horn, and beast.

Pillar of Fire's problems are few. Lantry should appear in a dark suit, greened with age; some ancient dinner attire, perhaps, badly spoiled by time. The rest of the cast should wear dark jumpsuits or body stockings, cheaply purchased. In the Hearth scenes, the performers should be draped in sun-colored, orange-colored scarves, and the man in charge of the Hearth itself should be uniformed brightly, to reflect the burning optimism of that place. Beyond that, where indicated, the play needs few props, a decent soundtrack to let us hear the huge whisper of the Hearth, a few good bars from a sombre and then a heartier Bach, and imaginative lighting on an almost empty stage. Two coffins should be available, one very dark and of no particular singularity for Lantry to come out of. The other, utilized later in the Hearth, should be as bright and fantastically painted as an Egyptian sarcophagus, the sun-symbol being repeated a dozen times or more upon its surfaces. The Hearth itself can be a brightly illuminated red maw at stage rear. Borrow one of those roller-rung-ball-bearing ladders from a van-and-storage truck to put your coffins on. When it comes time to slide them into the Hearth, they shoot along splendidly on the swift rolling rungs, and vanish into the "fire" with a grand effect.

Kaleidoscope, it can be seen immediately, could be staged thirty different ways, from Peter Pan grandiloquent, with invisible wires and flying harnesses costing thousands, down to Simple Simon poor, which means standing three or four actors on one level, with others on tables or step-ladders or risers painted black against an all black background behind them.

Variations on this might be large black wheels spotted here and there about the stage, to which the actors might cling to be turned roundabout upside down at various times during the play.

But something like an immense book-shelf, or series of shelves, painted black, could be knocked together cheaply for your best effect. The actors could lie flat out on this, with their heads toward the audience, speaking their lines. Then if you wish an effect of men briefly spinning in space, the actors could achieve this by just rolling on their sides or over on their backs. In this fashion, the actor would be in complete control of his actions at all times. The entire crew, arranged at various levels on such a large, dark, and, therefore, invisible book-case, would surely suggest the Space that we utilize in the play. Stars could be projected all about them without necessarily revealing the construction you have put up.

The children need not appear at the end of this play. Their voices could be heard as the small trace of fire moves across the night sky.

There. I have said enough, no, more than enough about these plays.

Run grab them. Do them with great zest and fine gusto. Celebrate their terrors and delights. Get you to New England's coast, Poe's fiery tomb, and all of universal Space.

But . . . a last reminder.

Build me no Bogs!

Ray Bradbury
Los Angeles, California
Spring, 1975

Pillar
of Fire

At rise of curtain, darkness. Shadow shapes of tombstones here and there (projected), but in the main, darkness. We make out a coffin disposed alone amidst the graves. The lid opens slowly. We see only a hand. After a long moment, a very pale man in a dark suit sits up, slowly, achingly, half-blinded by sleep or that which is deeper than sleep. He feels himself. He climbs from the coffin and looks about, stunned.

LANTRY: I am dead. But . . . I am not dead.

He is examining himself incredulously.

LANTRY: I am reborn. In what place, to what time, for what reason?

His hand falls upon a tombstone, which he sees.

LANTRY: Wait. . . . Lantry? Yes . . . William Lantry. My name! Why? Lord, *someone* speak! Tell me! *(He almost weeps.)*

Voices approach. He pulls back in shadow.

Two men enter in dark jumpsuits, with a single symbol of fire on their breast-fronts. They carry spades and some peculiar kind of laser device, and are immaculate for all their being workers.

SMITH: Come on, Harry, this is it.

HARRY: They been waiting hundreds of years. Another ten seconds won't sweat them.

SMITH: This is special, though, this grave, this is history. I mean there should be newspapers here, television, radio. Photographers should take pictures! Listen, this is the *very last one.* In all the world, Harry, there are no more dead people! In all this country and all the countries of the world at long last there are no dead, no bodies, no corpses, no cemeteries, no graveyards. Think of it!

HARRY *(sits on coffin):* I'm thinking.

SMITH: That's your trouble. Nothing gets through to you. We've finally *done* it! Cleaned the earth, tidied up the soil, cleansed mankind of flesh and bones, of ribs and skulls. All gone except . . . er . . . Lazarus here. *(Nods to box.)*

LANTRY *(aside):* Lazarus . . . yes, Lazarus, *that's* my name. Called forth from the tomb, to do . . . *what?*

SMITH: A historic occasion, Harry! Celebrate!

HARRY *(dryly; waves hand weakly):* Hurrah.

SMITH *(peering at coffin lid):* What's *this* one's name again?

HARRY *(without looking, rises):* Plumtree.

LANTRY *(sotto voce; angry at this):* Lantry! Lantry!

SMITH: Well, good soul, lone Christian or whatever, he's the last dead 'un in history, the last actual flesh-and-blood corpse lying in the ground. He is extra-special. In a way he should be put in a museum like a mummy. *(Bends, opens coffin lid.)* Hold on . . . ! We didn't *finish* last night, did we?

HARRY: No.

SMITH: There *was* one more coffin, wasn't there?

HARRY: Yes.

SMITH *(peering):* It's empty!

HARRY: You've got the wrong hole . . . here . . . *(Reads tombstone.)* L-a-n-t—Lantry.

SMITH: You see? That's him. He's gone. And his body was here last night.

HARRY: We can't be sure. We didn't look.

SMITH: People don't bury empty coffins. He was in his box. Now he isn't. Smell that smell? He was here, all right.

HARRY: Nobody would have taken the body, would they?

SMITH: What for?

HARRY: A curiosity, perhaps? He was *special,* eh?

SMITH *(almost as if by rote, mechanically):* Don't be ridiculous. People just don't steal. Nobody steals. *Nobody* steals.

HARRY: Well, then, there's only one solution.

SMITH: And?

HARRY: He got up and walked away. Yes. That's it. He *got up* and *walked away! (Beams at his own joke.)*

SMITH: Harry, we're in big *trouble.* What will the Officials say if we show up empty-handed?

A siren wails, interrupting. A light flares on the sky. They turn and look and blink.

SMITH: There goes Lazarus-But-One. Into the old Fire. So long. Good-bye.

LANTRY *(sotto voce; aside; moves off, afraid):* The incinerator! That *Fire!*

SMITH: Good old Fire Place, Fine Hearth, great bonfire. I wish *I'd* thought of that, Harry.

HARRY: What, the Incinerator?

SMITH: Death pays fine cash, son. The man who built the first one, a millionaire. And all the rest since. Every city, town, village, you name it. They all got an official and therefore special Holy Incinerator. Where we all wind up.

HARRY: *You* before me, sir.

LANTRY *(aside):* The Incinerator. That light on the hill. Yes, yes. In the town a man dies. No sooner is he cold than his relatives pack him into a car and drive him swiftly to—

HARRY: The Incinerator. You're right. We grew up as Diggers. *Should* have been Officials. Hey, what do we do after tonight? Why . . . we're . . .

SMITH: Out of work. True. Out of work.

LANTRY *(slowly inspired, but still unsure; aside):* Not if I have anything to say about it.

HARRY *(shrugs; a beat):* You ever been inside the Incinerator?

SMITH *(snorts):* Sure! Haven't *you?*

HARRY: I never knew anyone *died. Yet.*

SMITH: Oh, it's a beautiful place. Gorgeous. You *must* see it!

HARRY: I will, soon enough.

They bend to hoist the coffin.

LANTRY *(picking it up; aside):* Soon enough.

LANTRY *steps forward into the light.*

LANTRY: Gentlemen! I bid you welcome!

Startled, they let the coffin fall.

HARRY: Hey, what are you doing here?

SMITH: Ah, shut up, Harry.

HARRY: How'd you *get* here?

SMITH: Harry. *(A beat.)* Sir, this is off-limits. No citizens allowed. You know the law.

LANTRY: I know the law.

SMITH: Well, then . . .

LANTRY: You're looking for a body?

SMITH: That's none of your affair.

HARRY: No, none!

LANTRY: I think I know where it is. I took it.

SMITH *(stunned):* You . . . *took* it?

HARRY: You got no right! How dare—

LANTRY: The right of first possession. It belongs to me.

HARRY *(pulls out pad and pencil):* All right. Let's just have your name for the Authorities!

LANTRY: Lantry.

HARRY *(writes, peering at pad; spells):* L . . . a . . . n . . .

He freezes. LANTRY *finishes it for him.*

LANTRY: . . . t . . . r . . . y. . . .

HARRY *(stunned):* It's a joke?

LANTRY *shakes his head.*

HARRY: Joe, isn't it a joke?

SMITH: A joke, sure, a joke! *(Laughs.)*

LANTRY: Well, you'll get your body, anyway.

SMITH: We will?

HARRY: Where is it?

LANTRY: Here.

>*He reaches out and strangles* HARRY. SMITH *watches, fascinated.*

SMITH: Here, now, what're you *doing?*

LANTRY: Getting you your body.

SMITH *(still fascinated, curious, watching):* But that's no way to do it . . . er . . . People don't murder people. Not anymore, they don't.

LANTRY *(holds* HARRY's *neck firmly):* They do *again.* There. *(Lets the body fall.)*

SMITH *(bends, peers):* What's wrong with him? He's not *really* dead? He *can't* be! People don't *do* that!

>LANTRY *moves calmly to put his hands around* SMITH's *neck now, as* SMITH *continues to comment, by rote, on the rules of this future society, as he is slowly strangled and his voice lessens, and finally he is still.*

SMITH *(sagging slowly, eyes wide):* People don't do that . . . why . . . people don't *do* that. They don't do that . . . they don't do . . . they don't . . .

>*Silence.* LANTRY *holds the dead* SMITH *by his throat a moment longer.*

LANTRY: What, not even a groan, a cry for mercy? Dear me. What will the Officials think? Two bodies instead of one. Ah, well.

He puts SMITH's *body in the coffin, then swiftly puts* HARRY's *body in on top of it and slams the lid.*

LANTRY: Peace. *(He turns, paces, eyes the sky, the land.)* Good. Good to walk again. Good to feel the wind and hear the leaves running like mice about my feet. Good to see the cold stars almost blown away in the wind. . . . Good even to know *fear* again. And . . . *(Feels himself.)* . . . I *am* afraid. Oh, yes. The very fact I *move* makes me the Enemy! An Enemy of all mankind. For there is not another friend, another *special* dead man just like me to whom I can turn for help, for consolation. So . . . War IS Declared! I know now why I was born back up out of the earth! It's William Lantry against the whole vampire-disbelieving, body-burning, graveyard-annihilating world. So, you there, city, people, customs, clean minds in clean bodies. You who cannot, *must* not, believe in me. Death has returned to your world. I will make more dead ones, more companions, so I won't be alone and lonely. . . . *NOW!*

A young man hurries through, whistling.

LANTRY: Oh . . . *sir!*

The man stops, turns. LANTRY *comes forward.*

LANTRY: Do you have a match?

The man strikes one into fire. LANTRY *looks at it. A beat. Leans forward. Blows it out.*

Instant blackout.

In the dark, a grand blast of Bach's Sinfonia from Cantata #29.

The colors change. All sun color now; oranges and yellows permeate the sky, the backdrops, the people. The music flows with summer sounds.

A VOICE *(gently whispering):* Welcome to the Hearth. Welcome to the Fires of God. Welcome to the place of the Sun. The Fire Place is always open. Summer and winter. Night and day. The Hearth is ready to welcome. The Fire is here to cleanse. The Sun is here to burn and make peace. Welcome, welcome. . . .

Enter AN OLD MAN *in colors of sun and summer.*

THE OLD MAN: Yes, welcome, welcome, come in, come in. . . . Put on the warm summer colors, brighten yourselves . . . that's it, yes, yes.

For THE OLD MAN *is being followed by* A YOUNG COUPLE, *who are pulling bright-colored capes over their darker clothes.* THE OLD MAN *helps adjust the capes.*

THE YOUNG WOMAN: We've been waiting so long.

THE YOUNG MAN: So long.

THE OLD MAN: Well, then, twice welcome. Put on summer, sir, put on summer.

He hands him a bright orange scarf to drape across his shoulders. An immense whispering sounds now.

THE YOUNG MAN *(listens, curious):* What's *that?*

THE OLD MAN *(listens, laughs):* That? Why, the fire, of course. The fire that rushes up the high round flue . . . the fire that burns all night, all day, forever, beyond that wall, within those stones, the fire, the sun, or the brother of the sun, you might say, a friend to all of us. *(Moves; points.)* Come into the bakery. Feel how warm. It's summer here all year. And the music? Have you *truly* listened?

*They all listen to the heavenly spheres in transit about
them on the air.*

THE OLD MAN: Bach rejuvenated! Bach made more alive
than he ever hoped or dreamed! Not music of death, but
music of life and fire, of all June, July, August, put away in
sweetest energies and flame. I—

A bell sounds. THE OLD MAN *shuts up, turns.*

THE OLD MAN: *Hist!* Watch. And know Joy!

The music rises. LANTRY *appears, surprised.*

THE OLD MAN: Oh, dear! Sir, sir, stand away. I mean . . .
oh, welcome . . . but . . . stand back! The Procession
of Joy begins!

LANTRY: The procession . . . ?

THE OLD MAN: Of Joy, of Joy! Wear summer, sir, put summer on. Here.

He gives and arranges the sun-colored scarf upon LAN-
TRY'S *shoulders, then pulls him aside and nods.*

THE OLD MAN: Music, begin again. Sound of children, *arise.*
And now, the procession!

*During the above, the music rises, the sounds of chil-
dren laughing, play all about.*

LANTRY *and the others stand waiting, intensely curious.*

THE OLD MAN *gestures, for the procession is obviously
late.*

THE OLD MAN: The *Procession!*

*In rolls a golden box on golden wheels, all to itself. The
box is covered with sun symbols.*

The box rolls to a slow halt, then creeps by at a snail's pace.

LANTRY *(stunned):* That is . . : a . . . *procession?*

THE OLD MAN: Yes! A procession through summer to the Sun!

LANTRY: And what's inside the coffin?

THE OLD MAN *(shocked):* Coffin? No, no. Sir, surely you know better.

LANTRY: Sorry . . .

For THE YOUNG COUPLE *are muttering, discontented, their faces shadowed.*

THE OLD MAN: This is the Hearthing Place.

LANTRY *(going along with it):* Of course, how silly of me!

THE OLD MAN: Which transfers souls to the New Life Beyond.

LANTRY: How *could* I have forgotten!

THE COUPLE *are smiling again.* THE OLD MAN *is satisfied.*

THE OLD MAN: In procession now. We shall accompany the exuberant soul of Minnie Davis Hopkins to the Hearth.

THE COUPLE *fall in behind the golden box.* LANTRY *moves into place, steered by* THE OLD MAN.

LANTRY *(to the couple; nods to the box):* Someone you know?

THE YOUNG WOMAN *(offended):* His mother!

THE YOUNG MAN: My *mother!*

LANTRY: Sorry . . .

THE YOUNG MAN: Nothing to be sorry about. I wish I were her, and knew Joy.

LANTRY *(dryly)*: Perhaps I can *arrange* it . . . ?

THE YOUNG MAN: What?

LANTRY *(shrugs; stands away)*: Move along to Joy.

THE OLD MAN: Yes, on to Happiness! So! . . . So! Music. Laughter. Oh, hear the children of Time!

> *Music, much childish laughter. The organ music rises.*

> *The light grows more intensely yellow. Suns appear everywhere on the backdrops. The box stops where the greatest sun-symbol fire-image burns toward the back of the area.* THE OLD MAN *takes hold of one edge of the box.*

THE OLD MAN: Minnie Davis Hopkins, who *still* lives, live only *more!*

> THE YOUNG MAN *and* WOMAN *hold the other corners, wait. They frown at* LANTRY. *He steps to hold the fourth corner.*

THE OLD MAN: You that were born of the Sun, return to the Sun!

> *The fire roars higher, as they stroke the bright box.*

THE OLD MAN: To live is a sweet burning,
To die is not to die,
But live in flame forever
And with God occupy
The time that's left for burning,
A billion years to sup!
So open wide God's laughter,
And let Him eat you up!

They tilt the carrier. The box slides off and down away, gone out of sight. An immense flux of flaming roar, as of a rocket almost, taking off! Music. Mixtures of children's laughter. The light fades.

THE OLD MAN *beams, smiles, shakes his head, pats one and all.*

THE YOUNG MAN *and* YOUNG WOMAN *smile and shake his hand, and turn to shake* LANTRY's *hand, but he is turned away, vastly puzzled and disturbed. They exit, leaving* THE OLD MAN *with* LANTRY.

THE OLD MAN *(gestures to the fire):* It burns ceaselessly, a solid golden river flowing up out of the earth toward the sky. Anything you launch on the river is borne upward, vanishing, forever!

LANTRY *(turned away; dryly):* You *do* go on.

LANTRY *turns and goes to look at the singing fires.*

THE OLD MAN: Is anything . . . er . . . *wrong?*

LANTRY: Wrong? How can anything be wrong in such a perfect world?

THE OLD MAN: True. *(Muses.)* When were you here last?

LANTRY: Never.

THE OLD MAN: Never?

LANTRY: Never in my life.

THE OLD MAN: But that's impossible. *(Thinks.) Isn't* it?

LANTRY: I exaggerate. I was here as a boy. But one forgets.

THE OLD MAN *(still not convinced; his face darker):* I shall be pleased to guide you on a tour.

LANTRY: No, no, thanks. Let me explain. No one in my family has died since I was a child. That's why—

THE OLD MAN: You have used the word "died," sir. We do *not* use that word!

LANTRY *(laughs, trying to make a joke of it):* We all have to die sometime.

THE OLD MAN *(steps farther back):* We do not, sir! Nothing ends, everything goes on, forever. Nothing spoils, nothing stops.

LANTRY: Have you never left a pound of cheese out in the sun?

THE OLD MAN: Sir!

LANTRY: Sorry.

THE OLD MAN: Sorry? *(starts off, turns, thinks)* But, then, oh yes. You *must* be one of those just returned from Mars . . . ?

LANTRY: Mars?

THE OLD MAN *(trying to convince himself, baffled):* Born and raised there? Used to *their* dread customs? People *do* die *there.* People *are* buried there? Things *do* spoil . . . on *Mars.*

LANTRY *(saved, and making use of it):* Yes, Mars, that's it!

THE OLD MAN: Which Apollo flight did you return on?

LANTRY: Why . . . the most recent.

THE OLD MAN *(not satisfied, suddenly wary):* And that would be . . . ?

LANTRY *(impulsively):* Last *month!*

THE OLD MAN *(suspicious now):* I see. *(Turns to go.)*

LANTRY: No, you don't see—wait!

THE OLD MAN *(turning back):* For what, sir?

LANTRY: You say nothing dies, nothing ends, nothing spoils?

THE OLD MAN: I do not say that, sir, the Program says it.

LANTRY: Then you are not afraid of ends, of finishes, of darkness.

THE OLD MAN: I look into the sun, sir, and am not blind.

LANTRY: Look further, then.

He has reached THE OLD MAN *and now takes hold of his throat.*

LANTRY: What do you see?

THE OLD MAN: Gah!

LANTRY *(insists, wild):* What do you *see?*

THE OLD MAN: Oh no, no, save me! *Darkness! (Dies.)*

LANTRY: You have passed the test, sir. The answer is correct.

He turns swiftly to haul the body to the carrier. As he deposits it, the music rises.

LANTRY *(inspired; calls out commands):* Music! Yes! Laughter of children! More, more! No, no, not *happy* laughter. Laughter that is somewhat . . . mad! Machines, do you hear? Leaning toward . . . *madness?*

The laughter changes, the light grows more somber.

LANTRY: How fine! Machines that listen and *obey!* Yes, *yes!*

The light is all earth colors now, and dusk. The laughter and music rise to insanity.

LANTRY: Man, born out of darkness, *return* to darkness.

He dumps the body. Organ tones: Bach, long after midnight.

LANTRY *starts to run out, stops, feels himself.*

LANTRY: Oh, this is . . . *fun!*

A WOMAN ATTENDANT *enters abruptly.*

THE ATTENDANT *(looks about):* Was there a service held just now?

LANTRY: There was.

THE ATTENDANT *(takes out pad):* There was one scheduled for ten o'clock . . . over, done. But it's ten *fifteen* now.

LANTRY: So it is.

THE ATTENDANT *(looks up sharply):* Who are you?

LANTRY: A fool full of wrong answers, who makes old men suspicious. Everyone *knows* mobs of children are brought here every year of their lives to teach them that fire is fine, going away is sunlight, leaving forever is flame, right?

THE ATTENDANT: I—

LANTRY: Right! But did I *say* any of those things? No. I said darkness, I said die, I said death.

THE ATTENDANT *(stunned and disgusted):* Unutterable, oh, most unutterable!

LANTRY: Isn't it? Darkness, die, death.

THE ATTENDANT: No, no! *(Puts hands to ears.)*

LANTRY: I'm done.

THE ATTENDANT: No!

LANTRY: I said I'm done.

THE ATTENDANT *takes her hands from her ears.*

THE ATTENDANT *(sniffs):* Wha . . . what's that smell?

LANTRY: Smell?

THE ATTENDANT: I walked in the fields once at dusk. That is the smell of . . . earth.

LANTRY *(nods, smiles):* Earth!

THE ATTENDANT: But, *more* . . . in the field, I found . . . a cow . . . a cow that had expired. A cow that had fallen away to eternity, but lay in the field for . . . a *week*. The smell, oh, the smell! And now . . . it's *here*.

LANTRY: Here. *(Holds out his hand.)*

THE ATTENDANT *(widens her eyes, sniffs):* You're so . . . pale.

LANTRY: Pale? *(Looks at hand.)* Yes, I never thought.

THE ATTENDANT *(as if reciting catechism):* People aren't pale. People are tan, sunburned, golden, brown.

LANTRY: People are, yes. But not the dead.

THE ATTENDANT *(motionless):* Dead?

LANTRY *(produces knife):* Do you know what this is?

THE ATTENDANT: A knife.

LANTRY: What would you say if I told you I was going to push it straight on into your chest?

THE ATTENDANT: People don't do that . . . people don't do that, people don't—

LANTRY: Yes.

THE ATTENDANT *(by rote):* You wouldn't do that, you wouldn't . . .

LANTRY *(touches her on her shoulder with knife):* Yes.

THE ATTENDANT *(reciting catechism):* People don't kill people. No one kills anyone. No one dies anymore.

LANTRY *(touches her on her brow):* I just killed your friend.

THE ATTENDANT *(by rote):* People don't kill.

LANTRY *(touches her on her chest):* Yours will be the fourth murder in as few hours in the past one hundred years.

THE ATTENDANT *(by rote, as if spelled):* I'm not going to be killed. I'm not going to be killed.

LANTRY: You're going to stand right there like a hypnotized chicken while I walk around you . . . *(Walks.)* . . . so. And now reach out with this knife.

THE ATTENDANT: You're not reaching out. People don't kill.

LANTRY: To shove in the blade.

THE ATTENDANT: It's not going in.

LANTRY: Die.

THE ATTENDANT: I'm not dying . . . I'm . . .

Her eyes shut. LANTRY *catches her as she falls.*

Darkness. Instant Bach-at-midnight. A great voice, like LANTRY's, *intones in the dark.*

LANTRY'S VOICE: Ashes to ashes, dust to dust.

There is a fantastic explosion, which lights up the night.

LANTRY *appears, warms his hands at the sight, holding them out upon the air as the lights rise again.*

LANTRY *(wildly to the Universe itself):* And what was that? Why . . . the Incinerator! The Hearth! The Grand Fire Place! Blown up and making more fire in the hills than all of autumn itself!

A final explosion, a dying of light.

LANTRY: Now, one by one, I'll blow up all the other Incinerator Fire Hearthing Places before anyone suspects they have a man of no ethics whatsoever loose in their midst. Long before they discover that this enemy-variable, this William Lantry, has run amok, I will have torn down and done murder across a world. For I am, after all, invisible. Since crime is impossible in this future world, who dares, who tries to see the obvious beast? *(Holds his hands out . . . gestures. An explosion!)* Delicious!

Blackout.

Lights come up on THREE MEN *in dark jumpsuits with bright suns blazoned on the jacket pockets, seated at imaginary computer electronic phone boards. Behind them, vast computer banks and electrical devices are projected on the scrims. There is a hum and moan of machines and soft bells sounding.*

A soft bell sounds above the others. One of the OPERATORS *pantomimes, palm-printing the air in front of him.*

THE OPERATOR *(crisply):* Central City Data.

LANTRY'S VOICE: Could you give me . . . that is . . . the telephone number of the . . . Police Department?

THE OPERATOR: The what?

LANTRY'S VOICE: Police Department . . . ?

THE OPERATOR *(crisply):* No such listing!

He "erases" the air with his hand. Disconnect sounds. A second bell rings. The SECOND OPERATOR *prints the air with his hand.*

SECOND OPERATOR: Central City Data.

LANTRY'S VOICE: Beg pardon, but . . . Police?

SECOND OPERATOR: Sir?

LANTRY'S VOICE: I'm simply trying to find the Police Department!

The FIRST OPERATOR *is looking over quizzically at the* SECOND, *who raises his eyebrows. The* FIRST OPERATOR *"plugs in," recognizes the voice, listens. The* THIRD OPERATOR *does the same.*

SECOND OPERATOR *(pronouncing it slowly):* Po-lice. Dee-part —ment?

LANTRY *(guessing):* Law Enforcement? Law Force?

SECOND OPERATOR: The terms you are using no longer exist, sir.

He gestures. The others begin an electronic trackdown.

LANTRY: Sorry, but I don't know—

SECOND OPERATOR: I will connect you with the Peace Control . . . ?

LANTRY: Yes! That's it! Peace! Peace Control!

SECOND OPERATOR: Control it is. One moment.

He "dials" the air, and nods to the THIRD OPERATOR, *who nods, winks, "prints" the air with his hand. A bell rings.*

THIRD OPERATOR: Peace Control.

LANTRY: Yes, well . . . put me through to Homicide.

THIRD OPERATOR: Sir?

LANTRY: Homicide Division. Investigation of Violence? Assault and Battery? Murder?

THIRD OPERATOR: Sir!

All three OPERATORS *are astounded. Their hands work overtime on the air, pantomiming circuit cut-ins.*

LANTRY: Is there no department to investigate . . . deaths?

THIRD OPERATOR: Sir, you are in much need of help. *(Checks imaginary circuits on air in front of him.)* You are in a phone station at Salem and Twelfth. Please remain there until the Quiet People arrive.

LANTRY: Quiet people? What! *Quiet* people, did you say?

THIRD OPERATOR: Do not leave that location, sir. Help is on the way.

LANTRY: Sir, sir . . . !

THIRD OPERATOR: Yes?

LANTRY *(takes a deep breath, holds it, explodes):* Wrong number!

Click-buzz. The system hums, moans. The men gesticulate. All talk into their phones at once.

FIRST OPERATOR: Peace Control, quickly . . . Unit Twelve.

SECOND OPERATOR: Quiet People Unit Seven. . . .

THIRD OPERATOR: Serenity Perimeter close to Salem and Twelfth. . . .

FIRST OPERATOR: Salem and Twelfth.

SECOND OPERATOR: Yes, Salem and Twelfth!

They reach up to "touch" the air a final time. Bells. Hums.

LANTRY'S VOICE: . . . wrong number . . . wrong number . . . wrong . . .

A final sizzle, a dance of light. A chord of music.

Blackout. Then lights up on LANTRY *lying asleep. He stirs.*

LANTRY: I wake at sunset with a dream of fire. I see myself pushed into the furnace, burned to ashes, then the ashes burnt to dust. God, can Dead men dream? *(Nods.)* And hate their dreaming. *(Listens.)* What? *(Raises his hand to touch out on the air.)* That building? It *"calls"* to me. I *must* . . . go there.

Exits into darkness.

The lights come up on: a library of the future.

A WOMAN *sits amidst the "stacks," which are projected images of strangely shaped "books," of objects which, when picked up, begin to speak in tongues, recite themselves.*

As A YOUNG MAN *enters and whispers to her, she points to one side. He goes to pick up a "book" from its place where it is hung like a strange harp, to her left. He touches his hand to it. A soft voice murmurs.*

THE VOICE: The square of the hypoteneuse . . . etc., etc.

A YOUNG WOMAN *enters and is directed to the right, where she picks up a voice-book and brushes her hands across it as on a stringed instrument. It murmurs:*

THE SECOND VOICE: The population of greater New York State, etc., etc.

ANOTHER MAN *has entered, and is directed to a place behind the woman, where his "book," touched, whispers:*

THE THIRD VOICE: At the age of thirty-three, Hector Berlioz went to live in Rome, Italy. At that time he . . .

Music rises softly: Berlioz. Amidst all these voices, sounds, whispers, musics, LANTRY *enters to the left, looks around, listens, ponders, turns.*

LANTRY: Yes . . . yes, can it be? Odd, very strange, *but* a library. And . . . I'm lonely. I need friends. Special friends. People like . . . myself. Are there any in all the world? Or am I, oh Lord, dead and buried flesh, alone . . . alone? This might be the place to find out.

He steels himself, then turns, walks straight up to THE WOMAN *at the desk amidst the murmurs and strange musics.*

THE LIBRARIAN: Yes?

LANTRY: I would like to read . . . I mean . . . *(Stops; to himself.)* Careful.

He looks, listens, waits.

THE LIBRARIAN: Beg pardon?

LANTRY *(to himself):* Careful. *Do* people read books, still? Or *watch* them like films? Or *play* them like toys?

He looks at the PEOPLE *"playing their harp books," entranced. He turns back to the* LIBRARIAN.

LANTRY: Ah . . . I would like, er . . . to *have* . . . Edgar Allan Poe?

THE LIBRARIAN *(puzzled):* Sir?

LANTRY: Er . . . Poe. . . . Edgar Allan?

THE LIBRARIAN: Oh, that would be fiction, wouldn't it?

LANTRY: . . . yes. . . .

THE LIBRARIAN *(sniffs):* Oh, we don't carry fiction, of course.

LANTRY *(stunned; aghast):* No *fiction!*

THE LIBRARIAN *(finger to lip):* Sh . . .

LANTRY *(lowering his voice):* No fiction . . . ?

THE LIBRARIAN: But of course you *knew* that? Wait. I see. You're one of those odd ones from Mars! *(Laughs.)*

LANTRY: Just got back. Been there forever.

THE LIBRARIAN: But surely, even up there, they *told* you?

LANTRY: About . . . ?

THE LIBRARIAN *(with sacred awe):* The Great Burning of Ten Years Back?

LANTRY: The Great Burning, of course.

THE LIBRARIAN *(proudly):* We burned Mr. Poe.

LANTRY: Burned?

THE LIBRARIAN: And Mr. Dickens, and Mr. Hawthorne, and Mr. Melville. Burned, burned, burned. Oh, it was most lovely. They deserved to be given their rest.

LANTRY: *Deserved?*

THE LIBRARIAN: They weren't *real.* Never *were.* Dreamers, the lot. Nothing to do with reality, data, information.

LANTRY: And so you just . . . *killed* them?

THE LIBRARIAN: No, no, *burned* is more like it.

From the shadows, POE *calls out softly.*

POE: No, not killed . . . !

LANTRY *hears, turns, wonders, sees nothing, turns back to the* LIBRARIAN.

LANTRY: Burned . . . ?

THE LIBRARIAN: *And* Mr. Dickens.

DICKENS *(calls from the shadows):* No!

THE LIBRARIAN: And Mr. Hawthorne!

HAWTHORNE *(as with the others):* No, not a bit of it!

THE LIBRARIAN: And Mr. Melville!

MELVILLE *(with the others):* Blast it, no!

THE LIBRARIAN: And Henry James, and Mr. Steinbeck, and William Makepeace Thackeray and—

A ghostly CHORUS *cries out: "No!" The four* AUTHORS *stand behind* LANTRY, *unlit, only shadows, half-seen. And behind them, projected perhaps, the* GHOSTS *of other authors, misting and reshaping, and reaching out. They sigh and murmur.*

THE AUTHORS: Please . . . please, no . . . !

THE LIBRARIAN *(sweetly, smugly):* Oh, it was most efficient-fine. They *should* have been put to rest centuries ago!

LANTRY: *Should* have?

THE AUTHORS: No . . . oh, no, no . . .

LANTRY *hears, and turns, half-sees.*

LANTRY: Yes, yes, there was a story once . . .

THE LIBRARIAN: A story?

LANTRY: Yes! A *fiction!* By a writer, can't recall . . . who wrote that all across Earth, the great names were burned. . . .

A sigh from the AUTHORS.

LANTRY: Most of their books, gone. . . .

THE AUTHORS *(whispering):* . . . gone . . .

LANTRY: And so, these authors' ghosts, why they flew away to Mars . . . And survived there as written dreams, as wondrous fantasies, strange figments of old and dear imaginations. . . .

The AUTHORS *stir and murmur, remembering.*

LANTRY: Until one day, a rocket arrived from Earth with the Burners, the Censors, the Data-Collecting Destroyers who lived only by fact, and not by Dream. And brought with them the final books, the final lives of these final ghosts, and burned them on the sands of old dead Mars. . . .

Thunder and fire in the sky. LANTRY *looks up, shades his eyes against the light, follows the fire and thunder down.*

LANTRY: The rocket . . . the rocket!

The thunder fades. A ROCKET CAPTAIN *stands forth out of darkness, an* AIDE *behind him carrying books. The captain himself has a list at which he glances.*

LANTRY: The captain of the rocket! Oh, look! He smells of menthol, iodine, and green soap. He is polished and manicured and oiled. His white teeth are dentrificed, his ears scoured to pinkness, as are his cheeks. His crisp hair is fresh cut and smells of alcohol. Even his breath is super sweet and new. There is no spot on him. And yet he comes to—

THE CAPTAIN (*cuts in; to himself*): Kill.

THE AIDE: Sir?

THE CAPTAIN: Kill, quite frankly. Lay the final ghosts. You have the books, let's check the list. *Tales of Mystery and Imagination,* by Poe?

THE AIDE: Check. (*Checks list.*)

THE CAPTAIN: *Dracula,* by Bram Stoker.

THE AIDE: Check!

THE CAPTAIN: *The Legend of Sleepy Hollow,* by Washington Irving?

THE AIDE: Check!

THE CAPTAIN (*swiftly*): *The Turn of the Screw,* by Henry James?

THE AIDE: Check!

THE CAPTAIN (*very crisply, swiftly*): *Frankenstein,* by Mary Shelley? *Rappacini's Daughter,* by Hawthorne. *Alice's Adventures in Wonderland,* by Carroll? *The Wizard of Oz,* by L. Frank Baum?

THE AIDE: Check, check, check, check!

THE AUTHORS' VOICES *murmur and lament softly.*

ALL (*whispering*): Oh, no . . . oh, wait, wait! No . . . no. . . .

THE CAPTAIN: Lovecraft, Wells, Huxley, check, check, check, dump them all.

THE AIDE: They're dumped. (*Does so.*)

LANTRY: Oh, lost souls, look at *us* . . . look at *them*. Two rocket men. *Two* men against a legion, yet we fail. All along the desert shelves of Mars tonight, beyond us, look. Shakespeare's armies alone are multitudinous . . . there the three witches, there Oberon and Hamlet's father's ghost! There Richard and his murdered court and mighty armies of imagination and strange Time against, count them, two clean men who smell of soap and righteousness! Let us move!

ALL *(whispering):* Move, yes, move!

THE CAPTAIN *(crisply):* The flame!

THE AIDE: The flame. . . .

> THE AIDE *pantomimes a match to the books. Bright flame-light bathes* THE CAPTAIN *only, with flickering fire-shadows.*

THE CAPTAIN *(warms his hands in the light):* So. So. So we dedicate ourselves to science and progress. So we destroy the dark past, and burn all superstition. So burn the monstrous names, the dreadful names of Cabell and Dunsany and Tolkien and Poe and Carroll and Lovecraft and Baum. So . . . so.

ALL: Oh! Oh . . . ! We die . . . we die . . . save us!

LANTRY: I will!

> *But he cannot move. Transfixed, he only "sees" the drama done.*

THE CAPTAIN *(dryly):* What, what was it the wicked witch said at the end of *The Wizard of Oz* when the bucket of water was tossed upon her?

THE AIDE *(tries to remember, and does):* I . . . I'm melting . . . ?

THE CAPTAIN *(pleased, points to the books):* I'm . . . melting.

ALL: Melting . . . melting. . . .

THE AUTHORS pull back into shadows, gone away, their voices fading.

LANTRY: No . . . please! Wait!

But they are gone. LANTRY *has moved toward their area, but stops, for he is isolated, and the colors and lights of the library come up again and the* PEOPLE *"play" their books and soft voices sing data.*

THE LIBRARIAN *(fades back in, reading her own list):* Lovecraft, Baum, Burroughs! That's the full list. Oh, and Mr. Melville, of course, whoever *he* was.

LANTRY *(to himself):* No! The man who birthed a whale, and now unknown! *(Turns and shouts at her.)* Do you know what you *are?*

THE LIBRARIAN *(startled):* Sir!

LANTRY: A murderer! A murderer!

THE LIBRARIAN *(stands):* Why, sir, I shall call the Peace Squad. You are in need of Peace. They will inject you.

LANTRY: Inject! Is there an injection, then, for my madness? *(Stops, gets hold of himself.)*

THE LIBRARIAN: You have been traveling, sir, a long way. The journey from Mars has tired you. I will *not* call the Squad.

LANTRY: Thanks. I'll be back. What day is this?

THE LIBRARIAN: Why, October 29, of course.

LANTRY *(snorts with the irony of it):* Oh, good! I'll be back in two days, on Halloween.

THE LIBRARIAN: Halloween? You know there *isn't* any.

LANTRY *(a beat):* No? They . . . burned *that,* too?

> THE LIBRARIAN *smiles and nods smugly. There is a great roar and crackling as of a huge and special fire, toward which* LANTRY *looks, stunned.*

LANTRY: Murderers! Oh, yes . . . *murderers!*

> *He wanders off into darkness.* THE LIBRARIAN, *having jumped up at this last outburst of his, waits a beat, then sits and "dials."*

THE LIBRARIAN: Q-112? Library here. . . . Peace Squad, please.

> *Blackout. Sirens. Motors. Voices. Then lights up again as* LANTRY *runs in, stops, looks back.*

LANTRY: Oh, now, one *must* be careful. How strangely I am balanced in this world. Like some kind of dark gyroscope, whirling with never a murmur, a very silent man. *(Peers around.)* The street lights! How *dim* they are. And how *few!* It can't be—

YOUNG MAN *(passing by at this instant):* Can't be what? *(Stares at* LANTRY.*)*

LANTRY: Could you tell me, I mean . . .

YOUNG MAN: Tell you what?

LANTRY: Why there are so few street lights, and those so dim, and none in the middle of the blocks?

YOUNG MAN: Why?

LANTRY: You see, I'm a teacher. Merely testing your knowledge.

YOUNG MAN *(blankly):* A teacher.

LANTRY: And it's *dark.*

YOUNG MAN: So?

LANTRY: Aren't you afraid?

YOUNG MAN: Of what?

LANTRY *(exasperated)*: The dark, of course, the dark!

YOUNG MAN *(calmly)*: Ho, ho!

LANTRY: Aren't *you?* Aren't *they?* Isn't *everyone!*

YOUNG MAN *(easily)*: Ho, ho, afraid, of the dark! Ha-hee!
Wow, oh boy.

LANTRY: But street lights were invented *against* the dark, to
prevent fear.

YOUNG MAN: Dumb. Of course that's not the reason. They
were invented so you could see where you were walking or
driving. But for no other reason. *(Shakes his head.) Real*
dumb.

LANTRY: You mean to say you could walk down that street
there, that unlit alley, and not be afraid?

YOUNG MAN *(snorts)*: Sure.

LANTRY: And go out in the hills and stay all night in the dark
with no light?

YOUNG MAN: Sure.

LANTRY: And go in a haunted house and stay alone and not
be frightened?

YOUNG MAN: A what?

LANTRY *(catches himself)*: Er . . . an empty house.

YOUNG MAN: Sure.

LANTRY: You lie! You lie! You lie! You must be afraid, I tell you, you *must!* You lie!

YOUNG MAN *(stops laughing; repeats as if by rote):* Lie? I've never lied in my life. People don't lie. People don't lie. . . .

LANTRY: You lie!

YOUNG MAN: Only genetic inequitables lie. Only glandular inefficients lie. Only . . .

He peers at LANTRY.

YOUNG MAN: Boy, are you pale. Boy, are you white. I never seen anyone so pale, so white. Boy . . .

LANTRY *(moves threateningly):* Aren't you afraid of me, for some reason?

YOUNG MAN *(calmly):* No.

LANTRY *(puts one hand on the boy's shoulder):* And . . . now?

YOUNG MAN: No.

LANTRY *(puts both hands on the young man's neck):* And . . . now.

YOUNG MAN *(calmly):* You may well be a genetic inequitable or most probably a glandular inefficient with the color of your skin, so . . . *(Shrugs.)*

A siren wails. LANTRY *turns, backs off.*

YOUNG MAN: Hey . . . wait. . . . I'll be darned. You're afraid. *You're* frightened. *You're* scared!

LANTRY: No! *(Runs; exits.)*

YOUNG MAN *(calls after):* Don't be, oh, please, don't be. *(Thinks, laughs, calls.)* Mind the dark, there, mind the dark!

Blackout.

Out of darkness, we hear CHILDREN'S VOICES *passing, laughing, crying.*

THE CHILDREN: Trick or treat . . . ha ha . . . trick or treat . . . ! . . . thanks. . . . Trick . . . trick!

The voices fade as LANTRY *enters, listening.*

LANTRY: Oh, no! All *that* . . . gone? All Hallow's dead? No more trick or treat? No more the happy children and the chase for sweets? The endless journeys in the rare autumn dusks of towns all spearmint and Baby Ruth rewards? Oh, *none* of that? Blind me! Of all the rank, gross, crawling, empty-mouthed stupidity. What fun is there in children, if you don't imagine things? Oh, unbrave new world that has such cowards in it. I am your enemy! And all men like me! Tell us you will burn us, we do not burn! Tell us we're forever dead, and then we move! Say there are no vampires in the world, and blood we seek! Tell me that I cannot walk, and walk I will. Put Murder by, and why, I'll resurrect it *whole!* I am, *en toto,* all impossible things come possible. You have birthed me with your damnable plain soda cracker and dumb tasteless stews boiled out of ignorances made new scientific faith. Sun is good, sun is all, say you? Well, so is night, so is dark, say I. Dark is horror, listen! Night is meant for contrast. You *must* be afraid, or, what use for life? There are no beginnings without an end, don't you see? Noon has no meaning without midnight, fools! Listen. Hear! *(Waits.)* No? Well, then, beware you stake-driving killers of Stoker and Poe, you burners of Tolkien who assassinate Santa Claus of a

Christmas Eve and crucify Christ forever. I will make night what it once was, the thing against which you futile, wise, smug, knowing men built and lit all your lanterned cities. I knock at your door. I wait. No Treats, no Fun in Scares and Frights? Well, then: immense and mighty Tricks from this Dark Child.

The lights dim swiftly as LANTRY *exits and the* GHOST CHILDREN *go by a final time, crying softly "Trick or treat." Fading.*

A light comes up on THE LIBRARIAN. THE SPACE-SHIP CAPTAIN *moves briskly in to confront her.*

BURKE *(the captain):* Good evening.

THE LIBRARIAN: Oh, yes, it's Captain Burke, isn't it?

BURKE: Burke, that's right.

THE LIBRARIAN: Just back from Mars. It's been quite a night for your people.

BURKE: Mine?

THE LIBRARIAN: The other gentleman, a friend of yours, he said—

BURKE: Other? Gentleman?

THE LIBRARIAN: Very pale. Said he'd come back with you two days ago, from Mars.

BURKE: But no one came with me. I came alone.

THE LIBRARIAN: Oh, dear. Oh, dear. He was lying, then? People don't lie.

BURKE: People don't lie.

THE LIBRARIAN: People don't lie. *(Dials phone.)* Peace Squad, please.

The light fades as she repeats.

THE LIBRARIAN: Peace Squad, please.

THE YOUNG MAN, *in his own light, speaks to a man in shadow.*

YOUNG MAN: Walking along here he was, yes, walking. Walking. Asked me if I was afraid of the dark, can you imagine? Walking, he was. Me, I was walking because, well, my car broke down. But him, why, he seemed to be walking, walking, yes, walking, *walking.* . . .

The light fades, and pinspots come up alternately on the various people: THE LIBRARIAN, THE YOUNG MAN, BURKE, *and* SMITH, THE FIRST GRAVEDIGGER.

THE LIBRARIAN: Pale he was . . .

YOUNG MAN: Walking . . . walking . . .

SMITH *(with one hand to his throat):* People don't kill. . . . People don't—

BURKE: People don't lie . . .

THE LIBRARIAN: People don't lie . . .

SMITH: People don't kill, people don't—

BURKE: People don't lie. . . .

ALL *babble their lines, fading.*

In a light to one side, PEACE SQUAD OFFICER MCCLURE *appears.*

MCCLURE: Peace Squad Officer McClure.

LIBRARIAN *(brightly):* Oh, yes!

MCCLURE: A man who *lied* was here?

LIBRARIAN: He said he came from Mars.

McCLURE: A man whose crime was being pale—

LIBRARIAN: Oh, very pale!

McCLURE *(to* BURKE*):* No friend of yours?

BURKE: He *said* he was.

McCLURE *(making notes on hand computer):* An odd man, not from Mars, and pale, and full of lies—

SMITH *(the gravedigger):* And killing, sir, killing, sir, *killing!*

McCLURE: Astounding thought. *(Writes.)* But, killing, *too.*

A vast explosion. ALL *turn.* ALL *look.*

McCLURE: And . . . going about . . . blowing up the Places of the Sun, the Hearthing Places, the Incinerators of Souls?

Explosions, explosions, explosions.

MCCLURE *waits a beat, eyes the reddened sky, then exits.*

Blackout.

LANTRY *enters among the strewn bodies in a make-shift morgue. We see the images of the laid-out dead, sheet-covered, on the scrims behind him, and on the floors about him.*

LANTRY: What's this? A temporary morgue? Yes, yes. With all the Incinerators blown up by me, nowhere for all the bodies, except here, a high school gymnasium. Well . . .

LANTRY *moves among the shadows and the forms.*

LANTRY: Yes. *(A beat.)* Yes! *(Gestures all about, fondly, as to his children.)* Only a moment, and you'll be good as new. Friends? *(Nods.)* Friends. Let me see some of you. . . .

Moves among them, reading names on tags or blouses.

LANTRY: Griswold, Hart, Remington, good. You'll rise and walk with me and make more dead. *(Bends, reads.)* Carruthers. An architect! Yes! Now, listen, Carruthers, when you awake and rise, we will rebuild the House of Usher! And build us anthropoids to prowl its midnight halls; sweet robot apes that, ticking madly, will find and keep the best learned sociologists of this clean time and stuff them up the chimneys! Even as that orangutan run wild in the Rue Morgue did fix a body up a flue! Red Deaths we will build and wind and wander free to spread a robot plague and teach men what's not been taught in years: to dread the dark, to fear a spider hand, to flee from daggers and from guns. . . . So at the end of all our building, with the grand gorillas, maddened black cats, stalking Plagues, we'll run the pack of brilliant teachers, learners, doers, to the android catacombs and there wall up their cries with bricks and casks of, oh, now, yes! Amontillado! And then stand back, and press the switch which breaks the dungeons down, lets water in! So Phantom of the Opera, Wax Works, murderers, dumb robot apes, and sociologists, psychologists, biting, yapping, snapping at their own tails, sink down, as Usher Two falls to rocks, and dust and oblivions lost to sight.

We hear the falling of the house into the lake, far off.

LANTRY *(a beat):* Will you build this with me? *(Nods, satisfied.)* I think you will. As for the rest? Soon enough, you'll know. . . . Now!

MCCLURE *enters unseen and watches as* LANTRY *busies himself with chalk taken from his pocket.*

LANTRY: Pentagrams, symbols, thus, and so. Symbols, pentagrams here, now there. And *there!*

He has marked the sheets of the dead. Now he draws a great circle on the floor to enclose himself and many of the forms.

LANTRY: Are we prepared? We *are!* So now, arise! Arise, ye dead. Arise, my brothers, sisters, stir, then go with me! Live! Live! By all that is unholy, or, why not? holy! live!

No motion. Nothing stirs.

LANTRY: You've been marked! I say the words! I do command! Rise up! Rise! *(Stunned now, and uncomprehending.)* No? But the mark is so—! *(Scribbles more symbols on the floor.)* And the words are thus: Be alive!

Nothing stirs. All is silence.

LANTRY: But you must! Why not! Why won't you rise to *be* with me? In all the years, the centuries, you *always* have! These signs, these words have done it! But *not* to *you?*

The sound of a jet flies over. He watches the sound move. A siren wails, a long way off.

Slowly LANTRY's *shoulders sag, his face grows bleak.*

LANTRY: Oh, plague take me for a fool. Fool. *(A beat.)* O ancient fool. This is the year . . .

McCLURE *(quietly):* 2274.

MCCLURE *has been standing to one side for a long while now, waiting, smoking.*

LANTRY *(startled):* What?

McCLURE *(quietly):* 2274.

LANTRY: Oh, yes, the year.

McCLURE: Very late in time. Very late for you.

LANTRY: How long have you been standing there?

McCLURE: Awhile.

LANTRY: You saw it all?

MCCLURE *nods, blows smoke slowly.*

LANTRY: *These* won't *move!*

McCLURE: Why should they? They're dead.

LANTRY: Once people shuddered when they heard the wind about the house, once people raised crucifixes and wolfbane, and believed in walking dead and bats and loping wolves. And as long as they believed, why, then, so long did the dead, the bats, the loping wolves exist. Mind made them flesh. But these . . . *these?*

He nods to the quiet forms, which MCCLURE *quietly regards.*

McCLURE: They don't *believe.* They never in all their *lives* believed. They had never read or talked or known of the walking dead, never traded superstitions, never shuddered in the night or doubted darkness. These were raised in menthol and cleansed with soap and salt and rinsed in medicines and spun dry-clean. They know no ghosts, they have no ghosts. Bones are simply bones to such as these. That being true . . .

LANTRY: . . . they cannot rise, or walk away.

McCLURE: No chalk can sign or symbol make them breathe. No lengthy diatribe can slap them, wind them up and run them to destruction. They are dead and *know* they are dead, and, *knowing,* stay cold forever. Which means— these are *not* your friends.

LANTRY: I hoped that they *might* be. . . .

A beat. McCLURE *considers his hand computer.*

McCLURE: You *are,* then, William Lantry?

LANTRY: I *was.*

McCLURE: Born 1973, died 2003?

LANTRY: The same.

McCLURE: We've been looking for you.

LANTRY: The Peace Squad?

McCLURE: No, no, oh, no. The Geriatrics Society, The Specialists in Suspended Animation, the Scientists who study Cryonics! You are special! You are amazing! And they all want to meet you!

LANTRY: After what I've done?

McCLURE: You've done nothing but sleep in suspended animation for two hundred years!

LANTRY *(stunned):* No!

McCLURE: Yes! Oh, we've known suspended animation with small animals, toads, frogs, insects, yes, but a mature man, hardly.

LANTRY *(stunned):* But you saw me mark the bodies?

McCLURE: I did.

LANTRY: I tried to raise the dead.

McCLURE: You did.

LANTRY: I blew up the Incinerators, killed people . . .

McCLURE: My dear Lantry, you acted in delusion! You're not a dead man, you're no kin to Dracula or Poe. Oh, I know the names. I have a few books put by in secret.

You're a common ordinary soul who has survived and slept out the years, and now, awake, was struck with a silly idea that somehow he represented the last of the dead!

LANTRY: But I killed people! Now you must kill me!

McCLURE: What? Destroy a singular medical miracle like you, the first man in history to survive underground for over two hundred years? You'll be in all the media! Films! Television!

LANTRY *(touches himself):* No, no! Even now, I don't breathe! My heart doesn't beat, my blood move, no, listen, *feel!*

McCLURE: Subliminal nonsense. *(Seizes* LANTRY'S *wrist.)* It's all there. You pretend it's not.

LANTRY *(feels his own heart and pulse):* Not? Not? But . . . I was so sure . . . ?

McCLURE: Just enjoy being a resurrected human being! Come along, come on!

LANTRY *(almost pitifully):* Then . . . I'm not a dangerous man . . . at *all?*

McCLURE: Dangerous? Naturally you deluded yourself, didn't know where to go, whom to turn to. Finding yourself in a graveyard that way, what else but you confused yourself. You made quite a trail. I knew you'd be here, tonight, in this morgue. Call it a hunch, a feeling . . .

LANTRY: But . . . but . . . it's very strange. *Why haven't I been hungry yet?*

McCLURE: Why, you're excited. Hunger will come in time. Come along.

LANTRY: Must I meet all your scientists, tonight?

McCLURE: No, of course not. Now I'm the one who plays the excited fool. Forgive. You'll come to my home, to rest, to sleep . . .

LANTRY: I've slept two hundred years.

McCLURE: Forgive. Well, then, it's food and drink and talk. You must *tell* me of the *Past!*

LANTRY: No. You must tell *me* of the *Future!*

Both laugh, and there is an embarrassed silence.

LANTRY *turns away suddenly, to himself.*

LANTRY *(to himself):* It's a trap! A trap!

McCLURE *(touches his elbows):* What's wrong?

LANTRY *(ducks his head, chafes his elbows: to himself):* A trap. He lies. He must lie. I *am* the dark thing that I *am!* Not the bright angel of resurrection that *he* says. *(Turns to look at* McCLURE *numbly.)* I think that I should kill you and escape.

McCLURE: What, still wallowing in graveyard worms and dust?

McCLURE *circles him slowly as he talks.*

McCLURE: All right, let's argue it from your angle. Suppose I *am* lying. Suppose you *are* dead, and I know you for dead. Suppose I did come up to you five minutes ago thinking you were some sort of glandular deficient, some inequitable citizen, eh? But then, watching you, saw you hold your breath, kidding yourself you were dead. Slowed your pulse, fooling yourself you were bad flesh, old corpse. Such delusions *are* known in history. And then, let us imagine, in watching you, I truly never saw you take one breath, and now close up, in the still night air, I sense, I know, your dead heart does not beat, not beat!

LANTRY: And? *Then? THEN?*

> LANTRY *reaches out and takes* MCCLURE *by the neck.* MC-CLURE *remains calm.*

MCCLURE: Well, then, *what* if you kill me?

LANTRY: It would satisfy my lust!

MCCLURE: For what? Simply to kill the nice efficient, un-hung-up people of a future time whose only crime is they are happy at midnight, and fear not closet shadows? And have let the Halloween pumpkin rot forever neglected?

LANTRY: Yes, that *is* a crime!

> LANTRY *tightens his hold on* MCCLURE's *neck, but* MCCLURE *refuses to panic, waits.* LANTRY *relaxes his grip some-what.*

MCCLURE: Let's take it one step further. You seek to kill to make friends.

LANTRY: Yes, friends!

MCCLURE *(points to the bodies nearby)*: And yet you've seen, you have no friends. These dead are dead forever.

LANTRY: I will kill more!

MCCLURE: And *they* will be dead forever.

LANTRY: You! *You*, I'll kill!

MCCLURE: And *I* shall be dead forever. I will not rise up to help you. I will not come to the aid of your single and singular party.

LANTRY: I will kill everyone on Earth!

McClure: To what avail or cause? Why, then you would be finally and completely *alone*.

Eyes shut, Lantry *shrivels at these words.*

McClure *(continues):* Kill one, kill all, kill millions, kill me, and you're no better off than you are this instant standing here wanting to throttle a man who throttles back with simple logics and inescapable fact. There is no winning, Lantry. You are lost now and you might be lost tomorrow. These dead have no dark corners in them. They have no superstition. I have none. You are friendless and unloved.

Lantry *(weakly):* I *can't* give up.

McClure *(simply):* Give up.

Lantry *opens his hands.* McClure *does not move. He nods a final time, this motion causing the hands to fall away.*

Lantry *stands, almost catatonic.*

McClure *(with sympathy):* Don't you see that hate is what brought you into the world? But now that you know yourself truly alone, loneliness is the thing that will kill you?

Lantry: Loneliness . . . ?

McClure: It kills everyone, finally, when they truly know themselves separate. One day it will even kill me.

Lantry: Will it?

McClure *(gently):* You know it will.

Lantry *has been examining his hands, touching his own body, trying to reconvince himself during all the above. Now he cries out and raises his fists, turning toward* McClure *as if to move upon and strike him.*

LANTRY: No! No! Shut up! Shut up!

At which point TWO MEN *enter and stop, curious, somewhat amazed.*

FIRST OFFICER: What's going on? A new game?

McCLURE: Yes, a new game! Catch him and you win!

LANTRY'S *fury explodes toward the* MEN. MCCLURE *steps back as* LANTRY *traps himself by plunging directly into their arms. They hold his arms behind his back as he struggles.*

SECOND OFFICER: We win.

LANTRY: Fools! Fools! Let me go!

McCLURE: Hold him tight!

FIRST OFFICER: A rough game, what? What do we do now?

McCLURE *(a beat):* To the Hearthing Place.

FIRST OFFICER: The Place of the Sun?

LANTRY *(shocked; almost to himself):* . . . the Incinerator!

They begin to move. LANTRY *holds back, but then gives up and moves along as* MCCLURE *speaks.*

McCLURE: Oh, it's been hard, hard to accept you. A man like me, a logical man, from my own age and time. But, shall I tell you something?

LANTRY: What? What!

They stop for a beat. MCCLURE *looks into* LANTRY'S *face.*

McCLURE: You almost . . . *frighten* me.

LANTRY *is shocked and almost pleased by this.*

LANTRY: You . . . me . . . ? *You* . . . ?

McClure *(nods):* Frightened.

He nods a second time to the MEN. *They move in a great circle through darkness now.*

Lantry: Well, then, that means, oh Lord, that means . . . I *am* Poe. I am all that is left of Edgar Allan Poe, and I am all that is left of Ambrose Bierce and Lovecraft . . .

A light appears behind them: the glow of the Furnace, the Incinerator, the Place of the Sun. They move in a great circle through darkness around the stage.

Lantry: . . . I am Osiris and Bal and Set. I am the Necronomican, the Book of the Dead. I am the House of Usher, I am the Red Death, I am a coffin, a shroud, a lightning bolt reflected in an old house window. I am an autumn-empty tree, I am a yellowed book page turned by a claw-hand . . . I am an organ played in an attic at midnight. I am a mask, a skull mask behind an oak tree on the last day of October. I am . . .

They have stopped now, and we see behind them the orange-yellow glow, the open maw of the Incinerator, the Place of the Sun. The TWO MEN *dance aside for a moment, leaving* LANTRY *to sway, fumbling at his own thoughts, supported for a moment by* MCCLURE. MCCLURE *pantomimes to the* TWO MEN *to go fetch something.*

Lantry: . . . I am a poison apple bobbling in a water tub for children's teeth to snap . . . I am a black candle lit before an inverted cross. I am a sugar skull with my name on it to be eaten . . .

The TWO MEN *are back with vast swatches of linen wrapping, which, as* LANTRY *watches, stunned, they begin to wrap around his ankles and then up along his legs as*

LANTRY *continues speaking, almost chanting, hypnotizing himself with his own recital.*

LANTRY: . . . I am a coffin lid, a sheet with eyes, I am the Legend of Sleepy Hollow and I am the Monkey's Paw and the Phantom Rickshaw. . . . I am the Pit and I am the Pendulum . . .

McCLURE *(gently, urging him on):* . . . yes . . .

LANTRY: I am the Cat and the Canary, the Gorilla, the Bat. I am Hamlet's father's dead and buried ghost. . . .

The MEN *move up, up, wrapping, wrapping him into a mummy. Now they are at his hips, circling the linen bandages around and around, passing it from hand to hand, efficient at their shroudwork.*

LANTRY: All of these things am I . . . while I lived, they lived . . . while I moved and hated and existed, they still existed. I am all that remembers them, and will *not* remember them after tonight. Tonight, all of us, Poe and Red Death and Roderick Usher, we *burn!* Like straw scarecrows at Guy Fawkes you will make a heap of all our panics and terrors and touch a match and burn!

The MEN *move steadily, calmly. They have bound his arms now around-about-around-about with the white linen mummy bandages, not even listening to him rave and chant. Only* MCCLURE *listens, nods, and quietly reaffirms it all.*

McCLURE: Yes . . . yes . . .

LANTRY: And oh what a wailing we will put up. The world will be clean of us, but in our going we shall say, oh, what is the world like, clean of Fear? Where is the dark imagination from the dark time, the thrill, the anticipation, the suspense of old October, gone, never more to be, smashed and burned by the rocket people, the Incinerator people, destroyed and obliterated, to be replaced by doors that open and close with no shrieks or cries and lights that go on and off without fear. Oh, by the dark gods, if only you *knew* how once we lived, what Halloween *was* to us! how we gloried in the dark morbidities! The time is *here,* those ghosts are *here,* in my head, my thoughts, my dreams! I *drink* to them! The Amontillado!

McCLURE: Yes, the Amontillado. . . .

They have finished with LANTRY's *body now and wrap steadily up about his face, his chin, and one swathe over his nose, and another over his brow, leaving his eyes wildly seeing, and his mouth wildly moving.*

LANTRY: Someone's at the door. Quick, oh quickly! The Monkey's Paw! Make the wish, the wish!

McCLURE *(gently):* The wish, yes, the wish.

The fire grows bright behind them. A great heart sounds, beats!

LANTRY: I am the Maelstrom, the Black Cat, I am the Telltale Heart, I am the Raven Nevermore, Nevermore.

The MEN *are done. They have put a last swathe across his eyes. But his mouth can be seen as he finishes.*

LANTRY: I am Dracula. I am the Phantom of the Opera.

McCLURE: Yes.

MCCLURE *nods to the* MEN, *who carry* LANTRY *backward toward the Fire.* LANTRY *senses this, twists his head left and right, blindly.*

LANTRY: I am in . . . the Catacomb?

McCLURE: The catacomb.

> MCCLURE *nods to the* TWO OFFICERS. *The* MEN *grasp and begin to hoist* LANTRY.

LANTRY: I am being chained to a wall, but there is no bottle of Amontillado!

MCCLURE: None.

LANTRY: Now someone is mortaring up the cell, closing me in!

MCCLURE: They are.

LANTRY: I'm trapped. A very good joke indeed. Let us be gone!

MCCLURE: Yes, gone.

> MCCLURE *nods a final time to the* MEN, *who hold the "mummy" suspended above the chute. The fire is bright. The great telltale heart pounds loud, louder, loudest.*

LANTRY: For the love of God, Montresor!

> *They tilt him swiftly over and down the chute, away, gone. The fire roars. The Telltale Heart stops pounding. Turned away, eyes shut, unable to watch,* MCCLURE *waits for the color of the fire to die behind him, two or three beats. Then he speaks.*

MCCLURE *(with compassion):* Oh, yes. For the love of God.

> *Lights dim swiftly. Blackout. Curtain.*

Kaleidoscope

At curtain rise: darkness.
Static, electronic sounds, radio impulses.

Then, a radio impulse, twice, three times.

HOUSTON RADIO VOICE: Signal RD Houston calling. Space Flight Apollo 99 respond.

HOLLIS *(on radio):* Apollo 99. Hollis here.

HOUSTON RADIO: Loud and clear. Medical checkout. Soma tapes running. By the numbers.

> HOLLIS *appears in silhouette, his face dimly illuminated. We can see that he stands amidst his* CREW, *all of them closely packed in a small crowd. Ideally these men should be located in the orchestra pit with their heads and shoulders above the sight lines, and the entire stage area free for later use. As each man speaks, his own individual illumination comes on until the entire* CREW *is seen compacted into what must be the interior of a space ship. As the men respond, they pantomime with their hands as if moving the controls or the radio equipment of such a ship.*

HOLLIS *(his spot comes on):* Hollis. Physical report to Houston medico/soma tapes. A-1.

STONE *(appears):* Stone here. A-1.

STIMSON *(appears):* Stimson. A-1.

APPLEGATE *(appears):* Good old Applegate here. In fine fettle.

HOLLIS *(curtly):* Applegate!

APPLEGATE *(ducks his head):* Hell. A-1.

LESPERE *(appears):* Lespere. Okay.

BARKLEY *(appears):* Barkley. Super A-1.

WOODE: Woode reporting. Fine, thanks.

APPLEGATE: All present and accounted f—

He stops, for HOLLIS *has given him a look.*

HOLLIS: All present and well. Nine days and three million, four hundred thousand miles out from Earth.

HOUSTON RADIO: Check. Psycho-balance tapes operative. Scramble thoughts. Word associate.

APPLEGATE: Stupid.

HOUSTON RADIO: Repeat, please.

APPLEGATE: Not only *how* we feel but *what* we feel, to a computerized psychoanalyst three million miles away! Stupid!

HOLLIS *(cuts in):* Applegate!

APPLEGATE: Now hear this: A for Applegate. H for Horse. S for Snowstorm. R.P. for Rabbit Pellets. Enough word association?

HOUSTON VOICE: Terminate, Applegate.

APPLEGATE: Terminate Applegate? *(Snorts.)* That's *poetry!*

HOLLIS *(cool and quiet):* Terminate. *(A beat.)* Hollis here.

HOUSTON RADIO: Scramble-associate, Hollis.

HOLLIS *(a beat; he swallows; then):* Sometimes I wonder why I am captain of a rocket bound into deep space.

The MEN *look at him, waiting.*

HOLLIS: And then I remember that not all of my crew members are named Applegate.

APPLEGATE *(mock miffed):* Hey . . . !

The CREW *laughs.*

HOUSTON RADIO: End of Hollis scramble?

HOLLIS: End.

STIMSON: Stimson here.

HOUSTON RADIO: Scramble-associate, Stimson.

STIMSON: It took me two days to get to the top of Saint Peter's in Rome. Three days to nerve myself to make it to the top of the Eiffel Tower. Sometimes I wonder what I'm doing, three million miles high in space.

The MEN *murmur.*

STIMSON *(shuts eyes):* End scramble.

WOODE: Woode here. I . . . I *never* made it to the top of the Eiffel Tower. I was . . . afraid.

HOUSTON VOICE *(mocking):* Now you tell us, Woode.

The MEN *laugh, gently, understandingly.*

WOODE *(nods, shrugs):* Now I tell you.

LESPERE: Lespere scrambling. Hot dogs. Apple pie. Mom.

APPLEGATE: Hey, what kind of word association is that?

LESPERE: Midnight. Open the icebox door. Reach in. Three-layer banana cake. Glass of milk. Yes, *sir!*

APPLEGATE: He's kidding.

LESPERE: Sand-lot baseball.

APPLEGATE: He's nuts!

LESPERE: Good cigars. Grandpa and Dad talking late at night on the front porch rocking chairs.

APPLEGATE: I may throw up!

LESPERE: Over and out scramble.

STONE: Stone in. I—

Bells, sirens, static, radio impulses.

HOLLIS: Stone, Woode, Lespere?

STONE: Meteor dead on! Impact! Impact! Prepare for collision!

The MEN *hold to each other, in one fierce wild crowd for an instant, then reach out their hands as if to hold off collision, and work, in pantomime, their various machines and computers. Bells ring. Rapid impulses run wild!*

HOLLIS: Crew to stations. Oxygen helmets! Helmets on! Helmets on!

We see them, in pantomime, clap on their helmets and oxygen equipment. Sirens blare.

HOLLIS: On stations, all?

LESPERE: On! We . . . Oh, my God! Impact! Im—

Instant darkness. The MEN *vanish.*

A fearful explosion. Static and radioactive sounds. Voices cry and shout. ALL *fade in and out.*

VOICES *(on radio, rising, fading):* . . . Oh, God, falling, falling . . . ship . . . where's the rocket? Explosion! Gone! Where, where? . . . Captain? . . . Stone? The men, the men, where're the men? . . . Captain? . . . Gone, gone . . . Oh, falling, falling!

One face, that of CAPTAIN HOLLIS, *appears, pinspotted, higher now, up on stage left in a kaleidoscope of shifting lights, shadows, stars. He looks all about, terrified, then gradually regains his wits and his speech. Slowly, he pieces it together.*

HOLLIS: Oh, the concussion! Like a giant knife had cut it, the rocket just . . . split wide! The men, oh . . . thrown out in space. Like, like a dozen wriggling silverfish. Scattered in a dark sea. And the rocket, in a million pieces, there it goes, a meteor-swarm seeking a lost sun . . . gone . . . oh, gone.

VOICES *(over radio):* Barkley, Barkley, where are you? . . . Woode, Woode . . . ? Captain?

HOLLIS: Voices . . . calling like lost children in a long night. . . .

VOICES: Captain . . . Barkley . . . where, where? Woode?

STONE'S VOICE: Captain Hollis, Captain . . . ? This is Stone!

HOLLIS *(quickens):* Stone, Hollis here. Where are you? *(Stops.)* Stupid, stupid question! Where?

STONE *(his face appears floating in the dark off to one side):* God knows, I don't! Which way is up? I only know I'm falling, falling . . .

HOLLIS: Yes, we fall. Like pebbles down a well. We're not men anymore, not captain, crew . . . only voices . . . voices without bodies . . .

STONE: We're going away from each other . . . !

HOLLIS: Oh, yes, that's for sure. At one hundred thousand miles an hour! Here's your hat, what's your hurry? We *do* move.

STONE: What happened?

HOLLIS: A meteor strike. The rocket blew up. Rockets *do* blow up.

STONE *(numbly)*: They do, oh, they do. Is . . . is there any way for us to get back to one another, get together?

HOLLIS: Not unless you strapped on your force-fly unit just before the blowup?

STONE: No. You?

HOLLIS: There wasn't time. So here we are, seven men dropped in space, with no way to maneuver, turn, fly. All we can do is . . .

STONE: . . . fall . . .

STIMSON'S VOICE *(on radio)*: . . . fall . . . fall . . . Oh, it's a long way . . . long way . . . a long, long, long way down . . .

STONE: Who's that?

HOLLIS: Stimson, I think. *(Calls.)* Stimson!

Now STIMSON's *pinpoint light fades up. We see him floating above and beyond the other two.*

STIMSON: . . . long way down . . . long way . . . I'm going to die. I can't *believe* that. I—

HOLLIS: Stimson! Let's get organized here!

Now APPLEGATE's *face light flashes on as he hoots with laughter. He floats, moves, now up, now down, only his face visible.*

APPLEGATE: Organized? Organized! Listen to the man! Organized!

HOLLIS: Applegate, is that you?

APPLEGATE: Applegate, scared gutless but reporting. Boy, you're funny, Captain.

HOLLIS: What do you *want* me to do, let us all go to Hell?

APPLEGATE: You're not in *charge* anymore, Captain. We go where we *go*.

HOLLIS: Roll call, anyway, damn it!

APPLEGATE: Roll call! *(Hoots again.)*

HOLLIS: So help me, we're going to die decently. By the names, check in! Stone?

STONE *(nods):* Stone here.

HOLLIS: Lespere?

LESPERE *(whose light comes on now):* Lespere here.

HOLLIS: Barkley?

BARKLEY *(his light comes on):* Still alive. Barkley.

HOLLIS: Woode?

> *Silence. We see* WOODE's *face, alone, illuminated, above the* MEN, *floating. But his eyes are tight shut, his teeth gritted. He is shut away in himself, in panic.*

APPLEGATE: *Make* him answer, Captain.

HOLLIS: Woode?

> *Static and far electronic angel voices in space.* WOODE *drifts off, as his light slowly fades.*

APPLEGATE: Like I said, Captain, you're not in charge.

HOLLIS *(cuts across):* Stimson?

STIMSON *(numbly):* Stimson, who's *he?* Oh, yes . . . *he's* . . . falling . . .

APPLEGATE, *hearing this, quiets, is moved by the sound of that far voice.*

APPLEGATE: I—

STIMSON *(numbly):* Falling, that's what *he* is, falling.

APPLEGATE *(quietly):* Take it easy, we're all in the same fix.

STIMSON *(dreaming):* I don't want to be here, I want to be somewhere else.

APPLEGATE *(dryly):* You can say that again.

HOLLIS: All right, Applegate.

APPLEGATE *(flaring again):* All right, *what?*

HOLLIS: We haven't much time.

APPLEGATE: Time, gah! We got all the Time in the world, and all of Space in the Universe. That's all we *do* have, Space and Time!

HOLLIS *(quietly, as calm as possible):* We're moving away from each other. We'll soon lose radio contact.

APPLEGATE: Can't happen soon enough for me. I won't have to hear any of your stupid voices.

HOLLIS: Why do you insist on being bitter?

APPLEGATE: Look around you, Captain. Where are you? Nowhere. Where'm I? Beyond nowhere. Where's everyone else? Falling to die. The rocket spun when it was hit. We were thrown off by centrifugal force, each man in a different direction. Some of us will hit the sun. Some of us will head out through the Universe and travel forever. Bitter? How can you *say* that?

STONE: Captain?

HOLLIS: Stone?

STONE: *Might* we get back together somehow? I mean—

APPLEGATE: For *what,* what, *what!?*

HOLLIS: To die in company, now that you ask.

APPLEGATE: You *do* that, then. I'll die alone, thanks, at one hundred thousand miles per hour.

STONE: If each of us released a certain amount of oxygen, we could maneuver—

APPLEGATE: Keep talking. Your hot air would fill a dozen balloons and save us all.

STIMSON *(numbly):* Please, someone help me, I don't want to be here. I don't want to be here.

HOLLIS: Stimson.

APPLEGATE: That's it, Captain, order him to shut up. *(Calls.)* Hey, Stimson, listen to the captain.

HOLLIS *(uneasily):* Stimson! We can't *talk* if you interrupt. I mean—

STIMSON *(like a child):* Help, oh, someone help, so far down, a long way down, falling, falling, oh, such a long way down. . . .

HOLLIS: Stimson . . .

APPLEGATE *(stares up, gasps):* Hold on! Oh, *now* . . . you're not going to believe this!

STIMSON: Help, oh, please, help, I'm afraid!

HOLLIS: Applegate?

APPLEGATE: Captain, he's *here!*

HOLLIS: What?

APPLEGATE: Stimson! He's floating nearby. I can *see* him! We're getting closer!

STIMSON: Oh, such a long way down, falling, falling, a long, long way. Help. Help.

APPLEGATE: Yes, I'll help you, Stimson.

HOLLIS *(apprehensive, guessing at* APPLEGATE*'s motive):* Applegate?

STIMSON: I don't *like* being here.

APPLEGATE *(softly):* You *won't* be much longer.

STIMSON: I want to be somewhere else.

APPLEGATE *(patiently, quietly):* You will, you will.

HOLLIS: Applegate!

APPLEGATE: Closer, oh, very close, Captain. He's floating almost in reach . . . almost . . .

STIMSON: Oh, I'm afraid, someone help. . . .

APPLEGATE *(gently):* Help, yes.

STIMSON: Someone . . . someone . . .

APPLEGATE: *Me.* . . .

HOLLIS: Applegate!

STIMSON: Someone, oh, please, someone . . . ?

APPLEGATE: *Me!*

STIMSON *(cries out):* Some—!

> In mid-cry, STIMSON*'s voice cracks to a complete shut-off. His light vanishes.*

There is a beat, and then HOLLIS *whispers in dread.*

HOLLIS: Applegate . . . ?

APPLEGATE *(eyes shut):* He's gone, Captain.

HOLLIS: Gone . . . ?

APPLEGATE: I smashed his helmet.

HOLLIS: You—?

APPLEGATE *(simply):* He wanted to be saved. *(Opens eyes.)* I saved him.

All the MEN *exhale in a moment of quiet.*

HOLLIS *(quietly):* Yes.

APPLEGATE *(a beat):* Approved?

HOLLIS *(a beat):* Approved.

Radio static swarms. There is a long moment when the MEN *move with their own thoughts, turning.*

APPLEGATE: Now we can talk more clearly, Captain. Now, if you want, we can get "organized."

HOLLIS: Applegate?

APPLEGATE: Sir?

HOLLIS: May you *burn* forever!

APPLEGATE: Why, sir, I'm on my way to burning now. From the way I fall, I figure in about half a year, I'll strike the Sun. How about you others, Stone, Lespere, Barkley? Where *heading,* for how *long?*

STONE: I . . . I think I'm going to hit the Moon.

BARKLEY: I'm . . . I think . . . I'm heading for Mars. Can't really say, but, well, Mars.

LESPERE: Mars and Beyond, Jupiter, Saturn, maybe visit Pluto, or go on into the Universe and travel forever, that's me—far-traveling. Doesn't that have a sound to it? Far-traveling.

APPLEGATE: Captain?

Silence.

APPLEGATE: Captain?

HOLLIS: I . . . I seem to be heading back toward Earth. When I hit its atmosphere . . . ?

APPLEGATE: You'll burn, long before me.

HOLLIS *(swallows hard, eyes shut):* I'll burn. *(A beat.)* Silence!

APPLEGATE: Order me some more. This is a mutiny of one. In just the few minutes since the rocket exploded, you and I have moved ten thousand miles away from each other. But we were *always* far apart! Come get me, sir. Shall I tell you some more that will make you want to come get me?

HOLLIS: Do your worst.

APPLEGATE: And the worst is this. Years ago, when we were at the Academy, your fiancée, that lovely girl, remember . . .

HOLLIS: No, it never *was.*

APPLEGATE: It was . . .

HOLLIS: No, Earth's *gone* now, I can't *see* it.

APPLEGATE: It's there.

HOLLIS *(turns head away):* No, it's like it never was. Green fields, towns, rivers, lakes, gone, all gone . . . so far away and only night now and stars, too many stars. . . .

APPLEGATE: No, there *was* this girl, and she left you, you want to know why, shall I *tell* you why?

HOLLIS: No, she never lived!

APPLEGATE: She lived.

HOLLIS: There is no Earth, no life, nothing.

APPLEGATE: There was life and earth and something. And I took it all away.

HOLLIS: You took nothing, nothing!

STONE *(cuts in):* Ah, no! No more, no more of this!

HOLLIS *(in an agony of remorse):* No more!

APPLEGATE *(shamed by their reaction at last):* No . . . more.

LESPERE *(a beat):* I'm amazed.

APPLEGATE: Eh?

LESPERE: I'm astounded.

APPLEGATE: What?

LESPERE: We're all going to be dead in a few hours, and you . . . go on like this? Can't you leave us to remember . . . ?

APPLEGATE: What?

LESPERE: Good things. Good, yes! The *best!*

APPLEGATE: What was ever best, what good?

LESPERE: My life, maybe not yours, but mine!

APPLEGATE: How was it better?

LESPERE: Let me make the list! A wife on Earth. Good friends on the Moon! My children on Mars!

APPLEGATE: And?

LESPERE: A wife on Earth, friends on the Moon, my sons and daughters safe on Mars!

APPLEGATE: What else?

LESPERE *(doggedly does the rote)*: My wife, my friends, my—

APPLEGATE: That's no *list!*

LESPERE: *Better* than a list, it's a *life!*

STONE *(calmly, almost to himself)*: *I'm* going to kill all of you in ten minutes.

APPLEGATE *(startled)*: Kill *us?*

STONE: Just by opening my helmet. I'll freeze solid in a millionth of a second . . . and you'll all disappear forever! Strange. The quickest death in the history of mankind . . . and invented not on Earth but a million miles out in space . . . I'll freeze and be frozen forever . . . think, think of it . . . if I should not hit the Moon but circle it for a million years, and a rocket came by and found me, I wouldn't have changed. Out in space, nothing ever changes. A billion years from tonight I'll be circling and young, still only this age, and my body frozen, not spoiled or grown old . . . a billion years from tonight . . . think . . . *think!*

APPLEGATE: I'm thinking: kill yourself now and cut the cackle.

LESPERE: I'm thinking that we should all say what we want to say in these last few minutes. I want to run my films, play my memories, say *there* was a good day, *there* a bad, there a good friend . . . Gah! You know what I mean.

APPLEGATE: No, I don't, because it never happened, like the captain says, once a thing is over it's like it never existed. *We* only exist now, a mob of voices floating half into nowhere and out of nothing.

LESPERE: No, I *count,* because I remember, I *do* remember!

APPLEGATE: Do you? *(Curiously.)* Do you really? Well. Maybe that's why I've gotten mean in my middle years. All my life, I kept waiting for something to happen. I mean *something.* But . . . it never did.

LESPERE: Man, man, you've been in space, you've circled the Sun, landed on Mars! What *more* do you want?

APPLEGATE: I don't know, isn't that funny? I just don't . . . Wait! *(Gasps; stares down in shock.)* Well, now, hear this. I . . . have no left hand.

LESPERE: What?

HOLLIS: Applegate!

APPLEGATE *(still in shock, but operative):* No kidding. Strange. I feel . . . it's happening to someone else. Oh, this is a course in sixth-grade philosophy. Someone else's left hand has just been cut off by a meteor. My left uniform sleeve has just automatically locked itself, sealed itself with self-sealant. I . . . *(Gasps.)* . . . lost some air, but the end of my wrist has frozen, frozen solid, scabbed itself with frost. *(Shuts eyes.)* Oh, oh!

HOLLIS *(concerned in spite of himself):* Applegate!

APPLEGATE: Come help me, Captain!

HOLLIS: I wish . . .

APPLEGATE: Come help me, Captain!

HOLLIS: If I could . . .

APPLEGATE: Oh, sir, the irony. Telling you to come order me around ten minutes ago, and now *really* needing you. Oh, burn me, burn me to ashes, then burn the ashes to dust!

Radio sounds are heard. APPLEGATE *begins to laugh quietly.*

HOLLIS: What . . . ?

APPLEGATE *(stunned, amazed):* Listen! You hear!? I . . . I'm in a meteor swarm, the very thing that cut off my hand is taking me with it, I'm being drawn away in space. Why, it's like being in a great big kaleidoscope. Those things, those toys, you held up to your eyes as a kid and looked in, and saw all the colors, shapes, sizes. A . . . a kaleidoscope. Look! Oh, beautiful. And taking me with it, me, *me*. . . . I don't deserve a trip like this. I never liked anything beautiful.

HOLLIS *(quietly):* Never . . . ?

APPLEGATE: Well, maybe when I was young. *(A beat.)* Hear the *voices?*

The radio sounds are more than electronic static now, but are beginning to "talk," with small soft bursts of music, voices from another time, long gone, old radio broadcasts.

STONE: Voices?

LESPERE: Yes. *(Listens.)* Yes!

HOLLIS *(remembering something):* No sound is ever lost.

APPLEGATE: What?

HOLLIS: Didn't we wonder, oh, years ago, what happened to sounds when they died, did they travel in space, forever, living their own lives? Well, here's your answer.

LESPERE: What, an electronic cloud that—

STONE: Traps old radio broadcasts, news, music—

APPLEGATE: Yes!

> *They listen to* CHURCHILL'S VOICE *in another year, talking out of World War II, and* HITLER'S VOICE *raging and* CROWDS *shouting "Seig Heil" and* ROOSEVELT'S VOICE *wandering in and out of hearing, and dance bands playing in 1930, 1955, 1974. . . .*

APPLEGATE *(immensely touched and moved):* Too much, too much. I'm the monster of all time, and I go out like *this*. You stay behind and die your plain vanilla deaths, and me, me, *me?* I go out in style, in a swarm of meteors so beautiful I can't move my tongue, and carried along by the voices of Churchill and Hitler and Roosevelt. Oh, friends! What *company!*

HOLLIS: Yes. . . .

APPLEGATE: Can you still *hear* me?

HOLLIS: Yes.

APPLEGATE: It's me and the whole grand bunch moving out and around the worlds for the next ten billion years. We'll be back, and Churchill will still be talking, and Hitler will still be mad, and Roosevelt will still be saying we have nothing to fear, nothing, nothing.

HOLLIS *(touched):* So it finally happened.

APPLEGATE: Eh? What?

HOLLIS: It. The thing you were waiting for. *Something!*

APPLEGATE *(thinks; looks around; beams):* Yes. . . . *(A beat.)* Yes! *(Nods wildly, happily.)* Yes! *(A long beat; then, slyly but warmly:)* So long. Burn, Captain, burn.

His light dims, fades, as does his voice.

APPLEGATE'S VOICE *(far away, happily fading):* . . . Burn,
burn . . .

The sounds of CROWDS, BANDS, VOICES, *fade and vanish.*

*Faint electronic hums displace the above and fade into
the background.*

HOLLIS *(quietly):* The same to you, Applegate.

LESPERE: Captain?

HOLLIS: Well?

LESPERE: Reception's fading for all of us. Why don't we get it
over with and sign off?

HOLLIS: Good idea. Can you see the meteor swarm that took
Applegate with it?

LESPERE: Oh, yes, yes, lovely. There . . . there.

HOLLIS: Can you see any of us?

LESPERE: No. . . .

HOLLIS: *I* can.

LESPERE: Impossible.

HOLLIS: But I see. Or *think* I see. There you go home in the
dark, Lespere. And there you go off in the night, Stone.
And Barkley. *(Silence.)* Home *already? (A beat.)* Remember those summer nights when you were a kid and stayed
out in the middle of the street playing ball until you
couldn't see, it was so dark, not wanting to go home, and
at last all the mothers calling from blocks around, blowing
whistles, yelling, and at last, dragging their bats, scuffing
their shoes, all the boys went home, sad and hating it, as if

summer would never come again, even though summer was the next night and the next after that?

LESPERE: I remember.

STONE: Keep *on* remembering. Don't let anybody say otherwise. Lespere, Captain? So long.

His light goes off.

HOLLIS: Sleep well.

LESPERE: Captain?

HOLLIS: Lespere?

LESPERE: Last one in's an old maid.

HOLLIS: Here goes nothing.

LESPERE: Nothing.

His light vanishes.

HOLLIS: Alone. There goes Woode toward the sun. There falls Stone near the Moon. There flies Barkley out beyond Mars and toward far Centauri, forever. There moves Applegate and his meteors and fine company of ancient men. Pieces of the kaleidoscope, all of us, but flying apart. And myself . . . alone. Add it up, Hollis. What did your life mean? More than Applegate's, less than Lespere's? Did you do one brief, bright, lovely thing that might be remembered for one astounding instant by someone somewhere sometime somehow? What, what did you *do,* Captain, that was worth noting, worth remembering, worth the softest breath to tell? *(Looks around.)* Just this: In a few hours, I'll hit Earth's atmosphere. When I do, I'll catch fire and burn like a meteor. I'll flash across the sky in flames. All the world will look up and see me for . . . three seconds . . . yes . . . three seconds. I wonder.

. . . *Will* they look . . . *will* they *see? (A beat.)* Let's go
. . . find *out!*

*The electronic sound has been building beneath his last
few sentences. Now it rises to a crescendo, at the peak
of which, eyes shut, his light goes out.*

*A beat. Then, across the darkness of the starred night, a
burning light passes for a brief moment.*

A Boy's Voice *(in darkness):* Oh, look, there, look!

Another Boy's Voice: A falling star!

First Boy's Voice: Make a wish!

Second Boy's Voice *(in quiet awe):* Oh, yes. Make a *wish.*
Make a wish!

A beat. Then all the stars go out.

The Foghorn

Curtain up.

A lighthouse tower. A late-middle-aged man, MCDUNN, *crouched oiling some machinery in the darkening afternoon.*

McDUNN: There we are. Getting late. Sun'll be down in another half-hour. Fog's early. Here it comes. Welcome. *(He rises and casually salutes the mist.)* This place is yours. I live here by sufferance.

He rubs his hands and looks around.

McDUNN: All right, McDunn. Everything shipshape? Lighthouse, light, and your own creature well-being? *(Flexes his arms.)* Ready for anything? Ready! *(Breathes deep.)* Ah, I *do* love this.

He goes to a circular rail and looks down.

McDUNN: Damn me eyes, as the sailor-poets say. I'm really alone out here. No town for two hundred long miles that way north, no town for three hundred miles that way south, no town inland through that November mist for at least sixty fine lonely miles. There's just the empty coast, the empty roads, the empty land, the empty water, me, and one lone seagull, crying. All this considered, can I refuse the sea my love? I cannot. Why?

He lights his pipe, puffs, blows smoke.

McDUNN: Because man is the Bored Animal. We need change. But where find it? *(Looks up.)* In clouds, as a boy, laid out studying the high atmospheres and symbolic configurations, the widenings and closures of pure air and white substance. Or in hearthfires, winter nights. Never two flames the same arabesque, baroque, rococo. Air and fire! But! But the sea, the ocean, beats both! More original than clouds, stranger than all hell's furnaces. It prowls a thousand shapes and colors, and no repeats in the billion years since the first tides rolled. Here's my sky and my hearth, full fathom five, all spread below, and no dull bored brute animal this. Go on, entertain me, that's it.

He freezes as he looks up and off.

McDunn: Hello, more entertainment! A motorboat. Why . . . that looks like Johnny's . . . No, is he *back* then? *(Squints.)* But, it is, it is! Hi, Johnny! Hi! *(Stops.)* He can't hear you. Well. Not alone. That's all right. Company. Someone real to talk at, so you don't run off the rail. Curious. I wonder has he heard the rumors? The old man's daft. He sees things by night. Worse, in raw noon-light. Can that be it? Let's tread easy and find out. John! Johnny! Hello! Tie on. Come up! You're just in time for the grand illumination!

He turns and busies himself with last-moment details, storing things in a kit, brushing the brasswork. He turns suddenly and looks around and down, listening.

McDunn: He's on the steps. Let's give him a great hullo! Eh?

He presses a button and there is one huge cry of the foghorn as JOHNNY *steps to view, clapping his hands over his ears, beaming, panting.*

Johnny: When, my breath! Those steps! I'm an old man!

McDunn: No, *I'm* old. You're young as the horses in the May fields! Johnny! It's good to see you!

He bear-hugs the young man, who smiles, then laughs.

Johnny: I'm crushed to bits! Angus! You look fine!

McDunn *stands off and feels his own strength.*

McDunn: Ah, it's from running up and down ten thousand steps a day! Johnny, it's great you're here.

Johnny: I thought I'd surprise you!

McDunn: Is that all it is—surprise?

Johnny: What else?

McDunn *(catches himself)*: Nothing. You've been off away?

Johnny: California!

McDunn: But you had to come back, eh? I mean, I hear they have a different ocean there, not half as much fun as this one? They have, I hear, second-rate hand-me-down fogs and fourth-rate hurricanes. You simply *had* to come home!

Johnny: Dear Angus, if you had a choice between a theater play, a new motion picture, or the view from this tower—

McDunn: I'd choose the tower's view, no argument.

Johnny: But, you have no relief! You're out here seven nights a week, three hundred and sixty-five nights a year. I don't think I've seen you on the mainland in years! You deserve—

McDunn: Or is "need" the word you're looking for?

Johnny: Deserve, need. Wouldn't you *like* to head for town a whole weekend?

McDunn: And drink and swarm myself with locust plagues of trouble? It sometimes flits across my eyeballs like a speck of licentious dust, but it goes if I blink. And who would sit in for me here tending the great babe in the night?

Johnny: Me.

McDUNN: You!

JOHNNY: You raised me out here for two years when I was a kid, have you forgotten? You're next thing to my father. I worry—

McDUNN: Why should you, unless someone has stuffed it in your left ear and pulled it out your right?

JOHNNY: Oh, Angus, there *is* talk. What's gone on since I left?

McDUNN: It's not my doing. Ask the sea for answers. Johnny, I do *not* need relief, nor the town, nor drink. What's true is true. I *live* with reality, boy, at the foundation base of God's granite bulk himself. We came out of that sea a billion years ago, lost our gills, and put on manners, and things are still in that water which *do* rise up from time to time to frighten some and delight others. You've heard but the tail of the truth, and not the head and body.

JOHNNY: Fill in then, Angus. If I'm not to pile you in that boat and haul you back to the mainland, I got to have reasons to tell them there on the shore. Otherwise, they'll be out to relieve you of duty. Tell me everything.

McDUNN: First let's check a few last things. The infernal night is on, and us not ready. There.

He tinkers some machinery in the great box at their feet.

JOHNNY: I'm waiting.

McDUNN *(sighs):* Well . . .

He looks down at the ocean.

McDUNN: One night, two years ago, not long after you went away . . . Ah . . . you won't believe it.

JOHNNY: McDunn!

McDUNN: All right . . . one night, I was alone. But aren't I always? One night alone here like Hamlet's father's dear ghost in the tower, I *felt* something. Maybe *heard* something with the fuzz inside my middle ear. . . . I woke from a sound sleep to come look down there at the waters of old time.

JOHNNY: And you saw . . . ?

McDUNN: All the fish in the sea. All, every last one, they surfaced, they swam in billions, and lay out there, trembling, and staring up at the tower light going off, on, off, on, so I had swift flashes of their funny billion eyes. I turned *cold*. They were like a great peacock's tail out there, watching me, until midnight. Then, without so much as a sound, they slipped away, the billions of them was gone. I wonder . . . did they swim all those miles to worship? The light, the lighthouse, the tower high above the bleak waters, think how it must look and seem and be to the creatures, the dumb brutes there, the God-light flashing, and this tower declaring itself with its foghorn voice. They never came back, those fish, but don't you think for a while they thought they were in the Presence?

JOHNNY: They were, of a man with a wild tongue, and a taste for drink.

McDUNN: *I'm* full, and the *sea's* full.

JOHNNY: I can't tell that back on land, Angus! Come on, if we hurry—

McDUNN: Hurry, hell, boy. The night is on us. It's too late.

JOHNNY: It's only two miles to shore!

McDUNN: "Only" he says! Navigating in the dark, and the current gone wild in the last half-hour. No, boy, you'll stay the night, and float yourself in come dawn, God help you. For chances are you'll see tonight what I've seen and told no one of. Lend a hand, now. It's night, and fog, and much need of the light. There!

He turns a switch, and light comes on, turning behind them, misted, a shadowed motion of illumination.

McDUNN: And now—the horn itself.

He touches a second button. The foghorn cries.

McDUNN: Sounds like an animal, don't it? A big lonely animal set here on the edge of ten billion years calling out to the Deeps: I'm here . . . I'm here . . . I'm *here* . . .

The horn sounds again, not as loud.

JOHNNY: Angus . . .

McDUNN: Say nothing, for it won't make sense. You *don't believe.* But listen, Johnny, the foghorn calls, and the Deeps, they *do* answer. Why? Because one day years ago a man walked and stood in the sound of the ocean on a cold sunless shore and said, "We need a voice to call across waters and warn ships. *I'll make one.* I'll make a voice like all of time and all the fog that ever was. I'll make a voice that is like an empty bed beside you all night long, and like an empty house when you open the door, and like trees in autumn the first night the leaves have gone away. A sound like birds flying south, crying, and a sound like November wind and the sea on the hard, cold shore. I'll make a sound that's so alone that no one can miss it, and whoever hears will weep in their souls, and hearths will seem warm, and being inside best to all who hear in graveyard-distant towns. I'll make a sound and an apparatus to weep it with, and call it a Foghorn, and whoever hears it will know the sadness of eternity and the briefness of life."

The foghorn has blown at least three times, muted, during the above.

JOHNNY: Angus, you're right. The voice, just like you say. *You* might have invented it.

McDUNN: Flattery will get you nothing, save more soliloquies. Listen.

They listen.

McDUNN: That sound leads us the long way around to this night. We shall have a visitor! You'll *see!*

JOHNNY: Those billions of fish?

McDUNN: No.

JOHNNY: *One* fish . . . a *whale* . . . ?

McDUNN: Not a fish, and not a blood-warm mammal whale, but—Hist! Ah, yes! *There!*

He has come to the rim of the tower to peer out and point.

JOHNNY: Something . . . swimming   toward   our   lighthouse . . . ?

McDUNN: Aye.

JOHNNY: Something . . . big?

McDUNN: "Tremendous" is nearer the mark.

MCDUNN *lights his pipe and smokes, peering steadily. The foghorn blows, muted.*

McDUNN: It's a tide now, a motion to itself, hid down, and now rising, rising, a wave, a bubble, a bit of froth. Then, here, here, here it comes, boy.

JOHNNY: A head? A dark head? Eyes? One eye. Two? *Two!* And a neck, and more neck, and more—

McDUNN *(mightily pleased):* And *more* after that! Ten, twenty, thirty feet! And a body like an island of black coral and shells and crayfish, and all the subterrane. Ninety, one hundred feet in all! The monster! The beauty! It breaches! It breaches!

The foghorn cries!

The monster, in echo far off, cries.

McDUNN: You *hear?*

JOHNNY: No.

McDUNN: You *do!* Listen!

The monster cries, nearer.

JOHNNY: Impossible!

McDUNN: No, we're impossible! It's merely fantastic. It's like *it* was ten million years ago. *It* hasn't changed. It's *us* and the land have changed, and gone impossible! *Us!*

The foghorn blows. The monster echoes, nearer.

JOHNNY: The light! Its eyes!

McDUNN *(wonderfully enthused):* Our own lighthouse beam flashed back from it in fine Morse code! And what does it *say,* Johnny?

JOHNNY: It's . . . a dinosaur?

McDUNN: One of the tribe! And hear its lovely voice!

JOHNNY: But they died out!

MCDUNN: No, only hid away in the Deeps. Deep deep down in the deepest Deeps. Oh, hear the sound: Deeps. There's all the coldness and darkness and deepness in the world in words like that.

JOHNNY: What'll we do?

MCDUNN: Do? Why . . . enjoy the spectacle.

JOHNNY: It's circling around. Why? Why does it come here?

MCDUNN: Have you no ears?

The foghorn blows.

The monster cries.

MCDUNN: The foghorn *blows!* And the beast *answers!* There's a cry comes across a million years of water and mist. There's anguish that shudders the soul's marrow. Foghorn, monster cry, which is which? You might think that's another horn out there, lonely and vast and far away. The sound of isolation, a viewless sea, a cold night, apartness.

The monster cries.

JOHNNY: When did it first start coming here?

MCDUNN: Just a year ago. Think. Johnny, that monster lying far out, a thousand miles at sea and what . . . ? Twenty miles deep? Biding its time, maybe a million years old, this one beast, who can say? Not me. Think of it waiting a million years, could you wait that long? Maybe the last of its kind. And after all that waiting, here come men on the land and build a lighthouse and light a light and sound a horn and it cries out toward where you have been buried so deep the sound is no more than a whisper, an echo in your sleep, sea memories, no more, dim tides that remember a world where once you were young with thousands like yourself, all terrible beauties, but now you're alone, alone and no part of a world much changed.

The foghorn cries, muted. The monster cries, muted.

McDUNN: But the sound of the foghorn comes and goes and you stir from the muddy bottom of the Deeps, and you move slow, slow, and your eyes open like the lenses of five-foot cameras and the furnace stokes in your belly and you begin to rise slow, slow. You feed yourself on great slakes of cod and minnow, on rivers of jellyfish, and pick your teeth with whales, and rise slow through the autumn months. You got to rise slow; if you surfaced at once you'd explode from the change in pressure. So it takes you months or years to surface, and then at last there you are, the biggest grand monster in creation, and here's the lighthouse calling to you with a long neck like your neck sticking way up out of the water, and a body like your body, and a voice like your voice!

The foghorn cries, faintly. The monster echoes.

JOHNNY: Oh, the lost thing. Has it waited that long? A million years, for someone to come who never came back?

McDUNN: A million years. An insanity of time. While the skies cleared of reptile-birds and the swamps dried on the continental lands, the sloths and saber-tooths had their day and sank in tarpits, and men ran like white ants on the hills below Jerusalem. Last year, that creature swam round and round, round and round, all night. Not coming too near, puzzled. Afraid, too, maybe. And a bit angry after swimming all this way. But the next day, the fog lifted, the sun came out, and the beast swam away in the heat and silence and didn't come back. I suppose it's been brooding for a year now, thinking it over every which way. Maybe it only rises up once a year, on one night. I marked the date, anyway. And here it *is!*

JOHNNY: And coming closer!

McDUNN: Blast if it isn't!

The foghorn cries. The monster cries.

JOHNNY: It's rising up! It's rising up! Gah! Its head is *level* with us!

McDUNN: Stand back, boy!

JOHNNY: It's going to hit us! The light, Angus! The horn! If we shut them off, it'll go away!

JOHNNY *scrambles. The monster cries loud. The foghorn, in mid-shout, dies. The light goes out.*

McDUNN: Johnny, no! No!

The monster rages in fury.

McDUNN: No. *That's* worst of all! It thinks we're gone! Switch on. Ah, quick! Switch on!

The light comes on. The foghorn blows.

There is an earthquake shudder, and the cry of the animal.

JOHNNY: It's fallen against the tower, it's grabbed hold, it'll break! We'll fall!

McDUNN: Down the stairs! Below now! Quick!

JOHNNY: It's rising up again, up, up. No, no! So tall! Angus!

McDUNN: Down! Down, you idiot!

MCDUNN *pulls him. They drop through the stairwell.*

A fierce green light shines upon the tower. Then . . . a shadow! And darkness. The crash of glass. The splintering of wood, metal, and stones. All falls to ruin.

Silence for a time; then the green light rises enough to find the two men sprawled flat, eyes tight, waiting. And above and around them an immense breathing and moaning.

JOHNNY: Angus?

McDUNN: Alive. Thank God for this cellar. Listen. Sh. It's him, folded over and above us, not a stone's thickness away.

JOHNNY: The smell. It's terrible. I'll die.

McDUNN: You'll live. But will *he?* Listen. The lament. The bewilderment. To him, the tower is gone. The light gone. The thing that called to him across a million years gone. So there's just him calling now, like the Foghorn come alive again, sending out great keenings, again, again. And ships at sea, passing late at night now, do they hear him cry and think: There it is, the lonely sound, the Lonesome Bay horn. All's well. We've rounded the cape. We're beyond the reef?

The gasping dies. The sound dies. There is a great tidal stir. We hear waves.

JOHNNY: Is he gone?

McDUNN: He is.

They both sit up. The light begins to clear.

McDUNN: Oh, wasn't that wonderful?

JOHNNY: Wonderful?

McDUNN: And wasn't it sad?

They begin to get to their feet, and stop, for, far off, there is a cry.

JOHNNY: It's coming back!

McDUNN: No. Going away. Going back to the Deeps. Having learned what? It doesn't pay to love anything too much in this wild, strange world? Or it's best to love anyway, even if it turns out to be no more than mere lighthouse, light, foghorn in a fog, and two mere anthill men in charge of it all?

JOHNNY: Do you think it knew what we were?

McDUNN: As much as we know what *it* is; not much. Oh, Johnny, tomorrow get into the land, marry well, live in a warm house with bright windows and locked doors far away from the sea, come visit each year, but leave the ocean to me.

JOHNNY: It won't ever come back. I feel. It's gone back to wait another million years.

McDUNN: Poor thing. Waiting out there. Waiting. Yes. While man comes and goes on this pitiful small world. Waiting . . . until . . . I rebuild this tower? And then, maybe . . . Johnny . . . if it *did* ever return? If the monster came to visit, and with its terrible sad voice reared up again to ask ancient questions?

We hear a lonely cry from far away.

McDUNN (*slowly*): To those questions, Johnny, what *answers* have you ready? What might you possibly . . . *say?*

They look at each other a long silent time, then look out steadily at the sea.

The light dims. The voice of the sea beast fades.

The curtain comes down.